Trifecta of Murder

A Booker Falls Mystery

by

Kenn Grimes

For information, email **Cozy Cat Press**, cozycatpress@aol.com or visit our website at: www.cozycatpress.com

COZY CAT
P R E S S

ISBN: 978-1-946063-30-4

Printed in the United States of America

Cover design by Paula Ellenberger
www.paulaellenberger.com

1 2 3 4 5 6 7 8 9 10

Acknowledgments

To my readers,
Linda Miller
and
Judy Grimes

and

To my editor,
Madge Walls,

who does her best to keep me
on the straight and narrow
when it comes to my grammar,
especially my use of commas.

(NOTE)
Dear reader, if you should
run across a comma where
there shouldn't be one,
or see a place where there
should be one, but isn't,
please do not blame the
editor.

It just means I chose to
disregard her advice.

Dedicated to
my daughters-in-law

Didi, Denise, Whitney and Melanie

whom our sons were lucky enough to meet
and
smart enough to marry

CHAPTER ONE

Rachel Steinmyer's eyes focused on the barrel of the biggest gun she had ever seen, a gun pointed straight at her head.

"Puh a mun n a bog," growled the man holding the gun, as he shoved a dirty, crumpled-up Eagle brand flour sack across the counter towards her.

A bandana, even dirtier than the flour sack, covered the lower part of the man's face. A floppy hat was pulled down over his forehead.

"What?" asked Rachel, knitting her brow. Her hands started to shake and she felt a knot forming in her stomach.

The man lifted up the bandana. "I said, put da money in da bag."

Even without the bandana, his words were slurred, and Rachel smelled the distinct odor of rye whiskey.

Twenty-eight-years-old, she had worked at the bank all her adult life, and knew everyone in town. The man on the other side of the teller's window was not familiar to her.

"What did he say?" came a voice from behind her.

Rachel turned to her father, Isaiah, who was sitting at a desk in one corner of the room. From where he was, he couldn't see the bank robber, nor could the man see him.

"He says he wants money," said Rachel.

"Who's zat?" asked the man. "Who you talking to?"

"The janitor," said Rachel, thinking quickly, not wanting to put her father in danger.

"Tell him get out here," growled the man.

"He can't—he's . . . he has a broken leg."

"Does he have an account with us?" asked Isaiah.

Rachel looked at her father. "No. I think he's robbing us. Are you sure you want to do this?" she asked, turning back to the robber.

She was beginning to feel a little bit calmer.

The man pulled his bandana up again and moved the gun closer to her head. "Now! Put da money in da bag."

"Okay, okay," said Rachel, her anxiety starting to rise again.

She began stuffing dollar bills into the flour sack. "You'll never get away with this, you know."

"Did you say he's robbing us?" asked Isaiah. He hadn't moved from his desk.

"It's all right. He won't hurt us." At least, she hoped he wouldn't. The man didn't appear to be too steady.

"Beh bills—I wan beh bills." The bandana was down over his mouth again.

Rachel emptied the two teller drawers, about a thousand dollars in all.

"That's it," she said. "That's all I have."

"Geh a muny outa da safe."

"I don't have the combination," Rachel lied. "And my father's not here."

The man frowned and started to back away towards the door. "Don folla me," he said, as he stumbled out onto the sidewalk.

Rachel slipped out from behind the teller's cage and hurried to the door in time to see the man duck into Alton Woodruff's barbershop—an establishment that, along with tonsorial services, also provided libations in the back room for thirsty patrons, an amenity much appreciated and employed during this first year of Prohibition.

"What's he want?" asked Isaiah. "Is he going to kill us?"

"No, father, it's all right. He's gone. I'm going to call the constable."

Rachel ran to the back office where she lifted the earpiece from the phone box, took a deep breath, then cranked the handle.

"Well, hello, Rachel," came the voice on the other end of the line.

"Maribel," said Rachel, "no time to talk right now. Can you put me through to the constable's office, please?"

"Yah, I could, honey, but I know he's not dere."

"How do you know that?"

"'Cause he just called Mayor Salmon a few minutes ago from da boarding house."

"Okay, then," said Rachel, "put me through to Mrs. Darling's."

"Well, okay, den," said Maribel. "Will do."

A few minutes later, Rachel heard, "Hello?"

"Mrs. Darling, this is Rachel Steinmyer at the bank. Is Constable de la Cruz there?"

"Well, hello, Rachel. Yah, he is. I'll go fetch him."

"No, please, just tell him the bank has been robbed, and the thief is down at the barbershop right now, I'm sure, celebrating by getting even drunker than when he was in here."

"Oh, my!" said Mrs. Darling, her eyes getting big. "I'll go tell him right now."

When Rachel returned to the front office, she found her father slumped over his desk, the ink well he'd been using tipped over, black liquid spilling out onto the tiled floor.

*****

In the sixty-five years of its existence, The Booker Falls Bank and Trust had survived the financial panics of 1884, 1893 and 1907; three earthquakes in 1905, 1906 and 1909; and a fire in 1915 that had barely been extinguished before the whole building went up in flames.

But it had never before been robbed.

In fact, in the past several decades, only two robberies had been committed in the town of Booker Falls, Michigan. The first occurred in 1898, when a tramp passing through town on a local freight train decided to help himself to the pie Rosemary O'Leary left to cool on her kitchen windowsill. The culprit was captured and put on the next train out of town, but not before getting rid of all the evidence—by eating it.

In 1909 a more serious theft occurred when John Littlejohn got away with a fine palomino that belonged to Ezra Hitchfield. Neither John nor the horse, Eliza, was ever seen again.

*****

Twenty-nine-years-old, Henri de la Cruz had been the county constable for the past four years, since the death of the previous constable, Richard Barnoble, in 1916. Before that he had been Barnoble's part-time assistant for three years, at the same time teaching history and science at the local high school.

He often wished he could go back to his old job. He didn't feel he was cut out for law enforcement. He hadn't been trained for that sort of work.

But there'd been a robbery at the bank, Mrs. Darling had said. Come right away.

He strapped his gun belt around his waist, slipped on his uniform coat and hurried out the door.

*****

In addition to Henri, three other boarders called Mrs. Darling's Boarding House home: Myrtle Tully, Daisy O'Hearn and Pierre Longet.

A year ago, after having served eighteen months in France as one of General Pershing's "Hello Girls," working as an operator for the American Expeditionary Forces, Myrtle had returned to the United States, looking to start a new life. She had paid two hundred dollars for a twelve-year-old automobile, a green 1907 Model N Ford, and had then driven thirteen hundred miles in fifteen days from New Orleans to Booker Falls, to start her new job as the assistant librarian at the Adelaide College library.

During those twelve months, she'd been instrumental in helping solve a twenty-eight-year-old murder case, resulting in the killer now serving a life sentence in Marquette.

In her late twenties, Myrtle Tully was a woman ahead of her times, eschewing dresses and tailored white blouses with puffy sleeves and skirts that covered the ankles for shirts and trousers, including knickers, pants more suitable—at least to those who cherished fashion—for schoolgirls.

Instead of a cloche or turban headdress, a newsboy cap—black and green plaid to match her favorite pair of pants—usually covered the curly auburn locks that found their way down over her forehead.

She made a concession when it came to her work clothes. At the library she was more suitably attired in a skirt and blouse, giving in to Daisy's admonitions.

Since her arrival at Mrs. Darling's, Myrtle and Daisy, who worked as a reporter for *The Rapids*, Booker Falls' weekly newspaper, had become the best of friends. It was Myrtle who had seen Daisy through the death of her mother, and who had traveled with her by train to Chicago to attend the funeral. And it was Myrtle to whom she confided that she had killed her husband, stabbed him to death when he had attacked her, though it was discovered later he had survived, only to die a few years afterwards in a construction accident.

The two of them were sitting in rocking chairs on the front porch, discussing the newest boarder, Pierre, a professor at the college, who had recently moved to town from Boston, when Henri burst from the house and flew down the front steps, taking them two at a time.

"Henri!" Myrtle called out. "Where are you going?"

Without pausing, Henri turned his head and shouted, "Somebody just robbed the bank!"

Myrtle jumped up from her chair, nearly knocking it over backwards. "Can I come, too?"

Ignoring her, Henri climbed into his car and sped off.

"Come on," said Myrtle, heading for the door.

"Where?" asked Daisy.

"We're going to go see what's happening. You're a reporter, aren't you?"

*****

Henri stopped his car in front of the bank, where Rachel stood waiting, nervously wringing her hands as she watched her father being carried down the street on a stretcher.

"What happened?" he asked. He could see she'd been crying.

"The doctor says he thinks it's apoplexy. They're taking him to his office. They might take him to St. Joseph's over in Hancock."

Henri handed Rachel his handkerchief. "How would they get him there?"

"Carriage, I expect," Rachel answered, dabbing her eyes.

"Nonsense," said Henri. "If he needs to go, call George. He'll take him in his automobile. Now, you told Mrs. Darling this man who robbed the bank, he went into Alton's barbershop?"

"Yah." Rachel pointed down the street towards the shop. "He's wearing a dirty old floppy hat, and he had a bandana around his face."

"Did you recognize him?"

Rachel shook her head. "I've never seen him before, as far as I can recall."

Henri nodded and started off down the street. "Go be with your father," he said.

"You be careful, eh?" said Rachel. "He's got a gun."

*****

Holding his pistol behind his back, Henri cautiously entered the barbershop.

Alton Woodruff stood behind the barber chair, a straight razor in one hand. It was obvious, though, that the instrument was not intended for the customer seated in front of him, as the man's beard extended well down past his chin. Two men who had vacated the back room when the bank robber entered brandishing a gun, Joker Mulhearn and Lawrence Pollard, stood against the side wall.

Alton motioned towards the door to the back room and held his free hand out like a gun. "He's got a gun," he mouthed.

Henri nodded and approached the closed door. "Any more whiskey in there?" he said in a loud voice.

No answer.

"Hello?" said Henri.

Still no answer.

Henri's heart started to beat a little faster.

He pushed the door open slightly. Then a little further. He saw the man lying on the floor, unconscious, a gun and an empty bottle of Canadian Club whiskey next to him.

"You can relax," he called out to the men behind him in the shop. "He's passed out."

*****

Myrtle guided her car to a stop in front of J. P. Finnegan's Fancy Groceries and Fresh Meats in time to see Henri leading—half-dragging—an obviously inebriated man across the street.

"Is that him?" she asked.

"Yah," replied Henri. "I'm taking him to jail."

"Was there any gunplay?" asked Daisy.

Henri looked at her and frowned. "No, and I'm glad there wasn't."

"How's Rachel?" asked Myrtle.

Henri told them what Rachel had said.

"We should go see how she's doing," said Myrtle.

"Good idea," said Henri, as he continued to drag his prisoner across the street.

*****

"I heard you caught a bank robber."

Henri chuckled. George Salmon, his best friend, sat seated across the desk from him.

First elected in 1914 at the young age of twenty-five, George had served as mayor of Booker Falls for the past six years. Two years ago he had been re-elected when no one chose to run against him.

His parents were both deceased, as well as a younger sister, the latter tragically killed in an accident three years earlier. George did not hurt for money, thanks to a substantial inheritance, the result of his father's involvement in the early days of the area's lumber industry.

Six feet two, two hundred and ten pounds, he boasted an athletic build developed from playing amateur hockey, including three years for the fledgling Rensselaer Polytechnic Institute team of Troy, New York. Hair the color of wheat and eyes as blue as the unfiltered sky of Michigan's Upper Peninsula helped to qualify George as one of the most eligible bachelors the town had to offer. But he had shown little interest in women.

That is, until Myrtle showed up.

He'd been infatuated with her from the first time he saw her, the day she arrived in town. He had admired how she stood up to Henri when he berated her for the near accident the two of them had almost been involved in.

She had been rubbernecking, amazed at discovering an actual town in place of the wild and desolate outpost she'd been anticipating, when Henri came around the corner in his carriage. Myrtle had applied the car's brakes just in time to avoid a collision, but not to prevent Jessie, Henri's horse, from rearing up and nearly overturning the carriage, with Henri in it.

After a brief and less than friendly exchange of words, Myrtle had continued on her way. George had caught up with her and tried to strike up a conversation, but she had brushed him off, tarrying only long enough to ask for directions to Mrs. Darling's, where she would be taking up residence.

The next day he'd dropped by the boarding house and invited her to an ice cream social at the Lutheran church, but she'd declined his offer. That hadn't dissuaded him, however, and over the ensuing months they'd gone out together several times.

He was very much aware she had also dated Henri.

"Caught?" said Henri. "I'm not sure I'd use that word. The man was on the floor, passed out drunk. The hardest part was getting him across the street here to a jail cell. I practically had to carry him."

"Have you had a chance to question him, yet? Find out who he is?"

"Oh, I know who he is. Name's Mickey McInerney."

"Mrs. Folger's brother? I thought he was at Marquette."

"He got out a week ago. He's staying over at the Folger's, in the room above their carriage house."

"Did you recover the money?" asked George.

Henri laughed. "Well, I recovered *money*. Whether or not it's *the* money, is another story."

"What do you mean?"

"He had a little over a thousand dollars on him," said Henri, "which is about the same amount Rachel told me later was the amount taken in the robbery. When I asked Mickey where he got it he said his sister gave it to him."

"Mrs. Folger?"

"Yah. I asked him, I said, you sure you didn't get it at the bank?"

"What did he say?"

"Said he hadn't been in the bank. In fact, didn't even know where the bank was."

"Sounds pretty flimsy to me."

"We'll see what Mrs. Folger has to say when she gets here. I've called her."

"I heard he had a gun."

Henri patted his desk. "Safely locked up right here."

"Have you heard how Isaiah's doing?" asked George.

"I talked with Doc Sherman. Guess it's worse than they first suspected. In addition to the seizure, it appears he also suffered a heart attack. They decided not to take him to the hospital. Doc says it wouldn't have done any good. He's looking at a few weeks, maybe."

"Sorry to hear that. So he's at home?"

"He is."

"Is Rachel all right?"

"Myrtle went over to check on her."

"And Miss Wasserman?" said George. "How is she handling all this?"

"Their housekeeper? I understand they're going to bring in a second woman to be at the house during the day to help out."

"I should go by and see if I can be of assistance," said George.

CHAPTER TWO

George had barely walked out the door when Margaret Folger entered.

"Constable de la Cruz," she said.

Henri sprang up from his chair. "Mrs. Folger."

"You have Mickey here?"

"Yah, I do. He's back there." Henri jabbed his thumb towards the door that led to the two-cell jail.

"May I see him?"

"I'm not sure he's awake, yet. He was unconscious and pretty drunk when I found him. I managed to get him in the cell before he passed out again."

"You said he robbed the bank?"

"Yes, ma'am."

"Were there any witnesses?"

You can tell she's the wife of an attorney, thought Henri.

"Yes, ma'am—Miss Steinmyer. He had a gun on her."

Margaret's eyebrows arched. "Eh, a gun, you say? My brother had a gun? Where is it now?"

"Locked up safe in my desk, here," said Henri.

"May I see it?"

Henri unlocked the drawer and pulled out the gun, a Colt Single Action Army Cavalry model, with a seven and a half inch barrel—the one Rachel Steinmyer had stared down an hour earlier.

"Just as I suspected," said Margaret. "That is my husband's gun."

"Your husband's?"

"It belonged to his father—from the war."

"So Mickey took it from your house?"

Margaret nodded. "Evidently. And how much money was taken in the robbery?"

"Around a thousand dollars. Mickey had the money on him. He said you gave him the money."

Margaret smiled. "Gave it to him, eh? Was anyone hurt in the robbery?"

"Not directly. But Mr. Steinmyer suffered what the doc thinks was an apoplectic seizure, along with a heart attack. And Miss Steinmyer is pretty shook up."

"I am sorry to hear that. But Mickey is right about one thing—I did give him the money."

Henri's eyes narrowed. "You did? Might I ask how much? And why?"

"The answer to your first question is one thousand dollars, the same amount you found on him. The answer to your second question is—it's none of your business. Now, may I see my brother?"

Annoyed at Margaret's answer to his question, Henri nevertheless did his best to remain cordial. "Sure, right this way. But I have to leave the door open."

*****

Margaret Folger had not always been Mrs. Folger. In fact, she had not always been Margaret.

Born Maggie McInerney in 1862 in the rough mining town of Copper Falls, Michigan, she was one of eight children born to Ian and Fran McInerney, two of whom survived childhood: herself and a brother ten years her junior, Mickey.

Following the death of her father in a mine accident when she was twelve, and her mother running off two years later with a surveyor from Minneapolis, Maggie, along with Mickey, went to live with an aunt in Mohawk, where Maggie got a job clearing tables at one of the town's two restaurants, the Copper Pot. She reconciled herself to living the rest of her life right there, hopefully married to one of the mine workers who could provide for her and her little brother.

All that changed the day Rudolph Folger stopped for lunch on his way to Copper Harbor.

Thirteen years older than Maggie, Rudolph was a successful lawyer in Red Jacket, working for the firm of Waycross and Waycross. Struck by the beauty of the young girl scurrying from table to table, he was astonished when he found out she was only fifteen years old.

Over the next six months, Rudolph made it a point to schedule numerous trips north from Red Jacket. Each time he stopped at the Copper Pot, and finally worked up enough nerve to ask Maggie out. Three months later they were married on her sixteenth birthday.

Over the next seven years, Rudolph worked his way up the ladder at the law firm, eventually becoming its chief litigator.

But reality set in when it became clear he would never be named a partner.

Waycross and Waycross was a family affair, two brothers who took over when their father was shot to death by an unhappy client. Now, each brother also had a son, both of whom would soon graduate from law school at the University of Michigan and join their fathers in the firm.

Rudolph, a native of Marshall County, Kentucky, had attended the School of Law at the University of Louisville, not nearly as prestigious as the Waycross cousins' school.

So he'd left the firm and moved himself and Margaret to the small town of Booker Falls, where he set up his own practice. Within two years he had become the attorney of record for the Joshua Mining Company, Booker Falls' largest employer.

He and Margaret quickly blended in with the town's more socially prominent citizens, and were now considered pillars of the community. Once a skinny, young, unsophisticated mining town girl, Margaret Folger had grown, literally and figuratively, into her role as a society matron.

And then there was Mickey.

*****

Margaret glared at her brother in disgust. He lay curled up on the wooden pull-down cot, his back to her.

"Mickey!" she screamed.

In the outer office, even Henri jumped.

Mickey jerked up, turning and half falling off the cot.

"Wha . . . wha. . .?"

"Mickey, you idiot—what have you gone and done now?"

Mickey struggled to his feet and looked at Margaret, trying to acclimate himself to his surroundings.

He blinked his eyes twice. "Maggie? Whatchoo doing here?" Mickey glanced around the cell. "And where *is* here, anyhow?"

"First of all, it's Margaret, not Maggie. And I'm here because you've gone and gotten yourself thrown in jail."

Mickey's eyes scrunched up. "Jail? How come I'm in jail? Did I do something?"

"Robbed the bank, or so they say," said Margaret. "Come on, we're getting you out of here."

"Can't do it," came Henri's voice from the other room.

Margaret walked backed to Henri's office and glared at him. "What do you mean, 'can't do it?'"

"Not 'til his bail is set. That is, if the judge gives him bail. May not give him bail."

"Is Judge Hurstbourne upstairs in his chambers?" asked Margaret.

"Don't reckon so," said Henri. "As I understand it, he took off for a couple week's fishing trip yesterday. Won't be back until after the first of the month."

"Nonsense," said Margaret. "You can't hold my brother in jail until the judge decides to sashay back into town."

"Reckon I'll have to. I sure don't have the authority to let him go."

"Humph," said Margaret, straightening up to her full height of slightly over five feet. "We'll just see about that."

She turned and headed back to the other room where Mickey had made his way to the bars of the cell.

"Mag . . . Margaret, did I really rob da bank?"

"Let's not discuss that right now. Rudolph will be over to see you later. You can talk to him, then."

"I can't go back to Marquette." Mickey was shaking.

"Nobody's saying you're going back to Marquette."

Mickey reached one hand through the bars to touch his sister. She backed away from him.

"No," he said, "I mean I *can't* go back. I'd never get out alive. Dere's dis one guard dere—Big Olaf, they call him—he's out to get me. I'm lucky I got out when I did. If'n I go back, he'll kill me for sure."

"What did you do to make this . . . Big Olaf want to kill you?"

Mickey drew back his hand. "He was on me like fleas on a dog da first day I got dere." He hung his head. "And den I might of . . . you know . . . accidentally spit in his soup when I worked in da cafeteria."

"You idiot! You're hopeless!" Margaret shook her head. "Have you had anything to eat?"

Mickey looked up at the ceiling, trying to remember. "I don't think so. But I ain't hungry."

"I'll send some food with Rudolph when he comes. Try to stay out of trouble."

"I'm in jail. How much more trouble can I get in?"

Margaret walked back into Henri's office. "I'll take the gun now."

Henri looked at her, disbelief covering his face. "I can't give you the gun. It's evidence."

For a moment she stood there, scowling.

"Well, then," she said as she turned and headed for the door, "nothing better happen to it, eh? Not to Mickey, neither."

Before Henri could respond, she was out the door.

*****

At one time, Rudolph Folger worshipped the ground Margaret walked on.

That time was long past.

Their marriage now was more one of convenience than of desire or even intimacy. Margaret long ago made it clear she was no longer interested in engaging in any type of sexual relationship with her husband. She would fulfill all her other duties: accompany him to public activities, entertain his business associates—whatever it took to maintain her status as the wife of Booker Falls' most prominent attorney.

As much as he had once loved Margaret, Rudolph despised her brother.

When they had married, he reluctantly agreed to take the then six-year-old Mickey into his home, a decision he soon came to regret.

While Maggie was sweet, innocent, and a joy to be around, Mickey was sassy, hateful, and destructive, unwilling to obey Rudolph's orders, hitting other children, mistreating animals—it was impossible to have a dog or a cat as a pet—setting fire to the woodshed, destroying the whole winter's supply of wood.

Rudolph understood the child had had a rough life; however, he could not allow that to justify what the boy had become. Beatings became a regular routine until the day Mickey—then a strapping fifteen-year-old—took the thick leather belt away from Rudolph and beat him with it until Margaret intervened.

That was the last day Mickey lived under Rudolph's roof until he was released from prison a week ago and Margaret insisted he be allowed to stay in the carriage house.

Now she wanted her husband to represent him at trial for robbing the bank, something Rudolph had no intention of doing.

Henri looked up when Folger enter his office.

"Mr. Folger. I've been expecting you," said Henri. He nodded towards the door that led to the cells. "You can go on back."

Mickey jumped up when he saw his brother-in-law. "Rudy! God, am I glad to see you! How long 'fore you get me out of here?"

"Get you out, huh? If I had my way, they'd leave you here and throw away the key. Better still," added Folger, "they'd send you back to Marquette. Margaret told me about your love affair with Big Olaf."

Mickey's face turned ashen. "I ain't going back to Marquette! I ain't! I can't!"

"I'm not sure you have anything to say about it. Anyway, you're not getting out of here until Margaret can get old Judge Hurstbourne to grant you bail, and since he's out of town right now, that could be awhile."

Mickey slumped back down onto his cot. "But you're gonna defend me, ain't you? I mean, if they take me to trial?"

"Oh, you're going to trial all right," said Folger. "And you're going to be found guilty. And, no, I'm not going to defend you."

"You ain't gonna defend me? Why not?"

"For one thing," said Folger, "I don't like you. Wait—that's not right. I don't just dislike you—I detest you.

"And for another, I'm a corporate lawyer now. It's been years since I've handled a case at trial. But I will make arrangements for a friend of mine from Red Jacket to take your case. He'll be over in a day or so to talk with you. Here," he said, handing Mickey a brown sack. "Margaret sent you something to eat."

"Hey, Rudy, you don't suppose you could get me a bottle of whiskey in here, do you? Eh?"

Folger looked at him, shook his head in disgust, then turned and left.

*****

It was more than the rock-hard jailhouse cot that caused Mickey to toss and turn that first night in jail.

The nine months he'd spent behind bars at Marquette Branch Prison had not been a pleasant stay, thanks primarily to the meanest guard there, Olaf Jaworski, who, for some reason, had taken an instant dislike to Mickey and proceeded to make his life miserable, especially after the soup incident, which another inmate had told him about.

In his dream, Mickey saw the menacing face of his tormenter, the yellowed teeth, the broken nose with a scar that ran from its bridge over to one ear, and heard his words, more like growls from a mad dog.

"So, you, squish—what you in for?"

Mickey had taken a second too long to answer and had received a knee in the groin. He doubled over in pain.

"Stand up when I talk to you, squish!" barked Olaf.

Mickey put both hands on the hard tile floor and tried in vain to stand, but couldn't. A kick in the chest from Olaf propelled him back against the cell bars, sending a jolt like an electric shock up his spine.

Mickey spent his first three days in prison in the infirmary, the result of the beating he'd received.

That was the start of a daily ritual of being abused by his jailor.

Some days it was a mere punch to the gut. On others, Olaf worked Mickey over for thirty minutes or more. It seemed to be the guard's sole source of pleasure.

The day Mickey was released, Olaf came to his cell early in the morning.

"Getting out today, huh, squish? But you'll be back. Guys like you always come back. And the next time you're here, I ain't going to go so easy on you."

Then Olaf punched Mickey in the ribs one last time as a reminder.

Mickey jerked awake. He was shaking, his clothes soaked from perspiration.

No, he thought, *there was no way he was ever going to go back to Marquette Branch Prison, no matter what.*

He sat upright on the cot and looked up at the single barred window, some ten feet up the wall. He shook his head.

Whatever it took, he wasn't going back.

CHAPTER THREE

Nathan Steinmyer watched as the two small cubes released from his hand micro-seconds before floated through the air, seemingly suspended in space, carried along by some unseen force, occasionally brushing up against one another like strangers in a crowded room, or two butterflies performing an in-flight mating ritual.

Hovering over the green-colored table below that displayed a strange combination of circles and numbers and quadrangles, each cube revolved, slowly twisting, turning, allowing Nathan to easily read the various digits on each of their sides; numbers from one through six.

As he observed the dice in their flight, he thought back to the occasion that had brought him to this point—this moment—that, depending upon in what combination these two small plastic objects ended up on the table in front of him, would determine his future.

It had begun almost ten years ago, in a large meeting room in downtown Detroit.

He was seated next to his eighteen-year-old half-sister, Rachel, and their father, Isaiah, along with nearly a hundred other people: aunts, uncles, cousins, all descendants or relatives by birth or marriage of the late Israel Steinmyer, Nathan's grandfather. Nathan had waited impatiently, tapping his toe on the worn wooden floor beneath his feet, as the last will and testament of the family patriarch was read by the executor of the estate, Andrew Marshall.

The three of them had arrived the day before from Booker Falls following a seventy-two hour journey, first by rail to St. Ignace, then by ferry across the Straits of Mackinac to Mackinaw City, and finally by rail again to Detroit.

The ferry ride was an arduous trip at any time, but especially so in the dead of winter, tossed about by huge waves which threatened to swamp the boat they were on.

Rachel had not wanted to go, but Isaiah had insisted. Nathan, on the other hand, was anxious to discover how much his grandfather left him in his will.

Neither Nathan nor Rachel knew their grandfather, had never met him. Neither had accompanied their father months earlier for the old man's funeral.

Following token gifts to household staff and other individuals, as well as considerably more substantial bequests to the Shaarey Zedek Jewish Relief Society, the Phoenix Social Club, where the reading of the will was being held, and Israel's home congregation, Temple Beth-El, the time finally came to reveal what members of the family would receive.

In his lifetime Israel had sired twelve children, eleven boys and one girl. All, surprisingly enough, had survived him.

The one daughter, Naomi, who had never married and still lived at home, was left the family mansion in Brush Park, along with a generous trust fund.

The sons, as they came of age, had all been dispatched to various locations in Michigan and Wisconsin to manage one of the many Steinmyer family-owned banks. In the will, each received one hundred percent stock ownership of their respective institutions, plus cash amounts to compensate for the differences in the value of the various sites.

Finally it came time for the grandchildren, the moment for which Nathan had been waiting.

"And to each of my living grandchildren," read Marshall, "I leave a bequest in the amount of forty thousand dollars, such amount to be held in trust . . ."

Nathan hadn't heard the rest of what Mr. Marshall said. He had what he'd come for: the amount of his inheritance.

Later on he would discover a condition of the trust was that he could draw no more than five thousand dollars from it in any one calendar year. That didn't concern him; he knew his grandfather had a reputation for being a shrewd investor, and counted on the trust being comprised of stocks and bonds which would produce good dividends, earnings, and growth. It had but to deliver a return of a little over twelve per cent a year and it would never run out, even if Nathan withdrew the maximum amount each year.

One week after Nathan, along with his father and Rachel, returned to Booker Falls, he had made the break.

"I'm leaving," he told his father.

"Leaving? Leaving what?"

"This job. This place. This life. I'm tired of being stuck here in the middle of nowhere. I hate Michigan."

"Where do you plan to go?" asked Isaiah.

"California . . . San Francisco."

"San Francisco? And what will you do there?"

"Do there?" said Nathan.

"For work—employment. How will you make a living? Will you work in a bank?"

Nathan laughed. "Work in a bank? I think not! I've spent my life working in a bank. I'll find something far more interesting to occupy my time."

"And when do you expect to leave?"

"Tomorrow. I'm going to Houghton tomorrow to catch the train to Chicago."

"Well," said Isaiah, turning back to the ledger on his desk, "good luck to you, then."

That was the last time he'd seen his father or had any contact with him—almost ten years ago.

In San Francisco, Nathan moved in with his cousin, Abe, who had settled there two years earlier, and together they opened a restaurant. Unfortunately, neither knew anything about the restaurant business, and within three years it had gone bankrupt. Since then, Nathan had taken odd jobs, living mostly on his inheritance.

But by the fall of 1918, the stock market had lost over a third of its value of two years earlier; Nathan's trust no longer kept up with his level of spending. Two more years had passed and now he was essentially broke.

His eyes were fixed on the dice as they started their downward flight, still moving slowly, like feathers in the wind. It was as though the journey were taking place in slow motion. In fact, it seemed everything going on around him was happening in slow motion.

He'd arrived at the gambling hall ten hours earlier. He'd lost track of the amount of money he'd gambled away, as well as the amount of alcohol he'd consumed, but he was vaguely aware there'd not been one minute when he didn't have a tumbler of whiskey in his hand. At first, it was Huiliang who ensured he was never without a full glass. When she left to go home, Da-Xia had taken over the task.

He'd been lucky at first. At one point he was up almost five thousand dollars. He'd told himself he should stop, take his winnings, go back to his apartment and pay old lady Jepperson the three months back rent he owed her.

But greed got the better of him.

Ride the good luck out, he'd told himself. *Win enough to start over. Open another business. Become a success. That would show his father.*

And before he knew it, the good luck turned to bad. He couldn't win at anything: baccarat, poker, faro, blackjack, roulette—all proved to be losing endeavors.

Now, here at the craps table, he had laid out all he had left—all except for one chip he kept back—his lucky chip.

It was now or never.

He watched as the dice landed on the table, so gently it almost seemed as if they were afraid they might break. They bounced once, appeared suspended in air, frozen in time, as though reluctant to come back to earth again.

Slow motion.

Nathan thought back to when he was nine years old, and he had watched as the baseball, caroming off the bat of Willie Jones, headed straight for him. He'd stood, transfixed, as the object came closer and closer, but slowly, it seemed, so slowly he could count the stitches that held the cover on. He had watched the ball right up to the instant it crashed into him, knocking him unconscious. It was two weeks before he'd come out of the coma.

At the table, a shroud of silence hung in the air while the crowd watched, wordlessly, as the two dies appeared to languidly wend their way to the far end. Would they ever get there? Or would they stop in mid-transit, frozen in time?

But they journeyed on. Finally they hit the far wall of the table, almost reluctantly it seemed, bounced twice and leisurely rolled partway back down the green cloth.

Then . . . they stopped.

*****

When the cab pulled up in front of Nathan's apartment, a squalid tenement on Larkin Street in the Tenderloin district, he pulled out his pocket watch: five a.m. His hope was that Mrs. Jepperson might not be up yet, though he knew she was usually an early riser.

As quietly as possible he opened the outside street door and tip-toed in. But his first step on the squeaky stairs leading up to his third-floor room brought the landlady out into the hallway.

No bigger than a sprite, with a crinkly face and grayish hair that might have been another color had it ever been washed, Mrs. Jepperson was, nonetheless, not a woman to be trifled with.

"Mr. Steinmyer."

"Mrs. Jepperson. Sorry if I disturbed you."

"I been waitin' for you. You got some money for me, I trust."

"I do," lied Nathan. "In my room upstairs. I'll go get it for you."

"How much?"

Nathan hesitated. The dice had not fallen his way at the gambling hall. He was broke. He'd borrowed money from a friend for the cab ride. The question was: could he pack his belongings and get back out of the building without encountering Mrs. Jepperson?

"All of it," he answered. If he were going to lie, might as well make it a big one.

"Good," said Mrs. Jepperson. "Here."

She handed Nathan a folded piece of paper.

"What is this?" asked Nathan.

"How should I know?" said Mrs. Jepperson, a surliness in her tone. "I ain't one to read other people's mail."

Nathan nodded. She was *exactly* the one to read other people's mail.

He took the paper and opened it.

"It's a telegram," said Nathan.

"Good news, I trust."

"It's my father. He's seriously ill. They want me to come home."

*****

Nathan sat in the coach car of the Overland Limited, two hours out of Oakland. He'd managed to elude Mrs. Jepperson by going out his bedroom window and down the fire escape. He'd then walked the mile and a half to the Paradise Pawn Shop, where he'd waited around for two hours before the establishment opened. He'd been able to wheedle the young female clerk into giving him enough money for his diamond-studded cuff links to buy a train ticket to Chicago, with enough left over to travel on to Booker Falls.

He didn't need the cuff links anymore; the one shirt he had left to go with them had long ago been relegated to the trash, a casualty of blood and rips suffered in a bar fight.

He regretted the money he'd had to spend on a cab ride to the ferry, then the ferry ride to Oakland, and then another cab ride to the train station. And while he would have preferred to have a berth on the train, he opted for coach instead.

Now, he was on his way back to Booker Falls. What would he find when he got there?

CHAPTER FOUR

It had been four days since Mickey McInerney had been arrested and thrown in jail.

Margaret had been by to see him twice each day, so Henri was not surprised when she walked into his office Friday morning.

He glanced up, waved his hand, gesturing for her to go on back to the room where Mickey was being held, then returned to reading the latest edition of *The Rapids*.

He started when she plopped a wad of money down on his desk.

"What's this for?" he asked, looking up.

"Mickey's bail. Let him out."

Henri looked perplexed. "Bail? Why do you think he gets out on bail?"

"Here," said Margaret, handing him a piece of paper.

Henri took the paper and read it. It was a telegram. He looked up at Margaret.

"You got Judge Hurstbourne to authorize bail? How'd you get ahold of him?"

"Doesn't matter—there's the authorization: fifty dollars. Now, go unlock that cell and bring my brother in here, eh?"

Somewhere in the back of Henri's mind, he'd thought that he didn't care much for Margaret Folger. Now he knew for sure.

Minutes later, Mickey stood before Margaret. "You got me out!"

"Shut up," said Margaret, grabbing him by the shoulder and herding him out the door.

Out on the street, Margaret headed for her carriage. When she turned back to look, her brother was walking off in the opposite direction.

"Where are you going?" she shouted.

"Da barbershop," said Mickey.

"You're not going to go get drunk, not when I just got you out of jail," said Margaret, her face contorted in rage.

"Nope. I'm going to get a haircut."

Margaret frowned as she watched her brother continue on his way, his hair falling out of his hat, twirling onto his shoulders.

She knew damn well he wasn't going for a haircut.

*****

Alton Woodruff looked up when he heard the bell over the front door jingle, announcing someone's entrance. When he saw who it was he picked up his straight razor.

"What do you want?" he asked, an edge to his voice. "What are you doing here?"

Mickey looked at Alton. *What was he talking about*?

"What do you mean, 'What do I want?'" asked Mickey. "I want a drink."

Alton glared at him. "You sober?" he asked.

"Heck, yes, I'm sober," answered Mickey. "I just got out of jail. You tink dere going to let me drink in dere, no matter, get drunk? What's wrong with you, eh?"

"You got a lot of nerve showing up here after what you done."

Mickey shook his head. What he'd done?

"What'd I do?" he asked.

"Stumbling in here soused after you robbed the bank, waving that gun around and everything. Scared us all half to death."

Mickey looked down at the hair-covered floor, trying to remember.

He looked back up. "Did I really do dat?"

Alton, along with Jesse Billups, sitting in the barber chair, and Rancey Thornton, standing against one wall, waiting his turn for a haircut, all nodded.

"Jeez, guys I'm sorry. I sure din't mean to hurt nobody. Or scare nobody. Look, Alton, all I want right now is a drink. I promise I won't cause no trouble. I'm thirsty, dat's all, yah?"

Alton thought for a minute, then lowered the razor.

"Go on," he said, nodding towards the door that led to the back room.

Mickey started to go.

"But no funny business," said Alton, glaring at Mickey.

"Okay," said Mickey.

Mickey received no warmer welcome from Joker Mulhearn than he had from Alton.

"What the hell you doing back in here?" asked Joker, laying his hand on the shotgun he kept under the counter.

"Did I screw up here, too?" asked Mickey, beginning to wonder just what *had* he done?

"You mean busting in here, drunk as a skunk, waving that pistol around and demanding whiskey, scaring me and my other customers out? Yah, you sure enough did screw up in here. I think maybe you *threw* up, too."

"I'm sure sorry," said Mickey. "I sure din't mean to cause you no trouble. Look, all I want is a drink. I ain't even got a gun today, okay?"

Joker stared at him for a second. "Well, okay then," he said. "But you do anything stupid, I'll bust your head in and then throw you out, got it?"

Mickey nodded.

Joker set a glass on the bar and started to pour a drink.

"Oh, one ting," said Mickey. "I ain't got no money today, neither. I just got out of jail. I'll have to put it on my tab, eh?"

Joker pulled the bottle back before the first drop hit the bottom of the glass.

"Tab?" He shook his head. "You ain't got no tab."

"Maybe I could start one?" asked Mickey, trying to look as pitiful as possible.

"It's okay. I'll pay for it."

Joker and Mickey turned to see who had just spoken. It was J. P. Finnegan.

"You buying him a drink?" asked Joker.

"Let's take the whole bottle," said J. P. "Over to the table."

He laid a silver dollar on the counter.

"He's all yours," said Joker, picking up the money and handing the bottle to J. P.

"And two glasses," said J. P.

"How come you're buying me whiskey?" asked Mickey, when the two men were seated at a table at the far back of the room. "I don't hardly know you."

Nineteen years younger than J. P. Finnegan, Mickey did not run in the same social circles as the older man. Truth be known, Mickey didn't run in *any* social circles, at least none that could legitimately be called *social*.

He knew his benefactor owned the only grocery store in Booker Falls, located across the street from where the two of them now sat. Not that Mickey ever frequented the establishment; they didn't sell alcohol.

But he had made a few trips into town with Maggie in the carriage when she went there to shop, while he made his own purchases at Joker's place.

He also knew it was J. P.'s wife whom his brother-in-law was having an affair with, a fact that was no secret around town.

Not that Mickey cared. As mean as Maggie treated him, he thought it was good payback.

J. P. poured them each a drink.

"I may have need of your services," he said, handing one glass to Mickey, who took it, downed it in one gulp, and handed it back to him.

"My services, huh?" said Mickey, eyeing the bottle. He watched intently as J. P. filled the glass again and handed it to him. As before, Mickey downed it in one swallow.

"Yah," said J. P. "I hear tell you're handy with a gun."

Mickey laughed so loud the other four men in the room turned to look.

"Me? Handy with a gun? Where'd you hear dat?"

"You used it to hold up the bank," said J. P.

"And you tink dat qualifies me as being handy with a gun? Besides, I ain't sure I *did* hold up da bank."

"Can you shoot a gun?" asked J. P.

"Shoot a gun? 'Course I can shoot a gun."

"Then that's all that's required."

Mickey squinted his eyes. "Just what is dis 'service' you're a'wantin' me to do, anyway?"

J. P. looked around the room and leaned in close to Mickey. "I want you to kill somebody," he whispered.

Mickey jerked back.

"Kill somebody?" he said, in a voice considerably louder than that used by J. P.

"Quiet, you fool!" whispered J. P. "I'm not wanting the whole world to know my business, eh?"

"So, who is it you want killed?" whispered Mickey, pouring himself another drink. He'd decided he wasn't going to wait any more for J. P. to do it.

"Your brother-in-law."

"My . . . my brother-in-law? Rudy?" Mickey's eyes got big. "Wait . . . is dis because . . . he's . . ."

"Yah, because he's shagging my wife," said J. P., sitting back. "I want the bastard dead."

"Why me?"

"Because he's cheating on your sister. And because I'm pretty sure you can use the money."

"What makes you tink I need money?" asked Mickey. Of course, Mickey always needed money.

"To get out of town."

Mickey's brow furrowed. "Why would I want to get out of town?"

"'Cause if'n you don't, you're heading back to the penitentiary over in Marquette."

"Huh, uh," said Mickey, shaking his head firmly. "I ain't going back to dat hell hole."

"Look," said J. P., "you don't have a Chinaman's chance in Hell of not being found guilty of robbing the bank. Maybe even of murder, if old man Steinmyer kicks the bucket."

"No!" said Mickey, shaking his head even more emphatically. "Rudy's getting me a lawyer—he'll get me off."

Now it was J. P.'s turn to laugh.

"You really are stupid, you know it? The case is cut and dried. There's a witness—young Miss Steinmyer. The constable found you with the gun and the money still on you. Ain't no jury in the world's going to find you innocent. You stick around here to stand trial, I guarantee—you'll end up back in Marquette."

Mickey was quiet for a moment, taking in J. P.'s words.

"How much?" he asked, finally.

"How much what?"

"How much money? How much money you gonna pay me if I do da job?"

"Two hundred dollars."

"That ain't very much," said Mickey, frowning. "Not for killing somebody."

"I'm not looking to set you up in retirement," said J. P. "Just enough to get you out of town."

"What about a gun?"

"What about it?"

"I'll need one," said Mickey, throwing down another shot.

"What about the one you used to rob the bank?"

"The constable took it."

"Get it back."

"How?"

J. P. was beginning to wonder if Mickey was capable of pulling off the deed.

"He probably has it locked up in his office," said J. P. "Break in and steal it."

Mickey thought for a minute, then nodded. "I could do dat. When do you want me to . . . you know, do it?"

"Kill Folger?" asked J. P. "As soon as possible."

"I know Maggie's going to Houghton tomorrow, taking Rudy's secretary over dere to catch a train. And den she's staying overnight with Aunt Prissy up in Mohawk. I'll do it tomorrow night, while she's away."

"Then it's a deal," said J. P., reaching his hand across the table.

Mickey took his hand. "When do I get paid?"

"When it's done."

"I better," said Mickey, strengthening his hold on J.P.'s hand while looking him in the eyes. "'Cause I'll still have da gun if'n I don't."

CHAPTER FIVE

It took Nathan four days to travel from Oakland to Houghton, with transfers in Omaha, Chicago, and then in Bessemer and Nestoria, Michigan.

In Houghton he hired a carriage to take him to Booker Falls and arrived there late on Friday morning, the twenty third of September; nine years, seven months and twelve days after he'd left home for San Francisco.

Twenty years apart in age, Nathan and Rachel had never been close. His departure had not helped the situation, leaving a bitter taste in Rachel's mouth, as she felt her half-brother had abandoned both her and their father.

Mildred Wasserman, on the other hand, felt no such animosity. To her, Nathan was still the baby she had held in her arms since he was three days old; the nine-year-old boy she sat with for two weeks while waiting for him to awaken from his coma; the rebellious teenager for whom she served as a buffer between him and a demanding father; a grown man who struggled against the constraints of life in a small town.

When she opened the door and saw the carriage stop in the driveway, she flew to it like someone meeting one returned from the dead.

"Nathan!" she cried, wrapping her arms around him.

She held him tight for a few moments, then stepped back. "Too thin," she said. "You're too thin."

Nathan laughed and took her up in a bear hug.

"Miss Wasserman, you are the one thing I've missed from this God-forsaken place."

"Miss Rachel's waiting inside," said Miss Wasserman when Nathan finally let her go.

"How's father?"

"He's resting. Perhaps you should talk to Miss Rachel before you go see him."

When Nathan walked into the parlor, Rachel rose to meet him. She gave him a cursory embrace and kissed him lightly on one cheek.

"You need a bath," she said, stepping back and wrinkling her nose.

"Four days on a train will do that to you."

"Why don't you get cleaned up; then we can go see father."

Nathan nodded, picked up his bag and headed for the stairs.

*****

His room remained much as he remembered it: a painting by Thomas Satterwhite Noble of the pond at his home in Cincinnati, Ohio; a Chinese enamel box with pictures of peacocks his father brought back with him from a trip to Shanghai; the baseball glove he'd never used after his accident; the snowshoes with the elk binding and lacing he'd thought he'd never need again after moving to California—Miss Wasserman had done an excellent job keeping it ready for what she was sure would be his eventual return. She hadn't suspected it would be because of his father's imminent demise, however.

Nathan peeled off his grimy clothes and left them in a heap on the floor, to be disposed of in the trash.

He slipped on the robe Miss Wasserman had laid out on the bed for him and headed for the bathroom at his end of the hallway. He was delighted to find the bath had already been drawn.

Gingerly, he stepped into the slipper claw foot tub, at five feet seven inches in length two inches shorter than his own five foot nine frame. Sinking down to let the warm water swallow him up, he lay back, his head resting on the rim. He closed his eyes and allowed the weariness of the past four days to wash away.

*****

"You look much more presentable," said Rachel, when Nathan joined her in the parlor. "And I daresay you smell better, too."

Nathan had discovered that the last several years of frugal living, which included skimping on the amount he spent on food, had paid benefits. He was still about the same size as when he'd left home years before.

And just as Miss Wasserman had kept his room intact, so was the wardrobe he left behind when he moved to San Francisco.

He had chosen a pair of crimson-striped Bailey Pants, along with a brown Bailey Vest over a white, Sinclair Club Collar shirt. Had he been dressing for a day at the bank he would have added a silk puff tie. But this was to be a casual evening. A pair of black embroidered velvet loafers completed the ensemble.

"Are you ready to see father now?" asked Rachel.

"Not yet. Tell me what happened at the bank, while I get a drink. Do you want one?"

Rachel shook her head.

Nathan poured himself a brandy from the cut glass decanter on the Provençal Sideboard, and listened as his sister recounted the incident from earlier that week.

"And Mr. McInerney is now in jail?" he asked.

"No," said Rachel. "Constable de la Cruz called this morning to let us know he had just gotten out on bail."

"Out on bail?" exclaimed Nathan, almost spilling his drink. "How in the world did he get out on bail?"

"It seems he's the brother-in-law of Mr. Folger."

"Rudolph Folger, our family attorney?"

"Yes, and Mrs. Folger was able to persuade Judge Hurstbourne to allow her to post her brother's bail."

"That's outrageous!" said Nathan. "I've never heard of such a thing. I trust they did not give the scoundrel back his weapon."

"No, the constable said it was locked up securely in his desk. Let's go in now and see father, shall we?"

*****

Nathan couldn't believe the person lying on the bed before him was the same man he last saw nearly ten years earlier.

Those years had not been good to Isaiah. Once robust and uncommonly strong, at seventy-eight he was now a mere whisper of the man he had once been. To make matters worse, the excitement at the bank had taken its toll on him.

Just as Nathan had never been close with Rachel, a gulf existed between him and his father that he had never been able to bridge. The old man blamed his son for the death of Nathan's mother, Annie, who died giving him birth.

At the same time, Isaiah doted over Rachel, clearly favoring her over her brother, showering her with gifts of clothes and jewelry.

"Father," said Nathan, approaching Isaiah's bedside.

Isaiah opened his eyes and looked up.

"Nathan? Is dat you?"

"It is, Father. I came as soon as I heard what happened."

"Why are you here?"

"Rachel sent for me."

"Go away. You are dead to me," growled Isaiah, closing his eyes.

Nathan looked at Rachel, who shrugged.

"He was angry you left," she said. "He's never forgiven you."

"Why did you send for me, then?" asked Nathan, angrily.

Rachel motioned him from the room, leaving Miss Wasserman behind.

"Because he's dying. The doctor said it's a matter of weeks. I thought you should be here."

"He's asleep now," said Miss Wasserman, joining them in the hallway. "Let's go on down to da dining room. I got lunch ready."

"I'm not hungry," said Nathan, still visibly upset. He turned and headed down the stairs, not waiting for the women.

"Where are you going?" asked Rachel.

"To town," said Nathan, closing the front door behind him.

CHAPTER SIX

Margaret had agreed to drive Norma Pennyworth, her husband's secretary, to Houghton on Saturday, where the latter would catch a train to take her to Chicago. Norma's plan was to spend a few weeks with her mother, who was gravely ill.

The trip provided an opportunity for Margaret to go on to Mohawk to see the aunt who'd taken her and Mickey in when their mother abandoned them. The aunt, now in her late seventies, was in ill health, and Margaret wanted to see her again before the old lady passed.

Besides, Margaret had some things to work out in her head, and the time away from Booker Falls—and her husband—would allow her to do that.

Rather than travel all the way to Mohawk by carriage, she decided to go by rail. Dropping Norma at the train depot, she drove to Lindeman's Livery Stable where she arranged to leave the horse and carriage for the next two nights. From there, she walked the few short blocks to the Douglass House, where she had been told the streetcar made a stop.

The Houghton County Traction Company had not existed when Margaret last visited her aunt in 1898. Starting up in 1900, the interurban line now ran from Houghton, up through Laurium, all the way to Mohawk, with spur lines to Lake Linden and Hubbell, as well as Red Jacket and Wolverine, numerous stops dotting the route all along the way.

Margaret watched as the car glided to a stop and a few passengers got off. Then, along with about a dozen other people, she boarded.

Minutes later, the conductor came by, collected the ticket Margaret had purchased at the desk inside the hotel for ten cents, and handed her back a transfer ticket, for which she'd be paying several more times before she reached her destination.

The car made its way over the bridge crossing the Portage River into Hancock, through its sprawling commercial district and on out into the country.

Another half hour brought her to the first stop at Boston, where two men departed and a young couple with three children boarded. The conductor came and collected another ten cents.

"How far you going?" asked the woman as she settled into the seat across from Margaret.

"The end of the line," said Margaret. "All the way."

They passed a large building with a huge "ELECTRIC PARK" sign across the top.

"Do you know what that place is?" asked Margaret, bending her neck to see as the car rolled by.

"Oh, yah," said the woman. "Electric Park. They have dances and concerts and vaudeville shows, a playground for the kids—it's really a fun place to go, eh?"

"It doesn't look open."

"Nah, it's closed now—won't open up again 'til spring."

"Perhaps I'll come back some time when it's open," said Margaret.

"Yah, you and your husband would love it."

Margaret didn't say anything. She thought it unlikely she would still have a husband if she ever made it back.

She knew about her husband and Agnes Finnegan. And she was fairly certain it wasn't the first time he'd strayed. She had pretty much made up her mind she wasn't going to stand by and take it.

Margaret leaned back and closed her eyes. The question was: what, exactly, was she going to do about it?

*****

The sound of the conductor's voice stirred her from her nap.

"All exit," he shouted out. "End of the line. If you're a'goin' back, catch the next trolley."

Margaret looked at the watch she wore on a chain around her neck, a gold-filled, fourteen karat, seventeen jeweled "Riverside" Waltham that Rudolph gave her on their twentieth wedding anniversary. The outside of the front case had engraved lilies on it, Margaret's favorite flower.

Rudolph had ordered it through the Sears Roebuck and Co. catalog. It had cost him twenty-nine dollars and seventeen cents, a considerable amount, which he never let Margaret forget.

Five minutes after eleven. The whole trip, even with all its stops, had taken about two hours.

She smoothed back her hair, picked up the Cognac Victorian Touring Hat she had carefully laid next to her on the seat, and placed it on her head, adjusting it to make sure it rode at just the right angle. Picking up her canvas-covered travel valise, she exited the car and stood for a moment, taking in the town she had not seen in over twenty years.

She spotted a young boy of about ten or eleven and called him over.

"Boy, come here, please."

"Yes'm?" said the boy when he stood in front of her.

"How would you like to make a nickel?" asked Margaret.

The boy's eyes lit up. "Yes'm! What do I gotta do?"

"I want you to carry this valise for me."

The boy looked at the valise. "How far?"

"Not far. Half a mile, perhaps."

The boy shook his head. "I'd need a dime to lug it that far."

Margaret smiled and raised her eyebrows. "Oh, you would, would you?"

"Yes'm."

"Very well. I'm sure I can find another—"

"Oh, no, no, ma'am, I'll do it. I was just joshing."

"Well, okay, then," said Margaret. "Pick it up and let's be on our way."

Twelve minutes later they stopped in front of a weather-beaten house that had seen too many Northern Michigan winters. Margaret paid the boy his nickel, and he scurried off in the direction of Uncle Britch's General Store.

She knocked on the door. It was opened by a woman who looked as weather-beaten as the building.

"Aunt Prissy!" cried Margaret. She grabbed the old woman and held her close for a long time.

"My lands," said Aunt Prissy. "Let go of me, chile, 'fore you squeeze me half to death."

When Margaret released her hug, Aunt Prissy said, "Come on in, chile. From da looks of your letter we got us some discussin' to do, eh?"

Margaret followed Prissy into the house, set down the valise and looked around.

For two years of her life—possibly the two most important years, years when she had grown from a girl into a woman—this was her home. And as happy as she was to leave Mohawk, it had been difficult to say goodbye to Aunt Prissy and Uncle Wilbur, who had now passed on.

"Look da same?" asked Aunt Prissy.

Margaret smiled. It did, indeed.

"Set yourself down," said Aunt Prissy, "whilst I brew us some tea."

"Do you have anything stronger?" asked Margaret.

This time it was Aunt Prissy's turn to smile. "Yah, honey, I shore do."

She took a bottle of Old Granddad Whiskey from a cabinet, poured two glasses and handed one to Margaret.

"So, chile," she said, sitting down at the table, "how long you here for?"

"I was thinking 'til Monday, though I might go back tomorrow," said Margaret. "There's something I have to take care of. But if I do go tomorrow, and later on, anyone should ask how long I was here, you tell them I left on Monday, eh?"

Aunt Prissy nodded. "You do what you got to do, chile."

CHAPTER SEVEN

Myrtle knew she should feel guilty—but she didn't.

Once again, she had skipped Sunday Mass to enjoy a quiet morning on the front porch, snuggled down in one of the half dozen rockers that sat lined up there, like soldiers awaiting their marching orders. A warm shawl wrapped around her shoulders helped ward off the cool September breeze.

After a full year of living in Michigan's Upper Peninsula, she had come to appreciate the changes in season more than the subtle shifts of summer to fall to winter to spring of her native New Orleans. Today, even though there was a slight drizzle, the temperature was almost sixty degrees.

She opened the book she'd brought home yesterday from the library—*The Last of the Mohicans*—and began to read. Before she finished the first paragraph, she heard the front door open and Mrs. Darling's voice.

"Here you are, dearie," said her landlady as she set a steaming cup of tea on the small table next to Myrtle. "I saw you out here and tought dis might warm you a bit."

Myrtle looked up at Mrs. Darling and smiled. She so enjoyed the long, dangly earrings the old lady always wore, no matter what the occasion.

"Thank you, Mrs. Darling," said Myrtle, picking up the cup and taking a sip. Thimbleberry!

Mrs. Darling served two flavors of tea: thimbleberry and dandelion. Myrtle much preferred the former, as did the other three boarders in the house. But they would never tell Mrs. Darling for fear of hurting her feelings, as she picked the flowers herself that went into the dandelion tea—as well as dandelion jelly, dandelion salad, dandelion fritters and, in the spring, dandelion pancakes.

Myrtle asked Daisy once if the list included dandelion wine but was told Mrs. Darling was a teetotaler.

She picked up the book and resumed reading.

She wasn't sure when she fell asleep, but the sound of an automobile stopping out in front aroused her from her slumber. She looked up and saw Henri coming up the path. He'd been to church, but he didn't look like a man at peace with the world.

"Good morning, Henri," said Myrtle. "You look upset. What's wrong?"

"Someone broke into my office over the weekend," he growled, plopping down in the chair next to her.

"Oh, my! Was anything taken?"

"Yah, twelve dollars and seventeen cents . . ."

"That's not so bad."

". . . and the gun I confiscated from Mickey McInerney."

"Oh, my—that *is* bad!" exclaimed Myrtle. "Do you have any idea who might have done it?"

"Yah, I'm pretty sure it was Mickey," said Henri. "He and Margaret—and George—they were the only ones who knew it was there. I know George didn't take it, and I can't see Margaret breaking into my office, but Mickey? I drove over to the Folgers but there wasn't anyone home. I have to go over to Red Jacket this afternoon, so I guess I'll wait until tomorrow morning to get back out there. I just stopped by to pick up some papers. If I don't see Mrs. Darling, will you tell her I won't be here for lunch or dinner?"

*****

One thing that could be said about Mrs. Darling was that she fed her boarders well. And Sunday lunches—as well as Sunday breakfasts and dinners—were exceptionally plentiful, as that was one of the two days of the week—the other being Monday—that Myrtle, because of her schedule at the library, could be present for all three meals.

Today was no exception: two generous portions of fried perch; boiled potatoes; green beans; spinach salad; and cherry pie for dessert.

Myrtle stared down at the plate before her and shook her head. When she first arrived in Booker Falls, Mrs. Darling told her she would 'put some meat on her bones.' And the old lady had done her best ever since to do so. Still, Myrtle had gained no more than three pounds in all that time.

She envied Daisy, who was wolfing down her food as fast as she could and undoubtedly getting ready for seconds.

And the thing was, Myrtle realized, that evening's dinner would be no less ample.

Sighing, she picked up her fork and tackled the perch.

Twenty-five minutes later, after declining a second piece of pie, Myrtle excused herself.

"I think a nap is in order," said Pierre, patting his stomach. He was almost as voracious an eater as was Daisy.

"How about you?" Daisy asked Myrtle. "You going to take a nap, too?"

Myrtle shook her head. "No way. I napped this morning. What I need is to get some exercise. I think I'll take Penrod to town. Would you care to join us?"

"No, thanks. It's still drizzling outside. I'm going up to my room to work on my book."

"Perhaps I'll see you later, then," said Myrtle.

*****

When Myrtle arrived in Booker Falls, she hadn't come alone: she'd brought a dog with her.

She had spotted him tottering along on a road outside Mendota, Illinois, the saddest looking critter she'd ever seen. Though she'd been pushing to make Rockford before nightfall, there was no way she could leave him there.

She'd pulled the car over, picked up the poor mutt and deposited him in the passenger's seat. When Mrs. Darling saw him, she immediately took him under her wing. Her companion of fifteen years, a yellow lab named Alfred, had passed away a few weeks before.

So Penrod—named by Myrtle after a character in the books by Booth Tarkington—had, for all intents and purposes, become Mrs. Darling's dog. She fed him, bathed him and let him out to do his business.

Occasionally, though, on a Sunday afternoon, Myrtle would take him for a walk into town. They would window shop—though most shops were closed, it being the Lord's day and all—and almost always they stopped at Mr. Abramovitz's pawn shop, which *was* open on Sundays, and where Penrod was assured of getting a treat.

"Miss Tully," said Simon Abramovitz, looking up when he heard the little bell above the door ring, announcing the arrival of a customer—or, more often, merely a browser.

Unlike Isabell Dougherty's store, de Première Qualité Women's Wear, with its wide aisles and neatly arranged displays, Mr. Abramovitz's pawn shop looked as though a water spout had blown in off Lake Superior and had its way with the place.

Seven display cases, each four feet by two feet, sat jammed into an area no larger than four hundred square feet. A small counter that held a cash register sat near the entrance.

A pot-bellied stove, the sole source of heat not only for the shop but for the small room in back that Mr. Abramovitz called home, snuggled up against one wall. A wooden ice box sat opposite it against the other wall.

The shelves were stuffed with a potpourri of items relinquished by their previous owners, either through a need for cash or the realization they were no longer a necessity: jewelry; silverware; old paper money, some foreign, some confederate; coins, several that dated back to the time of Julius Caesar; musical instruments; knives, small and large; sporting goods; three cameras; locks and keys; fine place settings; a glass eye; tintypes, ambrotypes, daguerreotypes, union cases; eyeglass cases and eyeglasses, including a monocle; ladies combs and hairbrushes; board games and card games; a dancing ballerina music box; a jack-in-the box; a meerschaum pipe with a bear rearing up on it hind legs carved into the bowl; handguns; and hundreds of other items.

Three headless mannequins wearing various articles of clothing—pants, shirts, coats—were placed strategically around the shop; two racks on one wall held an assortment of both men's and women's hats.

Paintings and other larger items covered the walls along with a pair of skis, two pairs of snowshoes, flags, including a Confederate one, guitars, and mounted animal heads, among them three deer, an elk, and a moose.

Every time Myrtle entered the store she looked at the moose and hoped it wasn't the one she encountered the first day she'd come to Booker Falls.

"Good afternoon, Mr. Abramovitz," said Myrtle, responding to the old man's greeting.

"Und da little dog," said Mr. Abramovitz. He reached under the counter for a treat. "Come, Penrod, come und see vat I haff for you."

Myrtle let go of Penrod's leash and he dashed to the old man.

"Now zit, please," said Mr. Abramovitz, holding a Milk-Bone inches above the dog's muzzle.

Penrod promptly sat back on his haunches, his gaze fixed on the old man, waiting patiently until the treat was offered to him. When it was, he gently took it, lay down and began crunching. "Such a nice dog you haff," said Mr. Abramovitz. "So, Mizz Tully, vat can I interest you in today?"

He knew she rarely bought anything, but rather that the purpose of her visit was usually to satisfy her curiosity about the various items people were willing to part with, either permanently or temporarily, for a bit of cash.

She knew, too, it was her company he looked forward to most—hers and Penrod's.

"What do you have that's new and exotic?" she asked.

Mr. Abramovitz's eyebrows arched and Myrtle almost swore she saw a twinkle in his eyes.

"Ah," he said, raising one hand. "I tink I haff yust da ting for you."

He reached into a case behind him, removed a small brooch, turned and laid it on the counter.

"Vun of da students from da college brought dis in. Said it had been a gift from her fodder, but she needed da money for tuition. I hated to take it, but I could see she vas desperate. I told her I vould keep it so's she could redeem it later, but she said 'no,' she knew she'd never haff the money."

Myrtle picked up the piece and examined it—a lady pendant cameo brooch with the profile of an elegant, beautiful woman. "It's exquisite," she said. "I imagine it saddened that young girl to have to part with it."

"It is quite unique," said Mr. Abramovitz. "Da voman on it, I mean."

"Oh? Is she—was she—someone famous?"

"Not so famous, but she has a connection to da college."

"How's that?" asked Myrtle.

"Her name is Jeanne Francoise Julie Adelaide Recamier . . . vas—she's been dead many years now, eh?"

"Adelaide?" said Myrtle. "Like the college?"

"Yah, da college vas named after her."

"Really?" said Myrtle. "I often wondered where the school got its name."

"You don't know da story?" asked Mr. Abramovitz.

Myrtle shook her head. "There's a story?"

She leaned back against the icebox.

"Oh, yah," said Mr. Abramovitz, "dere's a story all right. Mr. Amyx told me it himself vun night ven vee vas drinking at da pub—'fore it had to close 'cause of da prohibition, ya know. Dis vas a few years after he started da college. He vas pretty much in his cups, uddervise I doubt he vould have told me."

"What?" asked Myrtle. The suspense was starting to get to her. "What did he tell you?"

"Vell, ven Mr. Amyx vas a young man back in France, he had dis affair vit dis Mrs. Recamier. I guess she vas quite a voman, high society und all. She vas in her fifties und Mr. Amyx, he vas yust nineteen. He vas in love vit her, but for her, according to vot he said, it vas yust a dalliance. Dat's vot he called it: a dalliance, votever dat is."

Myrtle sat, entranced, as Mr. Abramovitz went on.

"Anyvay, Mr. Amyx, he vas heartbroken, so he come to America to forget all about her. Den, ven he started da college—you know, after his vife died—he named it after her. Mrs. Recamier, not his vife. Und dat's how da college got its name."

"And Recamier Logement, where the girls live, that was named after Mrs. Recamier also?"

"Yah," said Mr. Abramovitz. "Dat, too."

Myrtle shook her head. "That's fascinating. Thank you for sharing with me."

"Vell, Mr. Amyx, he dead now, I don't s'pose he cares who knows anymore."

"Rainy today," said Myrtle, gazing out the window.

"Yah, yust like da almanac said."

"The almanac?" Myrtle turned back to the old man. "What almanac?"

"Da *Farmer's Almanac*."

Mr. Abramovitz took a book from under the counter and handed it to Myrtle. "You can alvays count on da *Farmer's Almanac*. Says here a big rain is coming dis Vensday. Und if da almanac says it, you can count on it."

Myrtle picked up the almanac and thumbed through it. "I think my father used to read this. But I never thought one could put much stock in it."

"Oh, yah. It's like da Bible. Vell, okay, not *da* Bible, but, yah, it hit da nail on da head every time—almost every time."

Myrtle laughed. "All right, I'll take your word for it. Wednesday, you say?"

Mr. Abramovitz nodded.

"How much for the brooch?" asked Myrtle. She picked up the piece and studied it.

"Oh, I'm afraid it is quite expensive. It is solid gold and has many jewels."

"*How* expensive?"

"Sewenty-five dollars."

"Wow!" said Myrtle. "You're right—that *is* expensive."

"I haff someting else you might could be interested in," said Mr. Abramovitz.

He walked to the back of the store. When he returned he was holding a small gun.

"You said a few months ago you vas tinking of getting a gun. I tink dis vun is yust right for you."

Myrtle took the gun from Mr. Abramovitz and examined it: a Remington, double barrel, 41 caliber, nickel-plated derringer, with a checkered rubber stock. Five inches in length, it rested easily in her hand.

"I like it," said Myrtle. "It feels very . . . comfortable."

"It is not new," said Mr. Abramovitz. "Ten, fifteen years old, maybe. But in wery good condition. It vas vell taken care of."

"How much for this?"

"For you—yust tree dollars."

"Oh," said Myrtle. "I think I could handle that. How about the bullets?"

"I trow a box of ammunition in for nutting," said Mr. Abramovitz, grinning.

"Sold," said Myrtle, taking a wallet from her purse. "Do I need a permit for this?" she asked as she handed the money to Mr. Abramovitz.

Mr. Abramovitz looked around furtively. "Dat's up to you. I vont say anyting."

Myrtle placed the derringer in her purse. She was pleasantly surprised at how well it fit.

CHAPTER EIGHT

Eighteen-year-old Penelope Wright fumbled with the key she was attempting to use to open the street door at Number Five, Main Street, located above Paige Turner's New, Used and Rare Books Store.

Although she had spent the previous week working with Norma Pennyworth, Rudolph Folger's regular secretary, learning the ins and outs of the office routine, she was still nervous: this was the first real job she'd ever had.

And Norma wouldn't be there to help. Mrs. Folger had driven her to Houghton where she'd caught a train to Chicago to see her mother, which was the reason Penelope was filling in for her. Her basic duties would consist of filing, greeting people as they arrived, and answering the few telephone calls that might come in.

She had arrived early, anxious to make a good appearance. She hadn't counted on being the first one into the building, and said a silent word of thanks that Norma had entrusted her with a set of keys.

Folger's office was on the building's second floor, one of six positioned along the hallway. When she reached the door to the office, she began looking for the appropriate key. Then she noticed the door wasn't locked or even closed all the way, but was ajar. She wondered if Mr. Folger had arrived before her, but left the street door locked.

"Mr. Folger!" she called out. She pushed the door all the way open and went in.

There was no answer.

Penelope glanced at the moose rack coat tree that stood in one corner of the room: no coat or hat on it.

Strange, she thought. *Perhaps Norma neglected to lock the door on Friday in her haste to leave the next day.*

She and Mr. Folger had both been there when Penelope left.

Removing her coat and the wool cloche cap she had bought expressly for her first day on the job, she hung them on the coat rack.

She walked over to Mr. Folger's office door, opened it the rest of the way and entered the room.

And screamed.

A loud, shrill scream that carried a long way.

Downstairs in the book store, Myrtle held Paige's cat, Ginger, stroking its long, soft fur. She and Paige were discussing a book the latter had just gotten in, *This Side of Paradise*, by a new author, F. Scott Fitzgerald, when the scream shattered the quiet of the early morning, followed closely by more screams.

The cat exploded from Myrtle's arms as though a firecracker had been set off under her, knocking over a stack of books from the nearby counter.

"My goodness!" exclaimed Paige, her eyes drawn instinctively towards the ceiling. "What was *that*?"

"That was a scream," said Myrtle as she rushed to the door.

Once outside, she entered the door leading to the upper level, taking the steps two at a time. When she reached the second floor hallway she stopped, then ran to the office from where the screams emanated.

Dashing first into the outer office, then into the inner one, she stopped short at the scene before her.

Sprawled out on the floor face down in front of the open Whitfield safe lay Rudolph Folger. A dark stain was visible on the back of his coffee-colored

Chesterfield top coat. His top hat sat perched on top of the safe.

Penelope stood over the body, still screaming.

Myrtle grabbed her and shook her. "Stop!" she said. "Stop screaming. I'm here. It's all right."

Penelope turned and looked at Myrtle. She still had a shocked look on her face, but the screams stopped immediately.

"Come on," said Myrtle as she ushered the girl out of the office and downstairs to the book store.

"What is it?" asked Paige. "What's happened?"

"Mr. Folger's been murdered," said Myrtle. "At least I assume it's Mr. Folger." She had never met Rudolph Folger, but noticed his name stenciled on the outer door when she entered the office.

"Here," Myrtle continued, handing over the now sobbing Penelope to Paige. "Take care of her and call Henri."

"Where are you going?" asked Paige, as she watched Myrtle head for the door.

"Back upstairs."

With the book store located across the street from his office in the court house, it took Henri only a few minutes to get there. Paige met him outside, where they were joined by Dr. Sherman, whom she had also called.

"What do we have?" asked Dr. Sherman.

"You said someone's been murdered?" Henri asked Paige.

Paige nodded towards the door leading to the upper floors. "Upstairs—Mr. Folger."

Moments later, the two men entered Folger's office and found Myrtle, kneeling and peeking into the safe.

"Myrtle?" said Henri, surprised to see her there. "What are you doing here?"

In spite of the fact that, on her first day in town, driving her Model N, she almost ran over Henri in his horse and carriage, the two had, over the past year, become more than good friends.

But he still harbored a modicum of resentment that it was she who had been instrumental in solving a twenty-eight-year-old murder case that had resulted with the killer sentenced to spend the remainder of his life in prison.

And now, here she was—at the scene of the crime before he was.

"What are you doing here?" he asked again.

"Checking to see if it looks like anything's missing," said Myrtle.

"No—what are you *doing* here?"

The tone of his voice left no doubt that he was obviously upset at her presence.

Myrtle explained how she'd been downstairs when they heard the screams, how she'd come up and found Penelope, then taken her back down to the book store.

"I thought I might be of some use with the investigation," she said.

"I haven't even *started* an investigation yet," said Henri, disgustedly.

"Then it's time you should," said Myrtle, turning back and continuing her examination of the safe. "And don't forget your gloves."

"Gloves?" said Henri.

"Fingerprints," said Myrtle. She stood and moved away from the safe. "It's possible the killer might have left fingerprints. We wouldn't want to accidentally destroy them, now would we?"

She held up her own gloved hands. "You do have gloves, don't you?"

"Just my regular ones."

"They'll do," said Myrtle, walking to the outer office.

Henri sighed, pulled a pair of gloves from his pockets and slipped them on.

Dr. Sherman looked at Henri inquisitively as though to ask *are you going to let her stay?*

Henri shrugged and lifted his hands in a gesture of surrender.

Dr. Sherman shook his head, then knelt down to examine the body.

"Looks like Rudy was shot in the back," he said. "Help me turn him."

Rudolph Folger was a large man. It took both of them, struggling, to get him over on his back.

"No exit wound that I can see," said the doctor. "So, yah, shot in the back, probably as soon as he opened the safe, eh?"

Dr. Sherman glanced at the safe. "I don't see any money. Some files, it looks like. Killer might have taken whatever cash was in there."

"Any idea how long he's been dead?"

"From the amount of rigor mortis, I'd say since late last night."

Henri checked Folger's pockets. "His watch is gone. So's his wallet."

"I'll call Andy Erickson and have him help me move the body down to my office," said Dr. Sherman. "I'm leaving tomorrow for Ishpeming, but I'll do the autopsy today before I go."

"When will you be back?"

"I'm attending a conference, but I should return by noon on Thursday. You can reach me at the Nelson House there, if you need to."

"The outer office door doesn't look as though it was jimmied open," said Myrtle, coming back into the room. "I'm betting whoever did this, Mr. Folger let them in."

"Come on," said Henri. "We're finished here. Let's go."

"Where?" asked Myrtle.

"First of all, to talk to the girl downstairs who found the body, then I'm going out to the Folger home to break the news to Mrs. Folger. Doc, will you make sure this place is locked up before you leave?"

"I'll go with you to the Folger's," said Myrtle.

"I don't think so," said Henri.

"Why not?"

"It's police business. You shouldn't be involved. You shouldn't have even been here."

"Mrs. Folger's going to be upset," said Myrtle. "Are you prepared to deal with that?"

Henri thought for a moment. "All right," he said, finally. "But you let me do the talking."

Myrtle smiled. "Of course."

CHAPTER NINE

As they drove the short distance from the court house to the Folger residence, Myrtle was, at first, unusually quiet.

Finally, she broke the silence. "She did it, you know."

Henri turned to her. "Who did it? Did what?"

"Mrs. Folger. She killed her husband."

"And what makes you think that?"

"She knew he was having an affair."

"An affair?" Henri's head jerked around. "Where in the world did you hear that?"

"With Mrs. Finnegan."

"Agnes Finnegan? J. P.'s wife?"

"Yep, that's the one," said Myrtle.

"And how do you know that?"

"Oh, come on, Henri, for the county constable, you sure don't get around much. It's all over town. Been going on for over a year now."

Henri sighed and shook his head. "I don't believe it."

"Believe it or not, it's true."

"Even if it is, what makes you think J.P. didn't do it?"

Myrtle turned to Henri. "You're right. It could have been him. Or maybe Mr. Folger was breaking it off with Mrs. Finnegan and she didn't want to let him go. She could have killed him, too."

"I don't know," said Henri. "It looks to me like robbery was the motive. That wouldn't seem to implicate either of the Finnegans *or* Mrs. Folger."

"That could be a cover, to throw us off the trail."

Henri looked at Myrtle. "Us?"

"You know you're going to need my help sorting this out."

Henri sighed. "So now we have three suspects."

"At least," said Myrtle, settling back into her seat.

*****

The Folger home was a two-and-a-half-story Victorian style, built by Folger in 1889, four years after he and Margaret moved to Booker Falls. By then he was one of the most sought after attorneys in town.

Constructed of red brick, the building was an exact replica of the house Folger had lived in in the old part of Louisville while a law student at the university. This home was located on the south side of Booker Falls, next door to George's residence.

Henri wasn't enthused about having Myrtle accompany him, and normally wouldn't have allowed it. But he had never before had to inform someone of another's death, a detail he wasn't keen to share with Myrtle.

"So the Folgers live next door to George," said Myrtle, as she and Henri walked from the car to the house.

Henri looked at her. "How do you know that?"

"I was here once—at George's, not the Folgers."

"Oh?"

"For dinner. It was an Irish feast, on St. Patrick's Day, prepared by Mrs. Delahanty."

"I didn't know you and George were seeing one another," said Henri, making no attempt at hiding the displeasure in his voice. But of course, he was well aware of it.

"That's because I don't clear my social calendar with you, Mr. de la Cruz."

By now they'd reached the front door.

The sound of the knocker on the wooden door brought the Folger's housekeeper, Jessica Parker, a young, black woman, to answer it.

"Constable," said Jessica.

"Miss Parker," said Henri.

Myrtle wondered if she didn't detect a hint of a spark between the two of them. Like Jessica, Henri was colored, a mulatto. And although Myrtle and Henri had dated—had even shared several kisses—she would have been surprised if he had not seen other women.

Jessica was certainly attractive enough to warrant any man's attention.

"Miss Parker," Henri continued, "is Mrs. Folger in?"

"No, sir, I'm sorry she is not. She drove over to Houghton this past Saturday—took Mrs. Pennyworth to catch the train to go see her mama. Then she was going to go on up to Mohawk and spend a few nights there with her aunt. But I believe she is planning on returning yet today."

"I see," said Henri. "When she does, would you please ask her to call me? I'm not sure if I'll be at my office or at Mrs. Darling's, but she could try both places."

"Yes, sir, I'll be sure to."

Jessica turned to Myrtle. "I like your coat, Miss. . .?"

"Myrtle," said Myrtle, "Myrtle Tully. It's skunk."

Myrtle was more than proud of her coat, unusual as it was, which she had purchased at Vertin's Department Store in Red Jacket on her first trip there with Daisy. "It's skunk—beautiful, isn't it?"

She ran one hand down the lapel and extended the other out to Jessica.

For a moment the housekeeper wasn't sure what to do. Then she took Myrtle's hand, but held it for only a second.

"You're the Miss Tully who helped put that Mr. Pfrommer in prison."

Myrtle beamed. "All I did was help Henri, here."

"I will ask Mrs. Folger to call you," said Jessica, turning to Henri.

As they walked back to the car, Henri said, "I guess we can scratch Mrs. Folger off the list of suspects."

"Perhaps," said Myrtle. "If she really was in Mohawk. Miss Parker is a beautiful woman."

"I suppose," answered Henri, without slowing his pace. "I really hadn't noticed."

*****

"I can't believe there was an honest to God murder upstairs, right over my store."

Myrtle had returned to the book store after Henri dropped her off back downtown so she could retrieve her automobile. He had walked over to J. P. Finnegan's Fancy Groceries and Fresh Meats store to question Mr. and Mrs. Finnegan. Myrtle begged him to allow her to go along, but this time he had adamantly refused.

Paige Turner, the bookstore's owner, had met Myrtle at the door.

"Believe it," said Myrtle. "Mr. Folger was shot dead sometime during the night."

"How awful," said Paige. "Do we know yet who did it?"

"Not yet. Henri thinks it might have been a robbery. He's going to call the state police over in Marquette to send someone to check for fingerprints."

"Can they do that?"

"Oh, sure, it's done all the time."

"Poor Mrs. Folger," said Paige. "I imagine she's devastated."

"She's out of town—won't be back until later today."

"What a terrible thing to come home to."

*****

Myrtle found Daisy waiting for her on the front porch when she arrived at the boarding house.

"You were there?" asked Daisy. "At the crime scene?"

Myrtle explained how she happened to be at the book store when the body was discovered, and how she rushed up to Folger's office, then accompanied Henri when he'd gone to the Folger's residence.

"Describe it to me," said Daisy.

"What?"

"Tell me what the crime scene looked like. I'll write an article for the paper."

Myrtle hesitated. "I don't know . . ."

"Oh, come on, what harm can it do?"

Myrtle shrugged. "Well, okay, I guess."

Twenty minutes later, Myrtle said, "And that's it. That's all I can tell you."

"Do you think Mrs. Folger did it?" asked Daisy. "'Cause, you know, she must have known about Mr. Folger and Mrs. Finnegan."

"Supposedly she was out of town," said Myrtle. "She's not scheduled to get back until later today."

"You don't sound convinced."

"No," said Myrtle, "I'm not."

*****

Henri had just returned to his office when the phone rang.

"Constable de la Cruz," came the voice on the other end, "this is Mrs. Folger. I just arrived back home from my trip. Jessica told me what happened. She heard it from Mrs. Dinsmore's girl."

Henri thought it sounded as though she'd been crying.

"I know you want to talk with me," Mrs. Folger continued. "Would you mind terribly if we put it off until tomorrow morning? I don't think I'm up for it right now."

"Yah, sure, that's fine," said Henri. "Around nine?"

"Ten would be better," said Mrs. Folger.

CHAPTER TEN

Sean Finnegan turned the key in the lock of the door to his room at Northern State Normal School in Marquette, where he was in his final year.

He entered the room, set his suitcase on the bed, and collapsed into the one chair the room held. His attention was focused on the piece of luggage in front of him.

Less than twenty-four hours earlier he had received a frantic telephone call from his mother, who said she was about to do something drastic.

"What, Momma? What are you talking about?" he'd asked her. "What drastic thing?"

"I can't talk about it, Sean," his mother said, her sobbing audible even over the phone.

"Have you talked to Poppa? Does he know what you're thinking of doing?"

"I can't talk to him anymore. I hardly see him anymore."

"What do you mean?"

"He's moved into da room above da store. And he told me he don't want me to come in to da store no more to help out."

"I'm coming home," said Sean. "Promise me you won't do anything until I get there."

After a slight pause, Agnes said, "I can't promise dat. If I do it, I don't want you here. Don't come."

"Momma, I'm—"

The silence on the other end told Sean his mother had hung up.

He tried to call her back but got not answer.

Using a friend's borrowed car, it had taken him over two hours to make the seventy-five mile trip from Marquette to Booker Falls. He didn't like to drive when it was dark, but he knew he had to go.

It was after ten thirty when he arrived home. The house was dark.

Entering through the door to the kitchen, he was immediately set upon by Boo, a golden retriever who smothered him with kisses.

"Down, Boo," said Sean.

Leaving his suitcase in his room, he went upstairs to his parents' bedroom, careful to avoid the fourth step, the one that creaked and his father had always said he would fix but never did. He pushed open the door and saw his mother in the bed, curled up in a fetal position. Tiptoeing over, he bent down and listened for her breathing.

It was slow and rhythmic. She was asleep.

Breathing a sigh of relief, Sean sneaked back out of the room, headed downstairs, and made his way to the parlor. Opening a drawer in the sideboard, he took out the gun his father kept there.

*****

The next morning when Sean went into the kitchen he found his mother humming.

"Good morning, dear," she said. "I was surprised when I saw you were here. Did you sleep well?"

Sean was confused. Yesterday his mother sounded upset, distraught, as if something bad were about to happen. Today she seemed . . . serene, happy even. "Momma, are you all right?" he asked.

Agnes poured a cup of coffee and handed it to him.

"I am very good, tank you." She poured herself a cup. "Mrs. Bunberry just left."

"Mrs. Bunberry from next door?"

"Yah. She had some news. Mr. Folger was shot and killed last night."

Sean had found out months ago from a childhood friend who now lived next door to the Folgers what was going on between his mother and Mr. Folger. He was surprised at how calmly his mother was taking the news of her lover's death.

"You're sure you're all right?"

Agnes took his hand. "I am fine," she said. "I hated dat bastard."

Sean nodded. "I hated him, too."

His mother wanted him to stay longer, but he told her he couldn't. Now that he knew she was okay, he had to get back to school. He had a big test on Tuesday.

He'd packed his suitcase, told his mother good-bye, that he'd be home for Christmas, then pulled away in the 1915 Model T he'd borrowed to get there.

Other than his mother, Sean doubted anyone else knew he'd been in town.

*****

He stood, unlatched the suitcase and removed the gun which he had brought back with him. He opened the bottom drawer of his dresser and placed the piece under a pile of underwear.

Then he unpacked the rest of his clothes.

*****

Agnes Finnegan wasn't surprised when Constable de la Cruz knocked on her door that afternoon. She knew all too well it was common knowledge around town about her and Rudy.

When he asked her about the last time she'd seen Folger, she said it had been more than a week. She had no intention of letting him know they had been together last night, in his office, where his dead body turned up this morning.

She had made up her mind the affair had to end, one way or another. Yesterday, in a panic about what she was thinking of doing, she had called Sean at school. He'd told her he was coming home, but she had hung up on him.

When Rudy called later and asked her to meet him at his office, she knew what she had to do.

And now, she was happy she'd gone through with it.

*****

The shooting was the topic of discussion that evening at the dinner table at Mrs. Darling's.

"Henri," said Pierre, "do you have any suspects yet?"

"According to Miss Tully here, we have three. Except one, at least, seems to have a good alibi."

"Really?" said Pierre. "Can you say who they are?"

"I'd rather not right now. It's a little too early to name anyone until we have more information."

"How did Mrs. Folger take the news?" asked Daisy.

"I'll speak with her in the morning. She arrived back in town earlier today, and when I talked to her on the phone she was too upset to see me. She'd already heard what happened."

"Right. Gives her more time," said Myrtle.

"More time for what?" asked Pierre.

"To come up with an alibi," answered Myrtle.

"She was out of town for the weekend," said Henri. "She already has an alibi."

"We've heard that one before," said Myrtle.

"What do you mean?" asked Pierre.

"We had a trial here in town this past summer where Paul Momet was found guilty of killing his girlfriend almost thirty years ago, after his alibi that he was out of town, fishing at Lake Kennekuk was debunked."

"But he was later exonerated when the real killer was found out," said Henri.

"That's not the point," said Myrtle. "An alibi's only as good as it can be proven to be."

"So do you think she did it?" asked Daisy. "Mrs. Folger?"

"I've told Henri what I think," answered Myrtle. "It's up to him now."

"If only it was," muttered Henri, knowing Myrtle's penchant for getting involved.

*****

Following dinner, Daisy excused herself to retire to her bedroom. Pierre decided to take a walk. Henri followed Myrtle out onto the front porch.

"Do you have a moment?" he asked.

Oh, oh, thought Myrtle, *I'm going to get a bawling out for something. Getting into Mr. Folger's office? Sharing all that information with Daisy?*

"The, uh, the Lutheran Women's Guild at St. James' is having its annual ice cream social tomorrow night," said Henri. "I was wondering if you would care to accompany me . . . after you get off work, that is."

That wasn't what Myrtle had expected.

It had been several months since they'd gone out together, when Henri took her to Houghton to eat at Marinucci's Italian restaurant, the night she'd kissed him in the parlor.

"Don't you have a murder to investigate?" asked Myrtle.

"I can't work twenty-four hours a day," said Henri, smiling.

"I remember the social from last year," said Myrtle. She didn't tell Henri that George had invited her to it her second day in town and she had turned him down. "I enjoyed it immensely. Yes, I would be delighted to go with you."

Henri grinned. "Well, okay, then."

*****

J. P. Finnegan sat at the table in the small room above his store that overlooked Main Street. A partially filled gallon jug of beer he had purchased across the street from Joker Mulhearn sat in front of him. J. P. was on his fourth glass.

The table, along with two kitchen chairs, a cot, a hot plate and a bucket for his personal needs were the room's sole furnishings.

He carried his water from the shop downstairs, and was able to take sponge baths in the large tub in the back room.

This had been his home for the last two weeks. He'd known much longer than that about the affair between his wife and Rudy Folger.

He was forty-one-years-old when he met Agnes. She was sixteen and had come to his store looking for a job. She'd dropped out of school because her father had been killed in a lumber accident, and their family of seven needed someone other than her mother bringing in a salary.

Nine months after she'd begun working there, they were married. Three years later Sean was born.

They'd been happy together for over twenty years. Then, eighteen months ago, it became clear J. P. was no longer able to perform his husbandly duties in the bedroom, a situation that did not sit well with Agnes. Within six months, she became involved in the affair with Rudolph Folger, twenty-nine years her senior and four years older than her husband. It didn't take long for the word to get around town and back to J.P.

At first, he tried to justify the state of affairs by rationalizing that since he couldn't provide for his wife's needs, she had every right to look elsewhere. The situation became unbearable though, when he discovered Sean, who was away from home at school, had found out about the affair.

J. P. insisted Agnes end it; she had refused. Said she loved Rudy, and she hoped he would leave his wife and marry her.

That's when he moved out of the house into the vacant room above the store, and prohibited Agnes from coming to work.

But he wasn't content to let the matter rest there. He had given much thought to what his next move should be, hence the meeting with Mickey.

Henri had been by earlier that day, asking questions about Folger.

J. P. hadn't been completely truthful with him. Though, to be fair, he hadn't exactly lied—he just hadn't told the constable everything about the night before—the night Folger was killed.

He'd been standing at the window, looking out onto the nearly deserted street below when, a block further up he'd seen his wife and Rudy Folger enter the building that held the latter's office. He'd hesitated for a minute, then turned and went downstairs to the store, where the gun he kept in case of a robbery sat on the shelf under the counter.

No, he hadn't told the constable any of that. There was really no reason to.

CHAPTER ELEVEN

Myrtle thought of calling Mr. Mitchell, the head librarian, to tell him she was too sick to come in, in order to accompany Henri to his meeting with Mrs. Folger.

Henri put a quick stop to that idea.

"I'll tell him you weren't sick—that you wanted to come with me. You know Frank—that would not make him happy."

Myrtle gave Henri a dirty look.

"All right," she said, resignedly. "But you're going to need my help somewhere along the way and—"

"—and I know you'll be happy to provide it," snapped Henri.

Myrtle made a sour face. "You're right. I will. But will you at least let me know what Mrs. Folger has to say? If you think her alibi is any good?"

"Maybe," said Henri.

And he was out the door before Myrtle could say anything else.

*****

Jessica met Henri at the door. "Good morning, Henri."

"Good morning, Jessica. I believe Mrs. Folger is expecting me."

Jessica nodded and ushered Henri into the house, then into the parlor, where Margaret, wearing a belted, canary yellow pullover frock, sat waiting, along with Mickey.

So much for wearing black for mourning, thought Henri.

"Mrs. Folger, I'm very sorry about your husband's death. Trust me, we will find whoever killed Mr. Folger."

"I have every confidence you will," said Margaret. "Please, have a seat. Do you have any suspects?"

"Not yet," answered Henri settling into an overstuffed chair. He wasn't about to tell her Myrtle considered her the prime suspect, nor the possibility that either Agnes Finnegan or her husband might also be considered. At the same time, he thought, *that situation, as distasteful as it might be, was where this interview should start.*

He cleared his throat and put his finger under his uniform collar in an unsuccessful attempt to loosen it.

"Mrs. Folger, there seems to be a rumor . . . that is, I've been told—"

"Rumor, hell," said Mickey. "It's true—Rudy was a' foolin' 'round with old lady Finnegan."

"Shut up, Mickey!" screamed Margaret, glaring at her brother. "Just shut up!"

She turned back to Henri. "Yah, it's true. Rudy was involved with that woman, though I can't imagine why. The few times I was around her she smelled like salami."

"She owns a meat market," said Mickey, laughing.

Margaret glared at him again.

He leaned back, his lips clenched.

"You were aware of the affair?" said Henri, speaking to Margaret.

"Yah, I was. That's why I was going to divorce the bastard."

Henri sat back, surprised not only at this bit of information but at Margaret's use of language.

"That's why I went to see my aunt over the weekend," Margaret continued, "to work things out. But it looks like someone took care of the situation for me."

"You were at your aunt's the whole weekend, and returned home yesterday?" asked Henri.

"I planned to stay both nights," said Margaret. "However, I changed my mind and decided to return home on Sunday. But then I stopped in Red Jacket to see a friend, the wife of a man Rudy worked with there. I changed my mind again and stayed the night at the Michigan House."

"Sunday night," said Henri. "The night Mr. Folger was killed."

"Yah, Sunday night, that's right." Margaret's tone had a sharpness to it.

"I see," said Henri. "And *then* you returned home yesterday."

"That is correct," said Margaret.

"And both your aunt and the Michigan House could verify that if need be?"

Margaret narrowed her eyes and looked at Henri. "Of course."

"Mickey," said Henri, "I have to ask—where were you Sunday night?"

Mickey glowered at Henri.

"Why? You tink I killed Rudy?"

"It's just a routine question. I'm not making any judgments—yet."

"Answer him, Mickey," said Margaret.

Mickey sighed. "I was here—out in da carriage house, where I'm staying—all night—never left."

"Did Miss Parker see you?" asked Henri.

Mickey looked even more sullen. "Din't nobody see me. Like I said, I was in my room—drinking, if you must know."

Henri looked back at Margaret. "Someone broke into my office over the weekend and stole your gun from my desk."

Margaret's eyes turned to Mickey. Henri followed her gaze.

"Hey, I din't steal no gun!" exclaimed Mickey. "I ain't even been near da court house since you—"

"Shut up, Mickey," said Margaret, disgustedly.

"Well, I din't steal no gun and I din't kill Rudy and I'm tru talking," said Mickey as he jumped up and rushed from the room.

"Was Rudy shot?" asked Margaret when Mickey was gone. "Is that how he died?"

Henri wondered if she was going to ask the question. He'd already decided not to volunteer the information.

"Yah," he said. "He was shot to death."

"Was it Rudy's gun that was used to kill him?"

"There's no way to know," said Henri.

"I apologize for my brother. But I'm sure he wouldn't have killed Rudy, even as much as he disliked him."

"And the gun?" said Henri.

"That I'm not so sure about."

CHAPTER TWELVE

Myrtle had asked Frank if she could leave work an hour early.

"Henri has asked me to the ice cream social at the Lutheran Church this evening," she said, "and it begins at five o'clock."

While he wasn't enthusiastic about the prospect of closing the library by himself, Frank had agreed to her request.

Promptly at five-thirty, Myrtle rushed home, changed clothes and had just gotten downstairs when Henri pulled up out in front.

"What did you find out from Mrs. Folger when you spoke with her?" Myrtle asked as she climbed into the car.

Henri told her what transpired at the meeting, including the fact Mickey was there, and that he couldn't provide a good alibi.

"And Mrs. Folger's alibi?" asked Myrtle.

"She claims she was at her aunt's home in Mohawk Saturday night, just as Jessica said. But then she went to Red Jacket on Sunday and spent the night there at the Michigan House."

"And you believe her?"

"Unless it can be proven otherwise."

"Henri, I was at the social last year, but I was so new in town I barely knew what was going on. St. James is a Protestant church, isn't it?"

"Finnish Lutheran."

"And that's a lot different from Catholics."

"Yah, a lot."

"Is there anything I should know before we get there?"

Henri turned to her. "Don't whistle."

Myrtle looked confused. "Don't whistle? Why would I?"

"I don't know that you would—but don't."

"All right, why should I not whistle?"

"These Finns are very conservative. For one thing, they don't play cards."

"My goodness, why not? Playing cards is quite enjoyable. And what does that have to do with whistling?"

"I guess they see playing cards as a form of sin, if they might have too much fun," said Henri.

"But what about the whistling?"

"Last spring, Mrs. Darling and I walked down to the park across from St. James. We had Penrod with us. When Mrs. Darling let him off his leash, he dashed across the street into the church yard and I chased after him. I whistled for him to come back. Just then the minister came out—"

"Pastor Albrecht."

"Yah, I guess that's his name; anyway, he came out and called me over and asked me not to whistle around the church building. He was very nice about it. He explained that whistling was the same as calling for the devil."

Myrtle laughed, but the look on Henri's face told her he wasn't kidding. "Wait," she said. "He was serious?"

"Quite serious. I apologized, told him I didn't know that and I would refrain from whistling. He thanked me and went back inside and shortly after that I came upon Penrod and put his leash back on him."

"Well, thank you for sharing that bit of information with me," said Myrtle. "And should I suddenly be overcome tonight with an urge to whistle, I shall restrain myself."

"By the way," said Henri, "you look very nice this evening."

Myrtle beamed. When Henri asked her the night before to go to the social and she'd said yes, she realized she didn't have anything to wear, other than the clothes she wore to the library and her normal outfits: pants, shirts, and so on.

She certainly wasn't about to wear the same dress she'd worn to this event last year.

She had taken her half hour lunch time to race downtown to the de Première Qualité Women's Wear shop where Isabell Dougherty, the store owner, convinced her to go with a patterned red dress that featured a dropped back, open sleeves, notched at the bottom, with fringe.

Since the weather had not yet turned too cold, a cream-colored, oversized shawl made of light velvet and decorated with intricate embroidery should be sufficient to ward off the evening chill, Isabell added.

Myrtle felt very pleased Henri had noticed.

A matronly type of woman who, Myrtle guessed, had consumed more than her share of ice cream in the past, greeted them at the side door of the church basement, where the social was being held.

"Good evening, Constable," she said. "And you, miss, you look familiar. Have we met?"

"I'm not sure," said Myrtle. "I was here last year at the social."

"Den dat's it," said the woman. "I never forget a face, eh? I am Mrs. Kangas. But you can call me Sofia."

"And I'm Myrtle."

"Well, okay, den, come in, come in. You can pay your turty cents over at da table dere, and den enjoy yourselves."

"Oh, there's Daisy," said Myrtle, spotting her housemate across the room.

"You go say hi," said Henri. "I'll pay our money."

"Oh, my," said Daisy, when Myrtle reached her. "Don't you look fabulous! Listen, Myrtle, you have to try this—it's scrumptious!"

Myrtle looked at the bowl Daisy held in her hand. It was filled with what appeared to be dark chocolate ice cream—*really* dark.

"Is that chocolate?" asked Myrtle.

"No, it's called salmiakki."

"Sal—what?"

"Salmiakki."

"If it's not chocolate, what is it?" asked Myrtle.

Daisy grinned. "Salty black licorice."

"You're kidding!"

"Nope. And it's delicious. Here, take a bite." Daisy held up a spoonful and slipped it into Myrtle's waiting mouth.

"Oh, wow, you're right!" said Myrtle. "That *is* delicious!"

"I was told it's not actually Finnish," said Daisy. "It's Swedish. But I guess the Finns love it enough they're willing to overlook where it comes from."

Myrtle had almost reached the table Daisy directed her to for the ice cream when she heard someone call her name.

"Myrtle!"

She turned and saw Paige Turner coming towards her.

"Paige! How are you?"

"I'm so glad you're here," said Paige. "Tervetuloa kirkostani."

Myrtle looked confused.

"Welcome to my church," said Paige.

"Oh, okay," said Myrtle. "So, you're a Lutheran?"

"I know," said Paige. "Hard to believe, isn't it? But not everybody in town is Catholic."

"No, I'm sure not."

"Oh," said Paige, "have you met our pastor?"

Myrtle saw Reverend Albrecht coming towards them. She remembered him from what she considered had been an eloquent meal grace he gave at the Fourth of July picnic.

"Pastor," said Paige, taking Reverend Albrecht by the elbow, "this is a good friend of mine, Myrtle Tully. Myrtle is the assistant librarian at the college."

Young, tall, blond with bright blue eyes, Robert Albrecht could pass for either German or Finnish. Regardless of which nationality might claim him, his winsome smile was what most impressed Myrtle.

"Yah, Miss Tully, I have heard of you."

"Oh, my," said Myrtle.

"It is all good," said Albrecht. "You are a hero of sorts here in Booker Falls."

"I am?"

"Yah, it is told you brought the murderer of that young girl to justice."

Myrtle blushed. "I was fortunate to come across information that led to his arrest."

"Oh, and this is my wife, Saija," said Albrecht, as a woman as beautiful as her husband was handsome, joined them. "Saija, Miss Myrtle Tully."

"Miss Tully," said Saija, "it is an honor."

"Myrtle, please," said Myrtle, becoming more embarrassed by the minute.

"Have you been here before?" asked Reverend Albrecht.

"Last year—here at the social. I'd only been in town two days."

"But not upstairs in the sanctuary?" said Saija.

"No. Not upstairs."

"Robert, why don't you show Miss Tully the sanctuary?" said Saija. "I need to steal Paige away for a minute."

"You have a beautiful wife," said Myrtle, as she and Reverend Albrecht climbed the stairs.

"Thank you," said Albrecht. "God has certainly blessed me."

"I'm not used to seeing priests who are married."

"No, I don't suppose so. But I am not technically a priest, although I am a minister. And, believe me, your priests don't know what they're missing."

They both laughed.

When they stepped into the sanctuary, Myrtle was as impressed by its starkness as she had been by the grandeur of St. Barbara's.

A lone stained glass window set at the front of the church above the altar, of a man draped in a gold cape, hands folded around a staff, and looking heavenward, broke the simplicity of the room.

In front of the window hung an empty cross crafted of downy birch which Myrtle learned later had been brought to the Upper Peninsula from Finland.

The walls, painted white, as was the ceiling, were devoid of any ornamentation: no statuary, pictures, or anything else.

"Is the window of Saint James?" asked Myrtle.

"Yah, it is. It's a reproduction of a seventeenth century painting done by Guido Reni: *Saint James the Greater*."

"It's beautiful," said Myrtle. "And the cross—it's empty."

"Different from your Catholic churches," said Albrecht, "which reflects a difference in theology between our two faiths. In the Catholic Church, great emphasis is put on the atonement of Christ, whereas in our church, and most Protestant churches, I think, the emphasis is on resurrection. Hence the difference between the crucifix and the empty cross."

"I never thought of it that way."

"We should rejoin the others downstairs," said Albrecht.

Moments later, Myrtle and Reverend Albrecht joined Henri, Daisy and Saija at a table in a corner of the room where they sat gobbling down different flavors of ice cream with abandon.

"Reverend Albrecht," said Daisy, between bites. "Albrecht sure doesn't sound Finnish to me."

"No, it's not. It's German."

"That's what I thought," said Daisy. "So how did you come to be the pastor of a Finnish congregation?"

"I've always been a Lutheran—a German Lutheran. I grew up in Hancock. When it came time for me to attend college, I just naturally went to Suomi. That's where I met Saija. When I graduated I knew I wanted to be a pastor, so I continued on at the seminary there. After I was ordained, I took the call here at St. James. That was five years ago."

"And your Finnish parishioners have no problem having a German minister?" asked Henri.

"They have been very gracious in accepting me."

"Tell them about Mrs. Järvinen," said Saija.

Albrecht chuckled. "Yah, that is a good story. Shortly after I arrived here, I paid a visit to Mrs. Järvinen. She was in her eighties and shut in. She was a founding member of the church back in 1900.

"We sat for a while and drank coffee—"

"We Finns are voracious coffee drinkers," said Saija.

"Yes, you are," said Albrecht. "Anyway, we were talking and Mrs. Järvinen cocked her head and said, 'Albrecht—Albrecht. That doesn't sound Finnish.' 'No,' I said, 'it's German.' 'I see,' said Mrs. Järvinen. Then, after a few minutes, she said, 'But your mother was Finnish?' 'No,' I answered, 'my mother is also German.' Another few minutes of conversation passed and then Mrs. Järvinen said, 'So you don't have a single drop of Finnish blood in you?' I laughed to myself, shook my head, and said, 'no, not a drop.' The look of concern on her face was very obvious as she leaned forward, looked me right in the eye, shook her head and said, 'Oh, I'm so sorry.'"

The table erupted in such laughter, others in the room turned to look.

"We need to be careful," said Saija, wiping tears from her eyes. "They might think we're over here playing cards, we're having so much fun."

*****

"I really enjoyed myself tonight," said Myrtle.

She and Henri were walking up the path from the road to the boarding house.

"I like Reverend Albrecht and his wife," Myrtle continued.

"They seem to be down to earth people," said Henri.

When they reached the front door, Myrtle started to turn the handle.

"Not yet," said Henri.

Myrtle turned to him, wondering why they weren't going in.

"It's too crowded in there for me to do this," said Henri, taking Myrtle in his arms and kissing her.

"That was very forward of you," said Myrtle, when he let her go.

"Well, it's not like we haven't done it before." He backed away. "But if you don't like it, I won't do it again."

"I didn't say I didn't like it," replied Myrtle, bringing Henri's face close to her and kissing him. "Actually, I like it quite a lot."

Henri took her in his arms and kissed her again—a long kiss this time.

"Perhaps we *should* go in," he said, when he let her go.

"No," said Myrtle, smiling. "I think perhaps we should go back to the car."

CHAPTER THIRTEEN

Myrtle's arrival in Booker Falls in September of 1919 had caused a stir, primarily because the sight of an automobile in town was a rare event, and partly because of the near accident involving Henri, his horse and his carriage.

The commotion this day also involved a car; a brand new—normally glistening, now dust encrusted—olive-green, 1920 Cadillac Phaeton. But as attention-getting as the automobile was, the driver behind the wheel was even more of an attraction.

Six feet four and weighing almost three hundred pounds, dressed in a dark, pinstripe suit and sporting a bowler hat, the man cut an imposing figure, made more so by the fact he was Chinese. A moustache drooped down a good six inches on either side of his mouth, accompanied by a goatee that extended twelve inches from his chin.

As the car passed through town, foot traffic on the sidewalks came to a standstill. Most residents of Booker Falls had never seen anyone of Oriental descent.

People gathered in knots, staring, speaking in hushed tones.

"Is he Chinese?" "He looks Chinese." "I ain't never seen a Chinaman before." "Man, he's a big 'un, ain't he?" "What's he doing here?"

Andy Erickson paused in his job of cleaning up horse droppings and watched as the man parked his car in front of the post office, got out, and went in.

Abandoning his wheeled barrel in the middle of the street, Andy rushed to Henri's office.

"Constable," he cried out, bursting through the door, "you gotta come and see dis!"

Henri looked up. "Wha . . .?"

"Come on, quick!" yelled Andy, running back outside.

Henri got up, slipped on his jacket and joined Andy on the sidewalk. He was surprised at the number of people standing around, talking, all facing in the direction of the post office.

"What is it?" asked Henri.

"Look!" said Andy, shaking with excitement and pointing down the street towards the Phaeton.

"A car? Whose is it?" asked Henri.

"Some Chinaman," said Andy.

Henri looked at Andy. "Some . . . what?"

"A Chinaman. A real live Chinaman. Right here in Booker Falls! He went in da post office."

Just then the newcomer exited the post office, turned right, walked across the street to the Walther Building and went in.

Henri took off down the street and minutes later stood across the counter from Hilda Littlefield, the postmistress.

Her eyes were big, and she looked as though she were in shock.

"Was some man just in here?" asked Henri.

"Yah, he was," said Hilda. "Near scared me to death when he walked in, I tell ya. I felt da hair on da back of me neck stand up."

"What did he want?"

"Wanted to know where he could get a room."

"A room?"

"Yah, a room. So I sent him 'cross the street to Walther's." Hilda nodded her head in the direction the

Chinaman had taken. "They rent out rooms on the top two floors, ya know."

"Is that all he wanted?" asked Henri. "A room?"

Hilda shook her head. "Nah. He also wanted to know where da Steinmyer home was."

*****

By the time Henri returned to the street, a number of people were gathered around the Phaeton. It was the most elegant conveyance they'd ever seen.

Sporting a wooden steering wheel, black leather seats and interior, the car could easily accommodate four people. A black soft top kept out the sun and most of the rain. Tilting headlights plus a spotlight mounted on one of the wind wings provided plenty of light to be able to traverse back country roads. A spare tire was mounted on the rear for that inevitable moment when one of the four regular tires blew out.

"All right, all right," said Henri, shooing everybody away. "What do you think's going to happen if this fellow comes out and finds all of you pawing over it?"

No sooner were the words out of Henri's mouth, than the car's driver emerged from the Walther Building and headed toward his vehicle.

Everyone scattered, except Henri.

"Welcome to Booker Falls," said Henri, extending his hand as the man approached.

The man stopped, bowed, then came forward and took Henri's hand.

"Thank you," he said in excellent English, but with a distinct accent.

"I'm Henri de la Cruz, the county constable," said Henri. "Are you in town on business or pleasure?"

"I am, what you say, sight-seeing?" answered the man.

"Sight-seeing, huh? We don't get many tourists here. What kind of sights are you looking to see?"

The man shrugged. "I do not know yet."

"I see," said Henri. "I'm sorry—I didn't get your name."

"My name is Yung Li."

"You're Chinese," said Henri.

Yung Li smiled. "Yes," he said, nodding, "Chinese."

"And you're staying at the Walther," said Henri, nodding toward the building from which Yung Li had come."

"The Walther, yes."

"How long will you be in town?"

Yung Li's eyebrows arched and his body assumed a slight defensive attitude. "I do not know," he said.

Henri nodded. "Well, okay, then. I'll see you around."

"Yes," said Yung Li.

They shook hands again, Yung Li bowed, and Henri turned and headed back up the street. When he reached his office, he found half a dozen men inside, waiting for him, including George and Andy.

"What's going on?" asked George. "Who is that fellow and what's he doing here in Booker Falls?"

Henri told the men what Yung Li had told him. But not what Hilda had said about the man asking about the Steinmyers.

"Sight-seeing, huh?" said Alton Woodruff, who was one of the men who had congregated in the office. "I bet he's up to no good."

There was a general murmur of agreement.

"You best keep an eye on him, constable," said Andy.

"I will," said Henri. "Now, don't you men have something better to do than hang around here? I know you do, Andy, 'cause I saw that plow horse of Izzy Labeuf relieve himself out in front of the courthouse as I came in."

*****

Henri parked his car in the driveway of the Steinmyer home and walked to the front door. Taking the Judaica brass and copper hamsa door knocker in his hand, he rapped several times.

Almost immediately, Miss Wasserman appeared.

"Constable de la Cruz?" she said.

"Miss Wasserman, good day," said Henri, removing his cap. "Would Mr. Steinmyer—Nathan—be around?"

"Why, yah, I believe he's in da study. Please, come in, come in."

"Mr. Steinmyer," said Miss Wasserman, peeking around the door of the study, "Constable de la Cruz is here to see you."

Nathan laid down the copy of *The Mining Gazette* he'd been reading and stood. "Show him in, please, Miss Wasserman."

"Mr. Steinmyer," said Henri, entering the room.

"Nathan, please," said Nathan, extending his hand. "Please, have a seat. Miss Wasserman, would you be so kind as to bring us some tea?

"What brings you around, Constable?" asked Nathan, when the two of them were seated.

"It's kind of funny—odd, maybe. But a fellow just arrived in town asking at the post office where your home was located."

Nathan stiffened. "Oh? Is that so?"

"Yah," said Henri. "And the thing what's odd is, he's a Chinaman."

Nathan stiffened more.

"I asked him what he was doing here," said Henri. "He said he was sight-seeing. But I don't believe he was telling the truth. Said his name's Yung Li. Do you know him?"

By now Nathan's color had turned ashen. He shook his head.

"No, don't believe I do."

His voice was shaky, and higher pitched than usual.

Henri couldn't help but notice the man's uneasiness.

Miss Wasserman appeared with the tea and poured a cup for each of the men.

Nathan picked up his cup, stood and walked over to the sideboard.

"Would you like a little something in yours?" he asked, picking up a decanter.

Henri shook his head. "Little early for me. Besides, I'm still on duty."

Nathan nodded. "I believe I will," he said, as he poured a generous shot into the cup.

"This . . . this Chinaman—what does he look like?" asked Nathan.

"Big," said Henri, sipping his tea. "Well over six feet, maybe six-four, and close to three hundred pounds."

"And what are you going to do about him?" asked Nathan.

Henri looked at Nathan. "Do? What do you mean, *do*?"

"You said you didn't believe him when he said he was here sight-seeing. Why do you think he *is* here?"

"I don't know, unless it has something to do with your family."

"Do you think he means us harm?"

"Would he have any reason to, that you know of?"

Nathan shook his head but didn't answer.

"Well, then, I don't know," said Henri. "But I would advise you to make sure your doors and windows are all locked at night. Maybe even during the day, too, eh? Are there any guns in the house?"

"Several, I believe," said Nathan. "I'll have to check."

"In the meantime, I'll keep an eye on him as best I can. But," added Henri, "unless he breaks the law, there's nothing I can do but watch."

"I understand," said Nathan. "We'll take precautions."

*****

When Henri got back to the boarding house that evening he was set upon by Myrtle, Daisy and Mrs. Darling.

"Okay, spill," said Myrtle. "We heard about what happened in town today. But what else can you tell us?"

"You know all there is to know," said Henri, "which isn't much. Fellow showed up in a fancy car, says he's here to do sight-seeing."

"Sight-seeing?" said Mrs. Darling. "What's to see 'round here?"

"My thoughts exactly," said Henri. "I don't think he's telling the truth. Now, I didn't tell the fellows downtown, but he'd asked Mrs. Littlefield where the Steinmyers lived."

All three women sat back in their chairs.

"Really?" said Daisy. "What did he want with them?"

"That's what I wondered," said Henri. "So I went by their place, talked with Mr. Steinmyer—Nathan. He said he didn't know the man, had no idea why he was interested in his family. But to be truthful, I don't think I believe Nathan any more about that than I do the fellow saying he's here for sight-seeing. He seemed really upset."

"And the man is Chinese, I hear?" said Myrtle.

"Yah, Chinese," said Henri.

"What are you going to do?" asked Myrtle.

"Same thing I told Mr. Steinmyer when he asked me the same question—basically, nothing. Not unless the man does something illegal."

"I know what I'm going to do," said Mrs. Darling. "I'm getting out dat old musket my husband carried in da war."

"Which war was that, Mrs. Darling?" asked Myrtle.

"Why, da one where we beat da South."

"That thing must be over half a century old," said Henri. "Does it still work?"

"I guess we'll find out if we have to," said Mrs. Darling.

CHAPTER FOURTEEN

Just as the *Farmer's Almanac* had predicted, the rain began a little after seven Wednesday morning, and steadily increased as the day progressed. By the time Myrtle left the library and headed home it was coming down harder than ever.

While she'd gotten minimally wet during the drive back to the boarding house, the quick dash from the road to the porch left her drenched.

"You poor dear," said Mrs. Darling, meeting her at the front door. "You get upstairs right now and get out of dose wet tings. I'll have a hot bowl of soup waiting for you in da kitchen when you get back down."

Ten minutes later, Myrtle sat at the kitchen table, downing spoonsful of lentil soup, when Daisy joined her.

"Wet out there, isn't it?" said Daisy.

Myrtle narrowed her eyes and gave Daisy a dirty look as drops of water slowly trickled down her forehead.

"Yah, okay, sorry about that," said Daisy. "Listen, Henri's home—wants to know if you want to go on a trip with us—him and me and Mr. Longet."

"A trip? What sort of trip? Where to?"

"'Round the world with Nellie Bly."

Myrtle's eyes lit up. She dearly loved to play the game of *Round The World With Nellie Bly*! She remembered when she had received it as a gift on her tenth birthday. Her mother had thought it too advanced for her, but her father knew she was ready for it.

"By all means!" said Myrtle. "Get him down here. Mr. Longet, too."

*****

Ever since the death of Angelina Steinmyer twenty-five years before in 1895, the big house at Fourteen Thimbleberry Road had been known locally as La Maison de Douleur: The House of Sorrow. Its more formal name, Steinmyer Manor, had been given to it by Isaiah, who oversaw its construction in 1872.

Seven years earlier, at the age of twenty-three, he had been fortunate enough to return unscathed from the just-ended War of the Rebellion between the North and the South. A year later, he had been sent by his father, Israel Steinmyer, one of the leading citizens of Detroit, and the owner of more than a dozen banks throughout Michigan and Wisconsin, to manage the Booker Falls Community Bank, which the elder Steinmyer had recently purchased, later renamed the Booker Falls Bank and Trust.

Five years after moving to Booker Falls, Isaiah married Annie Brown. By the following year, he had completed Steinmyer Manor. His dream was to fill its eight bedrooms with the children he hoped Annie would give him.

Unfortunately, such was not to be.

On a drizzly, cold morning in December, 1872, after a sixteen-hour labor, Annie gave birth to a son, Nathan. She did not survive the ordeal, breathing her final breath a few hours after the delivery.

Six years later, Isaiah's second wife, Arabella, died during a miscarriage.

In 1891, Isaiah married for the third time, to a twenty-year-old school teacher from Marquette, Angelina Fromme, who, nine months and four days later, bore him his second child, a girl, whom they named Rachel.

But, again, tragedy struck when, three years later, Angelina came down with tuberculosis. Within two months of being diagnosed, she died, the fourth person to die in the house.

Now, Isaiah himself lay near death upstairs, in the same bed that had claimed each of his three wives and an unborn child.

*****

Yung Li stood outside the Steinmyer mansion, seemingly oblivious to the drenching rain that fell on him, relying on the absence of any moonlight to shield his presence from curious eyes. He had walked the two miles from the Walther Building in order not to arouse suspicion by anyone who might have happened to notice his automobile parked on the street.

He'd left San Francisco four days earlier by rail, taking the same route that Nathan had taken, arriving earlier that day in Houghton, where arrangements had been made for him to pick up the Phaeton and continue on to Booker Falls. He had enjoyed the trip, his first outside of California since he'd arrived there from China five years earlier. The diversity of the places and people he'd seen as he crossed the continent had been a revelation to him.

But now it was time to take care of what he had been sent here for by his employer, Mr. Zhāng.

Nathan Steinmyer had left San Francisco owing Mr. Zhāng a considerable amount of money—money lost in the gambling hall Mr. Zhāng owned. And Mr. Zhāng was not one to allow such a debt to go unpaid.

So Yung Li had been sent to collect by whatever means were necessary.

He stood and watched, and waited—waited until the big house on Thimbleberry Road would go dark. Then he would make his move.

He leaned back against the oak tree and removed the bowler hat he'd purchased during the stopover in Chicago, a replacement for the Mandarin hat he had worn for years. He thought, mistakenly, the American hat might make him less obvious.

Taking a pack of Rooster cigarettes from his pocket, he lit one and took a long drag. He thought of his wife and three children back in San Francisco and wondered what they were doing. Having dinner right now, he supposed.

He turned his attention back to the house.

He knew Nathan Steinmyer from the gambling hall; even liked him. But a job was a job.

Yung Li was no stranger to violence. It took both hands to count the number of men he had dispatched. He hoped Nathan would be reasonable; that is—hand over the money he owed.

Yung Li sighed and took another drag. Before the night was over the situation would be resolved one way or another.

*****

Mildred Wasserman had been the housekeeper for the Steinmyer family for almost fifty years. Following Annie's death, Isaiah had hired her to care for his newborn son. She was twenty-three years old and newly arrived from England just the month before.

Six years later it was she who held Arabella's hand as she lay dying.

And, again, it was Mildred who sat at Angelina's deathbed and promised to take care of her three-year-old daughter, Rachel.

For most of those years, she followed the same nightly routine: turn down the beds of each of the Steinmyer clan; place a glass of water on each of their nightstands; close the shades on the windows to keep out the next morning's light; make sure all the windows and doors were locked; and wait patiently until every family member was in bed for the night before preparing to retire herself.

The routine gradually changed as the children grew older. When Nathan was old enough to be out at night, Mildred didn't bother to wait up for him. And Rachel was always in her room no later than ten o'clock.

The last two nights, ever since Mr. Steinmyer returned home from the doctor's office following his apoplectic seizure and heart attack, the routine had, again, become altered.

While a newly-hired woman was around during the day to help with the chores, Mildred had sat up with Isaiah through the night, in case he needed anything. But this day he had insisted he was fine, thank you, and she should sleep in her own room.

Tonight, as she had prepared to lock the front door, she'd hesitated for a moment, listening to, and watching through the glass side panel, the storm raging outside.

We'll be lucky if the basement doesn't flood again, she thought, as she climbed the stairs to her bedroom.

Dressed in a flannel nightgown and nightcap, she had just gotten into bed and pulled the covers up to her chin when she heard the sharp report of what sounded like a gunshot.

Jumping up, she quickly slipped on her robe and, barefoot, dashed out into the hallway where she saw Nathan running towards her from the other end of the passageway, headed for Rachel's room, located next to her own.

"What happened?" she asked.

"That was a gunshot," said Nathan. "It must have come from Rachel's room."

He opened the door, Mildred cowering behind him. As soon as he entered the room, he saw his sister lying on the Serapi carpet, her blood blending into the dark reds and purples.

"Stay there," Nathan said to Mildred. "You don't want to see this."

Ignoring him, Mildred raced into the room. When she reached Rachel's body, she gasped and made the sign of the cross on her chest.

Her mistress had been shot in the head.

"Quick—go make sure father is all right," said Nathan. "I'll notify the constable."

*****

"Yay!" Daisy's expression of joy was an indication that she was well on her way to winning *Round The World With Nellie Bly*.

While she was in Yokohama by her fifty-second day, Myrtle, Henri and Pierre were all mired back in Europe.

"I don't know how you do it," said Myrtle.

"Shrewdness," said Daisy, "and tenaciousness."

"And luck," said Henri.

"Luck is nothing more than opportunity meeting preparedness," said Daisy, puffing out her chest.

They'd been so engrossed in the game they hadn't heard the ringing of the telephone.

"Henri," said Mrs. Darling, coming into the parlor, "dere's a phone call for you."

Henri stood and walked into the hallway. Moments later he returned, looking distressed.

"What is it?" asked Myrtle.

"Rachel Steinmyer—she's been murdered."

"I'll go with you," said Myrtle.

Henri nodded. No sense in trying to dissuade her.

"What about the game?" asked Daisy.

Henri and Myrtle both stared at her. Was she serious?

"You're right," she said, scrunching up her mouth. "It can wait."

CHAPTER FIFTEEN

By the time Henri and Myrtle arrived at the Steinmyer home, the rain had picked up in intensity.

"You should stay here," said Henri. "It's raining too hard for you to get out. Besides, it's a crime scene; you shouldn't even be here. I don't know why I let you come."

Myrtle stared at him. "There is no way I'm staying in this car."

Without waiting for Henri, she opened the door and jumped out—landing in a puddle of mud.

"Darn!" she exclaimed as she headed for the door, feeling her boots melt down into the swampy path that had been just dirt the day before.

Hurriedly, Henri rushed around the car to join her, his boots sinking into the muck just as Myrtle's had.

Miss Wasserman met them at the door and waved them inside. Her eyes were red. She'd been crying.

"Upstairs," she said, leading the way.

As they made their way across the marble floor of the foyer, Myrtle stopped short.

"Oh, no!" she said.

"What is it?" asked Henri.

"Look," said Myrtle, gesturing back towards where they had just walked.

Henri turned and saw two sets of muddy boot prints: his and Myrtle's.

Miss Wasserman stopped to look also. She shook her head. "Never mind. Mr. Nathan did da same ting earlier. I'll take care of dat. Come on, now, he's waiting upstairs. Mr. Fitch is dere, too."

"Who's Mr. Fitch?" asked Myrtle.

"I know who he is," said Henri. "He's a student at Adelaide. He served overseas in the Army Ambulance Service before coming back to go to school. I remember now—Ambrose told me he was going to be filling in for him."

As they ascended the stairs, Henri couldn't get the thought out of his mind: two murders in three days.

The last time Booker Falls had experienced a murder had been almost thirty years ago, when the assistant librarian had been strangled to death. That perpetrator had been brought to justice a few months previously.

And now—*two murders in three days.*

When the three of them reached Rachel's room, Lewis Fitch was already examining the body.

Miss Wasserman excused herself and left.

"Who is this man?" asked Nathan, taking Henri aside. "And where is Dr. Sherman?"

Henri explained that Dr. Sherman was out of town at a conference, and would return sometime the next day. "Fitch is filling in while he's gone," added Henri.

"Does he know what he's doing?" asked Nathan.

Henri shrugged. "I'm sure if *I* don't know what he's supposed to be doing I couldn't tell you if *he* knows what he's doing. But I think it's obvious what the cause of death is. And we know when it happened. I doubt there's much more Ambrose could tell us if he was here instead of Mr. Fitch."

While Fitch continued his examination, Myrtle walked around the room, studying everything.

"I see no signs of a struggle," said Fitch. "And she was shot at close range, so either she knew her assailant, or he might have had a gun pointed at her from the start, and she was too frightened to resist. I'll get some men and we'll take her down to Dr. Sherman's office."

"What about the autopsy?" asked Henri.

"I'm certainly not qualified to perform one," said Fitch. "We should keep the body cool until the doctor returns tomorrow."

"How do you plan to do that?" asked Henri.

Fitch shrugged. "I have no idea."

"Take the body to Finnegan's," said Henri. "He has a large, cold storage room."

Fitch hesitated. "You don't think he'll mind having a dead body in there?"

"I'm not giving him a choice," said Henri. "You tell him I said so."

Henri turned to Nathan. "Is your father all right?"

"Yes. I sent Miss Wasserman to check on him as soon as we found Rachel. She said he was sleeping soundly—didn't hear a thing."

Henri nodded. "Okay, tell me what happened, and then I want to talk with Miss Wasserman."

Henri and Myrtle listened as Nathan recounted how he'd retired for the night with a decanter of brandy and a book when he heard the gunshot and ran to Rachel's room, meeting Miss Wasserman in the hallway.

He hadn't touched the body, he said, but had immediately called the boarding house rather than Henri's office, sure that at that time of night he'd be there.

"Do you know of anyone who would want to harm your sister?" asked Myrtle.

"Half-sister," Nathan corrected her. "We had different mothers."

"Half-sister," said Myrtle. "Anyone who would want to hurt her?"

Nathan shook his head. "As you may know, I've been away for the last ten years. I returned home this past Friday. I didn't know much of what was going on in Rachel's life—except I know she was involved in the hold up at the bank. I'm afraid I can't help you."

"I should check all the windows and doors," said Henri, "to see if any have been broken into."

"I did that while I was waiting for you," said Nathan. "Everything was locked—except for the front door. For some reason it was not locked. But it had also not been broken or jimmied."

"But it wasn't locked?" asked Myrtle.

"No," said Nathan.

"Did you ask Miss Wasserman about it?" asked Myrtle.

"No, I was afraid it might upset her to think a moment of carelessness on her part might have contributed to Rachel's death."

"Mr. Steinmyer," said Myrtle, "I found this near the door. Do you happen to know what it is?"

She handed Nathan a round object that, at first, appeared to be composed of glass. But closer inspection had revealed to Myrtle that it was mother of pearl. The number 5 was stamped on one side and strange characters and figures, one of which was a dragon, on the other.

"Oh, no!" said Nathan, staring at the piece in his hand.

"You know what that is?" said Henri, taking the object from him, and turning it over, studying it.

Nathan nodded. "I didn't tell you everything."

"What do you mean, 'you didn't tell me everything?'" asked Henri.

"When you asked me about Yung Li. I told you I didn't know him. I do. He works for Mr. Zhāng."

"Who is Mr. Zhāng?" asked Myrtle.

"He is the owner of a gambling hall in San Francisco, where I used to live."

"And how do you know Mr. Zhāng?" asked Henri.

"I may . . . I may owe him some money."

"You *may* owe him some money?" said Henri.

"I do—I do owe him money; lots of money."

"How much?" asked Myrtle.

"Two thousand dollars."

Myrtle let out a whistle. "You're right—that *is* a lot of money. But what does this . . . this, whatever it is, have to do with anything? With Yung Li?"

"It's a gambling token—five dollars—from Mr. Zhāng's gambling hall. I assume it must have fallen out of Yung Li's pocket—which means he must have been in this room. Which means he must have killed Rachel."

"Why would he kill your sister?" asked Henri.

"As a warning to me, a warning to pay what I owe or else . . ."

"Or else you'll end up like your sister," said Myrtle. "I'm sorry—*half*-sister. But how do we know it didn't fall out of *your* pocket? You must have been in this room since you've returned home, haven't you? And if you frequented this . . . this *gambling* hall, you might have brought this back with you."

Nathan shook his head. "This is the first time I've been in Rachel's room since I've been back. And I'm sure I didn't bring any chips with me. I was broke when I left San Francisco."

Henri slipped the token into his pocket.

"I'll have a talk with Mr. Li after we leave here," he said. "For now, though, I'd like to speak with Miss Wasserman."

*****

Henri and Myrtle found Miss Wasserman downstairs, scrubbing the floor they had dirtied earlier.

"Miss Wasserman, I'm so sorry about that," said Myrtle.

When Miss Wasserman looked up, Myrtle saw that her eyes were still red; her cheeks were wet.

"Oh, it's okay. I had to do it earlier tonight when Mr. Nathan came in." She bowed her head. "I just can't believe she's dead."

The tears started up again.

"Miss Wasserman," said Henri, "I'm sorry, but can I ask you a few questions?"

Miss Wasserman put the scrub brush into the bucket and Henri helped her to her feet. She led them to a small room off the foyer. Other than eight chairs around a table some ten feet long that ran almost the length of the room, the only other furnishings consisted of a painting that hung on the back wall and a small table next to the door on which stood a menorah, some twelve inches high and twice as long.

"So you met Mr. Steinmyer coming down the hallway when you went to see what had happened?" asked Henri.

Miss Wasserman nodded. "We both got to Miss Rachel's room at da same time. He didn't want me to come in, but I did. It was horrible. Who would do dat?" She took a handkerchief from her pocket and wiped her eyes. "Who would shoot a beautiful woman like dat? And right in her face? It's horrible."

"It is," said Myrtle, not sure what else she could say to comfort the housekeeper.

"Miss Wasserman," said Henri, "do you know of anyone who might want to harm Miss Steinmyer."

"Yah," the old lady responded firmly, without hesitation. "Dat horrid Mr. McInerney, da one what stuck a gun in her face not ten days ago, he's da one— he's da one what shot her."

Henri nodded. "His name did come to my mind, too."

"Was Miss Steinmyer seeing anyone?" asked Myrtle. She couldn't imagine that a woman as attractive as Rachel Steinmyer had not had a suitor.

Miss Wasserman wrung her hands and looked down at the table.

"Miss Wasserman?" said Henri.

"I don't know it's for me to say," said the old lady.

"She *was* seeing someone, wasn't she?" said Myrtle. "You can tell us who. It can't hurt her now."

"Well . . . it was dat Mr. Jørgensen."

"Lars Jørgensen?" said Henri.

"You know him?" asked Myrtle.

Henri nodded. "Yah, I know him. He works down at the train station. Not much of a reputation. Miss Wasserman, are you sure it was him?"

"Yah, he was da one courting her. But her father didn't know."

"He wouldn't have approved?" asked Myrtle.

Miss Wasserman shook her head. "Nah. I know he was set dat Miss Rachel marry someone of her own faith."

"But there aren't that many Jews who live in Booker Falls, are there?" asked Myrtle.

"None others, 'cept this family. Well, and Mr. Abramovitz, who's got da pawn shop. But he's in his seventies if'n he's a day."

"Was Lars ever in Miss Steinmyer's room?" asked Henri.

Again, Miss Wasserman was not quick to answer.

"It's all right, Miss Wasserman," said Myrtle. "You can tell us. It won't go any further."

"Sometimes," said Miss Wasserman, "I could hear dem in dere."

"Was he here tonight?" asked Henri.

Miss Wasserman shook her head. "I'm not for sure. I heard voices coming from her room when I went to da bathroom, but I couldn't tell who was in dere with her. It did sound a little like an argument. I know Miss Rachel was going to break it off with him."

Both Henri and Myrtle became more attentive.

"How do you know that?" asked Myrtle.

"Miss Rachel, she told me. Said no matter how much she cared for Mr. Jørgensen, she couldn't go against her father's wishes."

"I'll definitely have a word with Mr. Jørgensen," said Henri.

"Mr. Steinmyer told us when he checked the windows and doors after discovering Miss Steinmyer's body," said Henri, "they were all still locked except for the front door."

Miss Wasserman's eyes got large. "Not locked? But dat's . . . dat's . . ."

"Is it possible you might have missed it when you locked up for the night?" asked Myrtle.

Miss Wasserman was silent for a moment, deep in thought.

"I 'member when I went to lock it, I stood for a bit, watching da rain outside. I suppose I...I could have... I could have...forgot to lock it."

She broke out in tears.

Myrtle stood, walked around the table and put one arm around the woman's shoulder.

"There, there," said Myrtle. "We don't know for sure anyone came in that way."

"Or went out that way," said Henri. "The killer could have left by the front door and not locked it."

"That's true," said Myrtle.

After a few minutes, Miss Wasserman regained her composure. She took a deep breath.

"I'm okay now," she said. "If you don't have no more questions, I should go check on how Mr. Steinmyer is."

"Oh, just one thing," said Henri. He took the gambling token from his pocket and handed it to Miss Wasserman. "Have you ever seen this before?"

The housekeeper studied the piece, then handed it back to Henri. "Nah, never have. What is it?"

"I found it in Rachel's room," said Myrtle. "You hadn't seen it there?"

Miss Wasserman shook her head. "Nah, and I'm pretty sure it wasn't dere when I brought Miss Rachel's water glass in, or I'd have seen it den."

As they started to leave, Myrtle noticed that the painting was crooked. She walked over and straightened it, then studied it for a moment. It was a rendering of the falls that gave the town its name, the colors so dark, particularly the greens, they almost appeared black.

"I know this style," she said. "This is Mr. Mitchell's work, isn't it?"

"Yah," replied Miss Wasserman. "Mr. Steinmyer gave a lot of money to da liberry a few years back, and Mr. Mitchell gave him dat in return. Mr. Steinmyer hated it, but he was a kind man, and he didn't want to hurt Mr. Mitchell's feelings, so he hung it in here."

"I wouldn't think people came in here very often where they could see it," said Henri.

"Dat's what Mr. Steinmyer tought, too," said Miss Wasserman, smiling for the first time.

*****

Back in the car, Myrtle turned to Henri. "What do you think? Did the Chinaman do it, like Mr. Steinmyer says?"

"I think maybe Mickey McInerney *did* do it, like Miss Wasserman said."

"What makes you think so?"

"When Mrs. Folger came to see him the day I arrested him, I overheard some of their conversation. I know he's terrified of going back to Marquette—thinks one of the guards there wants to kill him."

"What does that have to do with it?"

"Rachel was the only witness to the robbery. And Mrs. Folger's sticking to her story that she gave Mickey the money I found on him, but I know darned well she didn't. With Rachel dead, Jake may not be able to make a case."

"And if Mickey's the one who stole the gun out of your desk drawer . . ."

Myrtle didn't finish the sentence. She knew the loss of the evidence was a sore point with Henri.

"Yah, if he's the one, then that could be the gun that killed Miss Steinmyer," said Henri.

"What about this Mr. Jørgensen? Miss Wasserman said Rachel was going to end their relationship. That might not have sat well with him."

"I'll go past the depot tomorrow and talk with him."

"Henri," asked Myrtle, "do you think these two crimes are connected—Mr. Folger and Miss Steinmyer?"

"What makes you think that?"

"They were both shot."

"People get killed by guns all the time."

"Not in Booker Falls they don't," said Myrtle.

CHAPTER SIXTEEN

Miss Wasserman did not sleep well that night.

Tossing and turning, she kept seeing the image before her of her long-time charge, Rachel Steinmyer, lying dead on the floor, her once-beautiful face shattered by a bullet, blaming herself for possibly not locking the front door.

She was relieved when the alarm on the small oval clock on her nightstand went off at six a.m.

She swung her legs off the bed onto the floor, felt in the dark for her slippers, and slid her feet into them. She stood, then slipped into the wool bathrobe she had just removed from the closet to replace the cotton one she'd worn all summer.

*****

Miss Wasserman took down the box of Kellogg's Toasted Corn Flakes from the shelf and poured a generous amount into a bowl. She was about to add the milk when the realization hit her: Miss Rachel wouldn't be eating breakfast this morning.

Hand trembling, she set the bottle back on the counter, then sank into one of the chairs that sat around the table.

That's when the tears came—pouring out in torrents. Even more than last night.

Miss Rachel was dead. The little girl she had raised since she was three years old was dead. She wouldn't be eating any more Kellogg's Toasted Corn Flakes like she had every day of her life for the last twenty-seven years.

Miss Wasserman picked up the bottom of her apron and wiped her eyes, but the tears wouldn't stop flowing.

She laid her head down on the table, resting on her crossed arms, sobs wracking her body.

Who would do such a thing? It must have been that horrible Mr. McInerney.

For a few minutes she found herself unable to move. Finally the tears subsided and she quit shaking.

She stood and walked back to the counter, where she started the coffee percolating.

She placed the bottle of milk back in the new Kelvinator Mr. Steinmyer had purchased just that past summer.

But she didn't move the bowl of toasted corn flakes.

She gathered the ingredients she'd need for the biscuits she prepared fresh every morning: flour, buttermilk, butter, salt, baking powder and sugar.

Maybe keeping busy would help.

Mildred Wasserman's biscuits were noted for their lightness and flakiness, attained by shaping the dough into individual balls by hand, rather than rolling it out onto a sheet, then forming them with a cutter.

Once she finished this part of the operation, she popped the metal pan that held her handiwork into the oven.

She had objected when, two years ago, Rachel insisted on getting rid of the thirty-five-year-old Coldwater wood stove, replacing it with a brand new O'Keefe and Merritt gas model.

"Stoves should last at least fifty years," Miss Wasserman complained.

But she'd soon been won over by the angled mirror/glass window setup behind the burners that allowed her to check the contents without opening the oven door.

On the other hand, she hadn't complained at all when the subject of the Kelvinator came up.

She checked the clock on the wall, an advertising timepiece for the Connor Carriage Company out of Amesbury, Massachusetts. Isaiah had picked it up some twenty-eight years earlier at the Columbian World's Fair in Chicago, when he also purchased the buggy that still resided in the carriage house out back.

The carriage had been for him; the clock had been for Angelina.

In fifteen minutes the biscuits would be ready; time enough to take Mr. Steinmyer's medicine up to him.

"Mr. Steinmyer, it's me—Mildred," said Miss Wasserman, gently pushing the door open.

She walked over to the window and drew back the heavy, red velvet drapes, allowing the first faint rays of sunlight to penetrate the blackness of the room. Then she turned and moved toward the bed.

Isaiah's pale gray eyes stared up at the mural on the ceiling that rose fifteen feet above him, a replica of *The Creation of Adam* from Michelangelo's Sistine Chapel, that George Frederick Watts, a noted English artist, had been commissioned to paint some half century earlier, when the house was built.

A splotch of dried blood lay at the corner of his open mouth.

His expression was that of a man who definitely had not died peacefully in his sleep.

The house on Thimbleberry Road had claimed its sixth victim.

*****

The smell of smoke awakened Nathan.

He sat up, unsure for a moment what was happening. Then he jumped out of bed and slipped into the purple, silk, Chinese bathrobe he'd brought back with him from San Francisco. Rushing out into the hallway, he saw smoke drifting up from downstairs. He bounded down the steps, taking them three at a time and dashed to the kitchen, where he found the room filled with a gray haze.

He turned off the oven, then, grabbing a dishtowel from the counter, removed the smoldering tray of biscuits and dumped the whole mess into the sink.

"Damn," he muttered, placing one singed finger into his mouth.

"Miss Wasserman?" he shouted. "Where are you?"

No response.

Nathan returned upstairs and headed for his father's room, where he found a sobbing Miss Wasserman, stretched out over the dead body of Isaiah Steinmyer.

*****

For the almost thirty years Adolph Pfrommer had resided at Mrs. Darling's Boarding House, he'd insisted that breakfast be served precisely at seven o'clock every morning.

Although he was now gone—serving a life sentence at the Marquette Branch Prison for the murder he'd been convicted of two months ago—Mrs. Darling saw no reason to change the schedule, though she was no longer as firm about it as she had once been.

When Pierre arrived at the breakfast table a few minutes after seven, he found only two of his fellow boarders there: Myrtle and Henri.

He'd just sat down when the ringing of the telephone came from the hallway, followed minutes later by Mrs. Darling's voice.

"Henri, it's for you. You better come quick."

Henri stood and hurried from the room.

Moments later, he returned, wearing his constable's jacket.

"Mr. Steinmyer's dead," he said, to no one in particular.

Mrs. Darling stopped midway through pouring coffee into Pierre's cup.

"The old Mr. Steinmyer or young Mr. Steinmyer?" asked Myrtle.

"The old—Isaiah. Nathan says it looks like he died in his sleep. Probably another heart attack."

"Mrs. Darling, Nathan said Miss Wasserman is pretty upset. You suppose you could come along and be with her?"

"You go," said Pierre to the landlady. "I'll be fine here."

"I'm coming too," said Myrtle, getting to her feet.

"I don't think—" Henri started to say.

"I'm coming," said Myrtle, firmly. "I'll go call Mr. Mitchell and tell him I'm not coming in today."

"What will Frank say about that?" asked Henri.

Myrtle shrugged. "I don't really care," she said as she headed towards the stairs.

*****

Nathan met Henri, Myrtle and Mrs. Darling at the door and ushered them into the foyer. "Miss Wasserman is in the parlor," he said, showing Mrs. Darling the way.

As he rejoined Myrtle and Henri, there was a knock at the door. Nathan opened it to Lewis Fitch.

"This is a terrible time for Dr. Sherman to be out of town," said Fitch, visibly upset. "I'm not prepared for all this."

"You'll be fine," said Henri. He turned to Nathan. "Shall we go up to your father's room now?"

Nathan nodded and led them up the stairs.

For a brief moment, the four of them stood and stared at the lifeless body.

Then, Fitch spoke. "From the looks of it, I think it must have been a heart attack. He'd had another one recently, hadn't he?" he asked, turning to Nathan.

"Yes, a week ago this past Monday, the day the bank was robbed."

"You can tell it was a heart attack just by looking at the body?" asked Myrtle, who had moved to the bed and was bending over Isaiah's lifeless form.

"Not really," answered Fitch. "That's merely a surmise on my part. We won't know for sure until Dr. Sherman returns and does an autopsy, but based on the fact he just suffered one heart attack, it's not unreasonable he could have had a second one."

"I suppose you could be right," said Myrtle, straightening up and turning towards the men. "But I don't think so."

"What do you mean?" asked Henri.

"I don't think he died of a heart attack."

"You don't?" said Nathan.

"No," said Myrtle. "I think he was murdered—smothered with the pillow that's under his head."

The three men stood, stunned, not sure what to say.

"What makes you say that?" came a voice from the doorway.

Everyone turned to see who had spoken. It was Dr. Sherman.

"Doc?" said Henri. "Thought you weren't coming back 'til this afternoon."

"We wrapped up early and I got back in town late last night. Went right to bed. This morning I called Maribel—I swear, that woman knows everything that goes on in this town—anyway, I called to see if I had any messages. She filled me in on Miss Steinmyer and what happened this morning with Isaiah. So I came right over."

Lewis Fitch breathed a big sigh of relief.

"So, Miss Tully—smothered, you say," said the doctor. "And what leads you to that conclusion?"

"I'm sure you can give us a more professional opinion," said Myrtle, suddenly feeling embarrassed.

"No, no," said Dr. Sherman. "Go on, please."

Myrtle cleared her throat. "You see how white the skin around his lips is?" she said. "And those little red spots right there?"

She pointed to a patch of spots on Isaiah's cheeks.

"You can also see those little red spots in his eyes," added Myrtle. "That's from where blood vessels have burst. It's called petechial hemorrhaging."

Dr. Sherman looked at Myrtle with newfound admiration.

"And do you see this?" Myrtle continued, pointing to the splotch of blood at the corner of Isaiah's mouth. "Those are all signs something had been held tightly over Mr. Steinmyer's face, preventing him from breathing. Someone deliberately held something over his face."

"And you think it was the pillow?" asked Henri.

"Yes," said Myrtle. She removed a small bag from her purse and pulled out a pair of tweezers. Bending over the body again, she carefully removed an object from Isaiah's left nostril, holding it up for the others to see.

"A feather?" said Fitch.

"A feather," said Myrtle. "From the pillow. Pick it up and turn it over."

Henri slid the pillow from under Isaiah's head and turned it over. A spot of dried blood was clearly evident.

"This was no heart attack," said Myrtle. "Mr. Steinmyer was murdered."

"How do you know all of this stuff?" asked Fitch.

"While I was investigating—while I was *assisting* Henri with the Sinclair case," Myrtle added hastily, noting Henri's look of disapproval, "I became interested in the study of forensics. One of the books I ran across, a book in the library, by Alexandre Lacassagne, was *L'étude et la Détermination de Homicidal Asphyxiation.*"

"What?" said Fitch.

"The study and determination of homicidal asphyxiation," said Dr. Sherman.

Henri, Nathan and Fitch turned and looked at Dr. Sherman, who had been doing his own examination of Isaiah's body while Myrtle was talking.

"I believe I must agree with Miss Tully's conclusion," said Dr. Sherman. "Mr. Steinmyer was definitely murdered."

CHAPTER SEVENTEEN

When Henri arrived back at his office with Myrtle, he found a state trooper waiting for him.

"Leonard?" said Henri enthusiastically, grabbing the trooper's hand.

"Hello, Henri," said Leonard. "It's been a while."

"I thought you'd been transferred to Flint," said Henri.

"I was, but I'm back in Marquette now."

Myrtle cleared her throat.

"Oh," said Henri, turning to Myrtle. "Allow me to introduce you. Leonard, this is Miss Myrtle Tully. She also resides at Mrs. Darling's."

Leonard put out his hand and Myrtle took it.

"Miss Tully," he said. "My pleasure. I've heard so much about you."

"Mr. . . ?" said Myrtle.

"Captain. Captain Leonard Wysocki."

"Captain Wysocki." Myrtle nodded. "Are you by chance the Leonard who was Daisy's . . . her . . ."

"Her boyfriend? Yes, one and the same. How is she?"

It wasn't hard to see what Daisy had found attractive about Leonard—aside from the fact he had supplied her with confiscated liquor. At six foot two, he towered over both Myrtle and Henri. And although he was fifty years old, he still had the physique of an athlete who had played amateur ice hockey when that sport was still in its infancy.

As if that weren't enough, he had eyes that would have made the waters of Lake Superior envious.

"She's well. She missed you," said Myrtle. *Did you ever call her?*

"Perhaps I can see her while I'm in town."

"I'm sure she'd like that," said Myrtle, not sure at all that would be the case.

"So, what are you doing here?" asked Henri.

"I'm here to process the fingerprints for your murder."

"We weren't expecting anyone for another couple of days."

"We take murders very seriously, eh?" said Leonard, smiling.

"As do we, Leonard, as do we. Glad you're here. I'll walk you across the street to where the murder took place. But first I have a favor to ask."

"Sure. What is it?"

"I have to take someone into custody, and I'm not sure how it may turn out. I could use some back up."

"Glad to be of assistance."

Henri turned to Myrtle. "You should wait across the street at Paige's. I don't want you here when we bring him in."

"You're going after Mr. Li," said Myrtle.

"We are. And it's best if you're not here."

Normally, Myrtle would have objected to being excluded. But having heard a description of Mr. Li and Nathan's explanation as to why he thought the Chinaman was in town, she decided for once to accede to Henri's wishes.

"I'll wait for you there," she said.

Henri turned to Leonard. "It's not far. But let's take your car. I don't want to parade him down Main Street. I'll fill you in on our most recent murders from last night."

Leonard's eyes opened wide. "There's more than one?" he asked.

"Oh, yes," said Henri. "There is definitely more than one."

*****

As they drove the few blocks to the Walther Building, Henri told Leonard about the two Steinmyer murders and Yung Li's possible involvement.

"Sounds odd to me;" said Leonard. "the time in between the two, and one being shot while the other was smothered."

"Me, too," said Henri. "And while you're here, how about taking a look at that crime scene as well?"

*****

Henri knocked on the door of number 315 of the Walther Building.

Minutes later, Yung Li appeared. Leonard saw why Henri thought he might need his help.

"Mr. Li," said Henri, "I wonder if you would mind accompanying Captain Wysocki and me to my office."

A moment passed before Yung spoke. "Am I under arrest?"

"No," said Henri. "We just want to ask you some questions."

"About what?"

"Isaiah Steinmyer and his daughter were both murdered in their home last night. Yesterday, when you arrived in town, you inquired as to where they lived—where Nathan lived. I'd like to know why."

"I didn't kill them," said Yung.

He started to close the door, but before he could, he found Leonard's revolver in his face.

"This is not a request, Mr. Li," said Leonard. "We'll come in while you get your coat and then we'll go to the constable's office."

Yung backed away from the door as Henri and Leonard entered the room.

Henri saw it first: on the dresser lay a thirty-five millimeter pistol.

"We'll be taking your gun along, too," said Henri.

"I have a permit for that," said Yung.

"We'll see," said Henri.

Ten minutes later, Henri sat at his desk, Yung Li across from him. Leonard stood against the side wall, his hand resting on his pistol.

"Mr. Li, where were you last night?" asked Henri.

"In my room."

"No, no, you weren't. I inquired at the desk around eleven o'clock and Mr. Halderman said he hadn't seen you all evening."

"I came in through the back door. He didn't see me."

"There is no back door at the Walther Building," said Henri. In truth, he had no idea if there was a back door or not. He'd never noticed one.

"There is a back door. I came in that way."

"What time?" asked Henri.

"Around seven. I had dinner at the restaurant down the street, then returned to my room—by the back door."

"I'll check that out," said Henri. "I'm afraid, though, I'm going to have to detain you until we can get this straightened out."

"Detain me?"

"Keep you here."

"Here? In jail?"

"That's right," said Henri. "But only until we can confirm your alibi."

Yung shook his head. "I do not choose—"

"Mr. Li," said Leonard, drawing his gun, "if you would please precede me through that door."

He pointed his gun towards the door leading to the two jail cells.

Reluctantly, Yung stood and headed for the door. Minutes later he was behind bars.

"Let's go take a look at that first crime scene now," said Leonard. "And after that I can check out the other one."

*****

"Where's Captain Wysocki?" asked Myrtle when Henri returned to the book store to pick her up.

"He left for the Steinmyer home to check for fingerprints."

"Is he going to see Daisy while he's in town?"

Henri shrugged. "I have no idea. I didn't ask him."

CHAPTER EIGHTEEN

"Where is he? Where is the bastard? I'll kill him!"

Startled, Myrtle looked up to see a large Negro man charging towards her. Instinctively, she picked up the closest thing she could find: her ruler.

A lot of good this will do, she thought immediately.

The man stopped in front of the desk, towering over her. She still held the ruler in her hand, ready to strike him if necessary.

"Where is . . . never mind, I see him," said the man, taking off for Frank's office.

"Wai . . ." Myrtle started to say.

But the man was gone and in seconds had burst through the office door.

Frank's office, a small room, no more than nine by nine, was located against the west wall. Its glass windows afforded him a view of the entire main floor of the library. When he wanted privacy, he had shades he could pull down.

Today, the shades were all up.

Myrtle watched helplessly as the man began ranting and gesturing. Frank jumped up from his chair, knocking his glass of Southern Comfort to the floor, where it shattered, spilling its contents. He backed up against the wall, hands held out in front of him in a defensive gesture.

The man had slammed the door behind him, rendering it impossible to hear what was being said.

Myrtle looked around the room at the several dozen students who by now had stopped what they were doing to watch the scene unfolding before them.

What should she do? She couldn't call for Henri: the only phone was in Frank's office. Should she summon the few male students who were there to intervene? But she knew it would be wrong to put them in harm's way.

Just as she decided to get involved herself, Henri came through the front door.

"Oh, Henri, thank goodness you're here. That man–" she pointed towards Frank's office—"I'm afraid he's going to kill Mr. Mitchell!"

Henri ran to the office and rushed in. Like the Negro, he closed the door behind him: no reason for the students to hear what was being said.

The man turned to Henri and the two of them became embroiled in a heated conversation. The man looked at Frank, pointed a finger at him and spoke again. Then, turning, he brushed past Henri, out of the office, and out of the library.

Myrtle, along with the students, watched, stunned, as he left. She turned back to the office. Henri and Frank were talking, but so softly Myrtle still couldn't hear what was being said.

Moments later Henri emerged.

"All of you—" he said, gesturing to the students, "—back to whatever you were doing."

He walked over to Myrtle's desk.

"Henri, whatever was that all about?" she asked in a hushed voice.

"Where can we go to talk privately?"

"Downstairs—the vault."

The library vault ran under the entire length of the first floor of the building. It was Myrtle's least favorite place: dark, dank and just plain creepy. Fortunately, her trips there were few, as it was only used for storage. It was here last year where she found a cache of letters sent twenty-eight years earlier to Yvette Sinclair, a student at the college, shortly before she was found strangled to death in the stacks. She had held the same job Myrtle now held.

It was that discovery that had sent Myrtle off on the quest that almost resulted in her own demise.

"Okay, what's going on?" she asked when they reached the bottom of the stairs.

"It's Frank's girlfriend," said Henri, his face grim.

Myrtle stepped back, a shocked look on her face. "Girlfriend? What girlfriend? Mr. Mitchell doesn't have a girlfriend."

"Seems he does," said Henri. "And I guess it's no secret as far as the student body is concerned, though I've no indication anyone in town knows anything about it. I know I sure didn't."

Myrtle still couldn't believe it. "Well, who is it? And what does it have to do with the man who was in his office?"

"That was the girl's father and he found out about the affair a week ago."

"Affair? You mean they . . .?"

"No, nothing like that has happened—not yet, anyway.

"The girl's name is Eloise Blanchard. She's a first year student here, just started this past summer."

"Eloise Blanchard?" Myrtle remembered seeing the girl in the library on several occasions, one of the few Negroes who attended Adelaide.

She also remembered the time Frank had asked about her.

*****

"Miss Tully, could you come into my office, please?"

Myrtle looked around and saw Frank standing at his office door, beckoning her with his index finger.

He's probably taking off early again, *thought Myrtle. Frank had a habit on Fridays of leaving the library before it closed in order to have a good supper before he went to the weekly poker game at George's home.*

Dutifully, she rose and walked over to the office, where Frank met her at the door.

"That student, there," he said, pointing towards a group of five women gathered around one of the long oak tables that served as study areas. "Do you know who she is?"

"Which one?" she asked.

"The Negro—the colored one."

Myrtle looked back at Frank. Why did he want to know her name? But she didn't ask. "Eloise Blanchard," she said. "Her name is Eloise Blanchard."

"Thank you," said Frank. "That will be all."

Myrtle returned to her desk, shaking her head. Never before had Frank asked her about any of the students who frequented the library. In fact, as far as she could tell, he had absolutely no contact with any of them, nor did he want to.

She turned and looked back at Frank.

He stood where she left him, his eyes fixed on Eloise.

*****

"What did her father say to Mr. Mitchell?" asked Myrtle.

"He said if Frank didn't stop seeing his daughter, he'd kill him."

"What? Kill him?" Now Myrtle was *really* shocked.

"I don't think he would. But if I was Frank, I believe I would heed Mr. Blanchard's warning."

"Will he?"

Henri shrugged. "Who knows?"

"I don't know how this was going on and I didn't know about it."

"It's possible you're not as good a detective as you think you are," said Henri, grinning.

"You didn't know anything about it either," retorted Myrtle.

"Yes, but I'm not nosy like you are."

CHAPTER NINETEEN

That evening, when Myrtle walked into the office of Jake McIntyre, the county prosecutor, she was surprised to find not only him, but Henri and George as well. Jake had stopped by the library earlier that day and asked her to meet with him when she left work. He could use her assistance on something, he'd said.

The aroma of *Little Beauties*, Jake's favorite cigar, which he had shipped in from Kalamazoo, permeated the room. Myrtle found it a not altogether unpleasant smell; in fact, it reminded her of her father, who had also been a cigar aficionado.

Each of the men held a tumbler of scotch in his hand.

"Henri, George, Mr. McIntyre," said Myrtle.

"Miss Tully, I'm glad you could make it," said Jake, setting his glass down. "Please—call me Jake. May I take your coat? I believe this is skunk, is it not?"

"Yes, it is, thank you," replied Myrtle. "And I'm happy if I might be of assistance—to whatever it is you're about."

"We're here to solve three murders," said George.

"My," said Myrtle, arching her eyebrows. "That does sound ambitious."

"Please, have a seat at my desk," said Jake.

Myrtle sat down in the oak swivel chair and swung it around to face the three men. She nodded towards Jake's glass. "By chance is there any of that left?" she asked.

For a moment he was taken aback. He hadn't expected she would want a drink. "Why . . . why I suppose so. But didn't you just come from work? Have you eaten? It might not be a good idea for you to drink on an empty stomach."

"I can take care of that," said Henri. He handed Myrtle something wrapped in brown paper. "Mrs. Darling knew you wouldn't have an opportunity to eat before coming to the meeting. She sent this."

Myrtle unwrapped the paper. "A pasty!" she declared, enthusiastically. "It's perfect."

She looked at Jake. "It seems my stomach will not be empty."

Jake smiled and walked over to the cabinet where he kept the scotch. As he poured Myrtle's drink, she glanced around the office.

Twice as large as Henri's, it contained, in addition to the roll-top desk, a table some seven feet long, with eight chairs placed around it. It, too, was made of oak, similar to the chair on which she sat and all the other furnishings in the room.

Shelves filled with law books filled two walls.

A chalkboard, some six feet in length and five feet high, was mounted on a third wall.

She took the drink Jake offered her and sipped it. "Oh, my," she said. "This is amazing! What is it?"

"Johnnie Walker Black Label," said Jake. "Comes all the way from Scotland."

Myrtle lifted her glass. "Well, here's to solving three murders."

The men all raised their glasses and drank.

"I'm curious," she said. "What is the chalkboard for?"

"Oh," said Jake, obviously pleased she had asked. "When I'm preparing for trial I use it to write notes on, and questions I might want to ask jurors or witnesses, strategies I can employ."

"Is that why you win most of your cases?" asked Myrtle.

Jake beamed. "Yes, it is . . . that and the fact that I am an outstanding litigator."

They all laughed.

"He really is," said George, lifting his glass and taking another drink.

"Now, then," said Myrtle, "how are we to go about solving these murders?"

Jake lit a cigar and pointed with it towards the chalkboard. "With this."

"Your cigar?" asked Myrtle, playfully.

George and Henri both chuckled.

"No, no, the chalkboard," said Jake, oblivious to the teasing.

"Oh," said Myrtle, a bemused look on her face.

"Yes," said George. "It was Henri's idea."

Myrtle glanced at Henri, who was grinning broadly.

Myrtle settled back in the chair. "So, how does it work? How is this chalkboard going to solve three murders?"

"It won't actually *solve* the crimes," said Henri, "but it hopefully will help us figure out what's going on with them."

"And how can I help?" asked Myrtle.

"I insisted on you being involved," said Jake. "I know how much your insights helped solve the Sinclair murder, and I am sure they will be useful in our investigation."

Myrtle glanced at Henri, wondering if he might say anything. But he was studying the chalkboard.

Jake walked over to the board, picked up a piece of chalk and wrote three names across the top: RUDY,

RACHEL, ISAIAH. A bit further down and to the left of the names he wrote the word SUSPECTS.

"I believe in order to make some headway on figuring this out," he said, turning to the others, "we must determine what they all have in common, and what they do not. Let's us start with the suspects, eh? Henri?"

"I can think of three people who might have wanted to see Mr. Folger dead: Mrs. Folger, Mr. Finnegan and Mrs. Finnegan."

Jake wrote the three names—Margaret, J. P. and Agnes—under RUDY, leaving several spaces between each to allow for more information. "And the motives each would have had?"

"The same for all of them;" said Myrtle, "the affair. It was no secret. Mrs. Folger may have killed her husband out of a sense of betrayal or perhaps rage."

"And Mr. Finnegan might also have killed him out of anger," said George.

"I heard Mr. Folger broke off the affair recently," added Henri. "Which could have been a motive for Mrs. Finnegan—the jilted lover."

Under each suspect's name Jake wrote 'affair.'

"Anyone else?" he asked, looking around.

"We may be overlooking the obvious," said Myrtle.

"And what might that be?" asked Jake.

"The safe was open. We don't know what, if anything, was taken. What would any of these three suspects have wanted to steal badly enough to kill Mr. Folger. Was this a burglary by someone other than our three suspects or . . . ?"

"Or?" said Henri.

"Or was Mr. Folger indeed murdered by one of the three and the killer made it look like a robbery to throw off suspicion?"

For a moment no one spoke.

Then Jake said, "All right, then. That's something we'll have to sort out, eh? Now, how about Miss Steinmyer? Henri, I understand you and Captain Wysocki took Mr. Li into custody earlier today."

"Yah," said Henri, "but I'm not sure there's enough evidence to hold him on, let alone convict him."

"We'll see about that," said Jake, writing Li's name down. "Now, let's consider other suspects. The first one who comes to my mind is Mickey McInerney. With Miss Steinmyer dead and Mrs. Folger holding to her story that she gave her brother the money he had on him when Henri arrested him, I don't have much of a case. He'll almost certainly go scot free."

"And add Lars Jørgensen; Miss Steinmyer's boyfriend," said Henri.

"Ex-boyfriend," corrected Myrtle. "According to Miss Wasserman, Miss Steinmyer had broken off their relationship."

"Ex-boyfriend," said Henri, nodding.

"I don't think we can exclude Nathan," said George. "Miss Steinmyer was not married, had no children— Nathan could well have been the beneficiary in her will."

"Henri," said Jake, as he wrote down the three names, "would you see if you can obtain a copy of Miss Steinmyer's will—assuming she had one."

"And Isaiah Steinmyer's, also," added Myrtle.

"While we're collecting wills," said George, "shouldn't we be getting Mr. Folger's?"

"Yah," said Jake. "His, too."

"What about Miss Wasserman?" asked George. "Is she a viable suspect? She might also be in either of the Steinmyer's wills."

Jake shook his head. "I've known Miss Wasserman for all of my adult life. I can't believe she has it in her to hurt a flea, let alone murder someone, especially the woman she raised since she was three years old."

"Nevertheless," said George, "I think we should still put her name down. We can always take it off later."

"Okay," said Jake, adding the housekeeper's name to the list.

Under all the suspect's names Jake wrote down the corresponding motives: warning; get rid of witness; rejected suitor; inheritance.

"Now," said Jake, "how about Mr. Steinmyer?"

"Again, Mr. Li," said Myrtle.

"And Nathan," said Henri.

"And Miss Wasserman," said George.

"There's one thing I don't understand," added George. "The way I heard it, Mr. Steinmyer was on his deathbed, wasn't he? Why bother to kill him? Why not let nature take its course?"

"I've been thinking about that, too," said Myrtle. "In Miss Wasserman's case, it could have been done to put Mr. Steinmyer out of his misery. And in Mr. Li's case, if he did indeed want to send a warning to Mr. Steinmyer—the younger Mr. Steinmyer—just allowing his father to die a natural death wouldn't have sent the message he wanted to send.

"And there's another thing that bothers me about the Steinmyer murders," added Myrtle.

"What's that?" asked George.

"If they were both killed by the same person, that means the killer shot Miss Steinmyer, then hid somewhere in the house until after we left, and Mr. Steinmyer—Nathan—and Miss Wasserman, retired for the night."

"But Nathan said he checked the house," said Henri.

Myrtle shook her head. "No, he only said he checked the windows and doors. It's a big house: the murderer could have easily found someplace to hide. Then, later, he went into Mr. Steinmyer's room—the elder Mr. Steinmyer—and instead of shooting him as he did Miss Steinmyer, smothered him and then placed the pillow back under Mr. Steinmyer's head. But why smother him instead of shooting him as he did Miss Steinmyer? And why not kill Mr. Steinmyer *first*, which was done quietly, and *then* kill Miss Steinmyer, if he was going to shoot her—which undoubtedly would have aroused the household? Which it did.

"All of that might indicate another possibility: they were killed by two different people, possibly for different reasons."

"The killer probably put the pillow back under Mr. Steinmyer's head to make it look as though he died a natural death," said Jake.

"Which might have happened, had Myrtle not noticed the signs," said George.

"I'm sure Doc Sherman would have come to that conclusion on his own," said Henri, dismissively.

"Anyway," said George, "it makes me think it's the second scenario—that there were two different killers. If there was only one person, he sure didn't try to hide the fact Miss Steinmyer was murdered; why care about how Mr. Steinmyer's death appeared?"

The other three nodded, but no one spoke.

"Does that bottle have a hole in the bottom as well as the top?" asked Myrtle, breaking the silence.

Jake looked at her quizzically.

Myrtle held up her glass. "I seemed to have finished my drink."

Jake brightened. "Oh, oh, sure—here." He walked over to the sideboard, returned with the bottle and refilled everyone's glass.

"Better?" he asked.

Myrtle smiled and nodded.

"What about Nathan?" asked George.

"Maybe he wanted to get his inheritance sooner," said Henri. "He did say he owed money."

"He couldn't wait a few weeks?" said Jake, setting the bottle down and picking up the chalk. "If so, he must be pretty desperate. But let's go on."

Following each of the suspect's names listed under ISAIAH, Jake wrote: warning; will; will. Then under each suspect's name he wrote 'alibi.'

"Mrs. Folger was out of town," said Henri.

"So she says," said Myrtle, standing and stretching.

George looked surprised. "You don't think so?"

"She says she was at her aunt's in Mohawk. But even though it's a distance, I think she could have driven back here to Booker Falls that night and then back to her aunt's, maybe even to Hancock or Houghton, where she could have taken a hotel room. She's already said she spent the night in Red Jacket, so we know she wasn't at her aunt's."

"Has the aunt verified her alibi that she was there at all?" Jake asked Henri.

"I haven't been able to contact her yet," Henri answered. "She doesn't have a telephone. I've asked Constable Ayers over in Red Jacket to go up and check on it."

"But could you even believe her if she did confirm Mrs. Folger spent the first night there?" asked Myrtle. "I mean, she *is* her aunt."

"Let's see what she says, eh?" said Jake. "For now I'll put 'out of town.' Now, how about the Finnegans?"

"Neither of them has an alibi," said Henri. "Mrs. Finnegan claims she was home and J. P. says he was at the store."

"At the store? On a Sunday evening?" said Jake.

"He's been staying in a room above the store for the last several weeks."

"Ah, so no real alibi for either," said Jake, writing 'none' under the two suspects' names.

"But here's another thing," added Henri. "I asked Mrs. Finnegan if they owned a gun. She said they did, but when she went to get it, it was missing. She claims she doesn't know where it is. J. P. made the same claim when I asked him."

"That definitely sounds suspicious to me," said George.

"Yah, it does," said Jake. "So, now, how's about Mr. Li?"

"After Myrtle and I left the Steinmyer's," said Henri, "I dropped her off at the boarding house and drove back to the Walther Building. Marvin—"

"Marvin?" said Myrtle.

"Marvin Halderman, the night clerk at the Walther," said Henri, his tone suggesting annoyance at the interruption. "He said he hadn't seen Mr. Li since he checked in earlier in the day. I waited in the lobby until after three o'clock, then left. It seemed like I'd just gotten to bed when I received the call from Nathan about his father. When I questioned Mr. Li today he claimed he was in his room by a little after seven. Says he came in through the back door and that's why Marvin didn't see him."

"But no one can confirm that?" asked Jake.

"No," said Henri.

"So, no alibi for Mr. Li, either," said Jake, writing 'none' under the Chinaman's name. "How about Mickey McInerney?"

"Mickey has a pretty good alibi," said Henri. "I found out the night Miss Steinmyer and her father were killed, Mickey was in jail in Chassell."

"Wow," said Myrtle. "And he was my main suspect."

"Should we take him off the board?" asked George.

"Not yet," said Jake, writing 'in jail' under Mickey's name.

"And how about the ex-boyfriend?" asked George.

"I haven't been able to contact him yet either," said Henri. "He wasn't at work today. In fact, they tell me he hasn't been around for a couple of days."

"You think he left town?" asked Jake.

Henri shrugged. "Your guess is as good as mine."

Under Lars' name, Jake put a question mark.

"As far as Nathan and Miss Wasserman are concerned," he said, turning back to the group, "they have no alibis either, as they were both in the house when the deaths occurred. Now, there's one last thing—method."

Jake turned back to the chalkboard and under RUDY and RACHEL wrote 'gunshot.' Under ISAIAH he wrote 'smothered.'

"Do we know if the same gun was used to kill both Mr. Folger and Miss Steinmyer?" asked Myrtle.

"There's no way to tell," said Henri. "Although Doc Sherman says the same caliber of gun was used to murder both of them. He has the bullets from each of the crimes at his office."

"Could at least one of the murders have been done with the gun stolen from your office?" asked Myrtle.

"Again, no way to know," said Henri. "But, it *was* the same type of gun—that we know: a thirty-five millimeter pistol. That's also the same type of gun Leonard and I found in Mr. Li's room."

The four of them stood for a moment, studying the board.

"What do we have in common with all of this?" asked Myrtle.

With the chalk, Jake drew circles around Mr. Li's names under RACHEL and ISAIAH and connected them with a line. Then he did the same with 'Nathan' and 'Miss Wasserman,' and 'inheritance' under both RACHEL and ISAIAH, and connected the corresponding circles. Under Mr. Li's name for both RACHEL and ISAIAH he circled the word 'warning,' and connected them.

Finally, under RUDY and RACHEL he drew circles around the word gunshot, with a line that connected them.

"Looking at this," said Myrtle, "the only one who looks to have a solid alibi is Mickey—he was in jail. Mrs. Folger's alibi is yet to be corroborated, and the rest—at least for now—have no alibis that can be confirmed."

"And," said George, "while Miss Steinmyer's death and her father's have a great deal in common, the only thing Rudy's death has that connects him with either of the other two is that he was killed with a gun, the same as Miss Steinmyer; except we don't know if it's the same gun and there's no way to find out."

"Hmm," said Myrtle.

The three men turned to her.

"Do you see something else?" asked Jake.

"Maybe," said Myrtle. "There is one more thing both Mr. Folger's and Miss Steinmyer's murders have in common."

"What's that?" asked George.

Myrtle took the chalk from Jake's hand and walked over to the chalkboard. She drew a circle around both Margaret's and Mickey's names and drew a line connecting the two.

"Both of these suspects are related," she said, turning back to the three men.

"I'm not sure what the relevance of that is," said Henri. "Mrs. Folger had no reason to have Miss Steinmyer dead and, as far as we know, Mickey had no reason to kill his brother-in-law."

"Have any of you ever read the novel by Grégoire Dubois, *Assassiner par procuration*?" asked Myrtle.

George shook his head.

"What does that mean?" asked Jake.

"*Murder by Proxy*," answered Myrtle. "It's the story of two women, Genevieve and Adelphe, strangers who, by chance, find themselves sharing a sidewalk table at a small café in Paris. In the course of their conversation, they discover they have something in common: they each want to dispose of a man in their life; Genevieve, her husband, for the insurance, and Adelphe, her married lover, of whom she has tired but can't seem to get rid of. The problem is that they are both fearful of getting caught.

"So they come to an agreement: each of them will kill the other's man, allowing the other woman to establish an alibi.

"I think the same thing is possible here. If Mrs. Folger murders Miss Steinmyer while Mr. McInerney is in jail, he has a good alibi. And if Mr. McInerney murders Mr. Folger while Mrs. Folger is out of town, then she has a good alibi. Think about it: the one thing these two crimes have in common is that both victims were shot by the same kind of gun, the same kind of gun Henri took from Mr. McInerney, which Mrs. Folger identified as her husband's gun, which was later stolen from Henri's desk.

"How many people knew that gun was there?" she asked, turning to Henri.

"George, myself, Miss Steinmyer and Mrs. Folger," answered Henri.

"Either of them could have told someone else," said George.

Henri shrugged. "I suppose."

"All right," said Myrtle. "Another question: is there any chance all *three* of these murders are connected?"

Jake shrugged. "The Steinmyer's murders have a lot of suspects in common, and they were both killed on the same night."

"But by different methods," said George. "If the killer shot Miss Steinmyer, why would he—"

"Or she," Myrtle interrupted.

"—or she," said George, a wry grin on his face, "—use a different method to murder Mr. Steinmyer, as Myrtle pointed out earlier?"

"And the first two murders were done by the same method—a gun," said Myrtle.

"It is a puzzlement," said Jake. "We have a lot to think about. Let's call it a night, eh, and sleep on it? And Henri, you'll track down Lars and find out if he has an alibi? Oh, and check on the wills if you can."

As they put their coats on to leave, George turned to Myrtle. "The story—how did it turn out? Did both women get what they wanted?"

"Adelphe did indeed kill Genevieve's husband while she was out of the country," said Myrtle.

"And Adelphe's lover?" asked Henri.

"When Genevieve found Adelphe's lover at the bar Adelphe told her he frequented, she discovered it was her own father. She told him what she had agreed to do. He never saw Adelphe again."

George shook his head. "Murder by proxy. What won't they think of next?"

CHAPTER TWENTY

George shuffled the deck of playing cards and studied the other three men seated around the table: Clarence Hurstbourne, the local judge; Frank Mitchell, Myrtle's boss at the library; and Malcolm Middleton, who owned most of the homes in Greytown, that area of Booker Falls many of the miners called home. Conspicuously absent were two men who had been regular participants in the weekly game: Rudy Folger and Isaiah Steinmyer, both recent murder victims.

The game was a weekly event and, for some of the participants, had been for more than thirty years. George was the newest member, having been invited to join eight years ago following the death of Finn O'Halloran, one of the original members.

In the beginning, the game had rotated among the various players' homes. But the first time George hosted, the others were so impressed by his exquisite poker table, with its bright baize covering and its twelve wells—six for chips and six for drinks—they had continued to meet thereafter only at his home. The excellent spirits from George's pantry—Four Roses bourbon from Kentucky and Glenmorangie scotch from Scotland—made even Frank forego his usual Southern Comfort. The roast beef sandwiches and deviled eggs prepared with pickle relish by Mrs. Delahanty served as icing on the cake.

George pushed the pile of cards to Judge Hurstbourne, on his right, who cut them. Then George dealt out five cards to each player, including himself.

The game was five card draw.

It had always been five card draw.

Frank suggested once they might try something different, say, seven card stud.

"If you want to play a different card game," said Judge Hurstbourne, "I suggest you attend the Ladies Auxiliary over at the Lutheran Church. I understand they're into euchre."

That was the last time Frank suggested changing the game.

"Anybody given any thought as to who we're going to get to replace Rudy and Isaiah?" asked the judge, chewing on his cigar as he studied his cards.

"Good Lord, Clarence," said Malcolm. He was the only one who never referred to Judge Hurstbourne as 'Judge.' "The men haven't even been dead a week."

"Yah," said George. "They just put Isaiah and Rachel in the ground yesterday, and Rudy's funeral isn't until tomorrow."

"I didn't realize there was a required period of mourning for dead poker players," said the judge.

George shook his head.

"How about the constable?" asked Hurstbourne. "George, you're a good friend of his. Do you think he'd be interested in joining us?"

George scratched the back of his neck. "I doubt it," he said. "I don't think Henri has the kind of money it takes for our game."

"How about Isaiah's son, then?" asked Malcolm. "Nathan—is that his name? I heard he's back in town. And with his sister and father both dead now, he'll likely inherit the whole shooting match."

"I could ask him," said George, with little enthusiasm, knowing the other men weren't aware that Nathan was a suspect in at least one of the murders.

Malcolm turned to Frank, who had been silent throughout the whole conversation. "Frank, you haven't said anything. What do you think?"

"I think I'll bet a dollar," said Frank, pushing a chip toward the middle of the table.

*****

A lifelong bachelor, Frank Mitchell had three passions in life: painting, poker and reading dime mystery novels, such as *The New York Detective Library* and *Old Sleuth Library*, while imbibing in his favorite drink, Southern Comfort.

Unfortunately, he wasn't good at either painting or poker. In truth, he really wasn't all that good at holding his liquor, either.

Earlier that year, when Myrtle had been a dinner guest at George's home, she had been as captivated by the poker table as the regular Friday night players were. When she'd asked about the possibility of joining the group, George warned her that the stakes they played for were pretty high, undoubtedly more than she could afford.

She'd then posed the question of how her boss, Frank Mitchell, could afford it on his salary.

"When Frank first started at the library," said George, "he developed a close friendship with Louis Amyx—"

"The man who founded the college," said Myrtle.

"That's right," said George. "And when Mr. Amyx died, he left Frank a sizable bequest in his will."

"Is he a good player?" asked Myrtle.

George chuckled. "He's the worst I've ever seen. I don't know how he continues to be able to afford to stay with us."

*****

Frank was having trouble concentrating on his cards: the appearance of Eloise's father in his office the day before still had him on edge. No one had said anything about it, but he was pretty sure they had all heard.

Twenty-nine years ago, Frank had fallen in love with another woman: eighteen-year-old Yvette Sinclair, a student at Adelaide who worked for him as the assistant librarian. For a time, he had been a suspect in her murder, until the real killer was caught.

Following Yvette's death, Frank thought he would never find another woman he cared for as deeply; and certainly not one as young as Eloise.

It mattered not to him that she was Negro and nearly fifty years younger than he. And, much to his surprise, the difference in race and age apparently didn't matter to her, either. She seemed to enjoy his company as much as he enjoyed hers.

He was more than pleasantly surprised the first time she kissed him. It had been a long time since that had happened, and never when he hadn't initiated it.

He'd given no thought to what her parents might think of the relationship. Indeed, he had not given any thought to her parents, period. When her father showed up the previous day and threatened him, Frank had felt not only fearful, but humiliated that the confrontation took place in sight of Miss Tully and a roomful of students.

But he wasn't deterred by the threats Mr. Blanchard made: he was still determined to continue the relationship, and was relieved to find, when he told Eloise what had occurred, that she felt the same.

*****

"One dollar," said George.

"Call," said Frank. Only he and George remained in the hand.

"Three kings," said George, showing his cards.

Frank laid his hand down. "Full house," he said, raking in the pot.

Maybe this will be my lucky night, he thought.

Alas, such was not to be; it was one of only three winning hands the whole evening. By ten o'clock he had lost almost fifty dollars.

"I'm cursed," he said, throwing down his final hand, a straight, beaten by Judge Hurstbourne's flush.

"Maybe next time," said George, trying to sound encouraging.

"Yah, sure," said Frank, scowling. He stood and walked over to the small table on which sat the alcohol and glasses, poured a generous shot of bourbon, downed it in one swallow—then hurled the glass against the wall, where it smashed into a hundred pieces.

CHAPTER TWENTY-ONE

"Should we wait for her?"

It was Mrs. Darling asking the question.

She glanced at the grandfather clock sitting in the corner of the dining room: seven minutes after seven o'clock. Myrtle had been a few minutes late before for breakfast, but never this much.

Another few minutes passed. Then Daisy got up.

"Why don't you go ahead and serve Henri and Mr. Longet?" she said. "I'll go see what's keeping her."

A knock on Myrtle's door brought no response.

"Myrtle?" said Daisy. "You in there?"

Still no response.

Cautiously, Daisy pushed the door open until she saw Myrtle, lying on her bed, her back to the door, curled up, the covers pulled all the way up.

"Myrtle?" said Daisy approaching the bed, "are you okay?"

The only response was a slight shake of Myrtle's head.

Daisy went around to the other side of the bed. Myrtle's eyes, red from crying, were open, staring straight ahead.

"Myrtle, what is it?" asked Daisy, settling down on the bed beside her. "What's wrong?"

"My mother," said Myrtle, weakly.

"Your mother? What about your mother?"

"Today's her birthday."

Daisy took a deep breath. She knew both of Myrtle's parents were deceased.

"Today's her birthday?" she said.

Myrtle nodded.

"And you're sad because she's not here."

"Yes." The word came out strangled, as tears again began to flow down Myrtle's face. "I miss her so much."

Gently, Daisy lifted her friend up and put her arms around her. "I know, I know. I miss mine, too."

"She would have been fifty today," said Myrtle, burying her face in Daisy's shoulder. "That's special. She should have a birthday party to celebrate her fiftieth birthday."

"You're right—that's a special birthday."

Myrtle leaned back and propped herself against the backboard.

"We weren't that close when I was growing up," said Myrtle. "She and poppa were always so strict with me—at least I thought so then. I know that's why I am like I am now."

"Wild and free as a bird?" said Daisy, grinning.

Myrtle laughed. "I'm not sure I'd go that far. But, yes, independent, for sure. I don't want anyone to tell me what I have to do . . . what I have to wear . . . what I have to think or believe—or who I have to be. I'm me. I'm who I am. I'm who I want to be."

"And, all in all," said Daisy, "you're a pretty decent person—and a good friend."

Myrtle reached over and hugged Daisy. "And you're a pretty good friend, too." Then she laid back.

"I wish momma and I had been closer. Poppa, too. I could have been a better daughter. I didn't have to be as difficult as I was. But—even though I was—I know they both loved me. And I loved them. And now I can't tell them how much they meant to me."

"I'm sure they knew," said Daisy. "Look, I don't think you're in any condition to go downstairs for breakfast. Why don't I go down and have Mrs. Darling fix us something special. I'll bring it back up here and you and I can eat right here in your room?"

Myrtle nodded. "That would be nice. I suppose while you're doing that I should go wash my face and get dressed for work."

"You're sure you want to go in today? Maybe you should take the day off."

"No," said Myrtle, shaking her head. "Mr. Mitchell is already upset that I've missed so much time. I'll be all right."

"Well, okay, then," said Daisy. "And who knows? Maybe something good will happen today to cheer you up."

*****

Myrtle had just finished re-shelving an accumulation of two days of books and newspapers and sat down to continue reading a book the library had just received, *Ten Days That Shook the World*, when she heard someone call her name.

"Myrtle?"

When she looked up, she found a tall, attractive man about her age standing on the other side of her desk. Under a black, Chesterfield overcoat, he wore a beige-colored, tweed suit with a matching vest and a patterned silk tie. A black herringbone Cashmere wool scarf lay draped around his neck. His head was bare.

"Myrtle?" the man said again. "Is it really you?"

For a moment Myrtle was confused. The man looked familiar, and yet . . .

Then, in a flash, it all came back to her: that night in Paris three years earlier; the obscenely handsome Englishman she'd met at Le Chat Noir; leaving her friends behind and going with him to his apartment on Boulevard de Clichy—number eleven: she would never forget the address—and making love until the sun came up the next morning.

"Thomas?" she cried. "What . . . what are you doing here?"

"I might ask the same of you," answered Thomas, "except it is quite evident—you're the librarian."

"*Assistant* librarian," said Myrtle, smoothing the hair back from her reddening face. "But you—I never thought I'd see you again."

"Was that wishful thinking?" asked Thomas, grinning.

Myrtle shook her head—a little too vigorously, she realized after the fact. "No, no, it's just that . . ."

"It was wartime."

Myrtle nodded. "Yes, it was wartime. Who knew what the next day might bring."

She still couldn't believe Thomas was actually there, standing in front of her.

"Wait here a minute," she said. She stood and walked back to Frank's office. She knocked on the door and Frank beckoned her in.

"I'm taking my lunch break now," she said.

Frank glanced up at the solid oak Waterbury Regulator clock on the office wall above Myrtle's head.

"It's not even eleven o'clock," he said, looking back at Myrtle.

Myrtle didn't say anything; just stood and waited.

Frank shrugged. "Well, okay, then," he said, "I suppose it's all right . . . but I still expect you to close up at six-thirty."

Myrtle smiled. "Yes, of course."

When she returned to her desk, she said, "Come on, let's go."

Grabbing first her lunch from under the counter, and then her coat and hat from the hooks on the wall, she took Thomas by the elbow and ushered him out the front door.

Once outside, she led him around to the southwest side of the building where a small garden with a grotto and a pond was reluctantly beginning to relinquish its collection of summer flowers. Several benches and a picnic table afforded places for people to sit and talk. . . or think . . . or daydream.

They sat down at the table, where Myrtle opened her sack and brought out a sandwich, a hard-boiled egg, and one cookie.

"I'll share," she said, offering him the egg.

"As tempting as that is," said Thomas, "I shall pass. I had a large breakfast before I came here."

"So," said Myrtle, unwrapping the sandwich, "what *are* you doing here? How did you find me?"

Thomas smiled. "That's rather presumptuous, isn't it, assuming I came here looking for you?"

Again, a redness came to Myrtle's face. "Well, I thought . . . that is . . ."

"The truth is I had no idea you were here. Or where you were. It is strictly by chance I found you; which doesn't mean I didn't look for you. When you left that morning without saying goodbye, I thought I had lost you forever. I ran to the window just in time to see you get into a cab. I shouted, but you didn't hear. Or perhaps you did, and chose not to answer."

"I didn't hear you," said Myrtle. "I had to get back to the boarding house where I was staying."

"And you hadn't given me your last name—"

"Tully," said Myrtle. "Myrtle Tully."

"Tully—I like that."

"You hadn't given me your last name either," said Myrtle.

"Wickersham. Thomas Thurlby Wickersham."

"My, you truly *are* English, aren't you, Mr. Wickersham?" said Myrtle, grinning.

"I am. Not to brag, but my family goes back fourteen generations."

"Mine goes back further than that," said Myrtle, taking a bite of the cold, corn beef sandwich Mrs. Darling had prepared for her.

"It does?"

"Oh, yes; all the way to Adam and Eve. Of course, I'm not sure of all the names."

Thomas laughed. "Right, you have me there."

"You still haven't told me why you're here," said Myrtle. "Other than you didn't come looking for me."

"But as I said I *did* look for you—right after we were together. I tried describing you to all my friends and acquaintances, but all I knew about you was that you were American, and a nurse, and your first name. No one seemed to have the foggiest idea who you were or where I might find you."

"First of all," said Myrtle, "I'm not a nurse; never have been."

Thomas' eyes squinted; he was confused. "But you said you were with the Allied Expeditionary Forces. And I was sure you were not a soldier."

"I was a telephone operator," said Myrtle. "A Hello Girl."

"A Hello Girl?" said Thomas, more puzzled now than ever.

"You see, when the French girls answered the phone, they always said 'bonjour.' But we Americans answered 'hello.' So our men always knew when they got a 'hello' they had reached an American operator."

Thomas nodded. "I see."

"And the only thing I knew about you," Myrtle continued, "was that you were English, you were an art student at the École des Beaux-Arts, and your name was Thomas."

"I see we were both under a misconception."

"Oh? How is that?"

"I was not a student at the École des Beaux-Arts—I was a professor there."

"Ah, hah," said Myrtle. "I stand corrected."

"And the reason I am here now is that I heard of this tiny college library in some small town in Michigan named Booker Falls that contained not only an original Renoir, but a Cézanne as well, and I had to see them for myself."

"And you came here just for that?"

"Your town happened to be not too far out of my way. I resigned my professorship last year and joined the Chapellier Galleries in London. We specialize in works by American artists, and I am currently on a buying trip. I came here from Buffalo and am on my way to Minneapolis. So you see, this is not too far out of the way."

"You live in London now?"

"For now. But we are looking to open a New York office in the next few years, and I believe I will be transferred there."

"When do you leave for Minneapolis?"

Thomas pulled out a watch from his vest pocket. "I fear I must be on my way shortly. I have a reservation for a hotel in a town called Ironwood for tonight. But I do have time to look at the paintings."

"Come on, then," said Myrtle, gathering up the remains of her lunch.

*****

"You are probably familiar with these artists," said Myrtle, as she and Thomas stood in front of the first painting. "The only ones I know are Renoir and Cézanne."

"Yes, I am familiar with them," said Thomas as they walked past the six paintings on the west wall. "These are very nice, very nice pieces."

They crossed to the other side of the room where the remaining works hung.

When they came to the Renoir, Myrtle said, "I met Monsieur Renoir once."

Thomas looked at her. Was she serious?

"I was coming back home after the war and I'd gone to Paris on my way to Cherbourg. I'd been to Paris before . . ." She smiled at him. ". . . as you well know. But I had never been to the Louvre. I knew I might never get back, so I went.

"I was standing in front of one of Renoir's paintings—Mrs. Charpentier and Her Children—when this older man came and stood next to me. I was concerned at first, but he seemed harmless enough, so I said nothing. Then he asked me what I thought of the painting. I told him I thought it was wonderful, that I admired all of Renoir's work.

"He bowed and introduced himself as Renoir. I didn't believe him, of course, but I didn't want to offend him, so I pretended I did. We chatted for a few minutes, and then he walked on. When he was out of sight I went over to one of the guards and asked if he knew who the man was.

"And it actually *was* Renoir! The guard said he came in occasionally to see if anyone was admiring his work."

"That's amazing!" said Thomas.

"I know. I'll never forget it. What do you think of our collection?"

Thomas took a step back. "Impressive—even the forgery."

Myrtle's brow furrowed. "Forgery? What forgery? These are all originals."

"Most of them are," said Thomas. "But this one . . ." He pointed to a piece by Aurelio Montague, a cityscape, ". . . is a forgery—a good one, I'll give it that."

Myrtle stood still, shocked. "I don't know how that's possible. I'm sure Mr. Mitchell said they were all originals. I wish you could speak with him . . ."

She glanced towards Frank's office, but it was empty.

"Are you sure?" she said.

Thomas nodded. "I am. There's no question."

He took Myrtle's hand. "I have to go. It's been wonderful seeing you again."

"Will you be coming back this way when you're finished in Minneapolis?"

Thomas frowned. "I'm afraid not. When I head back, I'll go to Chicago and then on to Detroit before returning to New York."

Myrtle matched his frown. "That is disappointing."

"But sometime in the future, not before the year's end, but sometime, I could make it a point to come this way again."

This news brought a glow to Myrtle's face.

"When you do," she said, "make sure you are here on a Sunday or Monday. That way you can join us at the boardinghouse for dinner, when I can be there also."

Thomas thought for a minute. "I might consider that if . . ."

"If what?"

"If you were to allow me to paint you when I am here."

For a second Myrtle was stunned. Then she laughed. "Paint me? You mean, like a portrait?"

"Not only your face—all of you."

Myrtle stared at him. "Mr. Wickersham, now . . . you're not talking about something inappropriate, are you?"

Thomas grinned. "You mean, nude?"

Myrtle nodded.

"How would you feel about that?"

Myrtle smiled. "Tell you what. I'll agree to your condition to paint me. Let's let it go at that."

When they reached Thomas' car, he held out his hand. "Myrtle, it was great seeing you again."

"I'm not expecting a kiss," said Myrtle. "But we could at least hug, could we not?"

Thomas smiled and gathered her up in his arms. "Yes, we could do that."

Myrtle watched as Thomas' automobile hurried off down the road.

She could hardly wait to tell Daisy.

*****

"Thomas? The Thomas that lived in the same apartment Picasso once lived in? The same Thomas that you . . .?"

Daisy was almost as excited as Myrtle had been that Thomas had shown up in Booker Falls.

"Yes, *that* Thomas," said Myrtle. "One and the same."

"How in the world did he end up here?"

"He was just passing through." She went on to tell Daisy what Thomas had told her.

"And I've invited him for dinner the next time he's in town. I was a little concerned about what Mrs. Darling would say, but she thought it was a marvelous idea."

"Forget Mrs. Darling. What will Henri say? Or George?"

"Why should they say anything?"

"About meeting your old boyfriend?"

"First of all," said Myrtle, "Thomas is not my old boyfriend—I spent one night with him. And I have no intention of telling either Henri or George anything about what went on between Thomas and me. And you better not either!"

"My lips are sealed," said Daisy. "In fact, you can pour hot, burning candle wax on them to keep them sealed. Okay, not really. But I promise—I won't say anything. What's the second thing?"

"What second thing?"

"You said, 'first of all,' so there must be a second thing."

"There is no second thing. Just you mind you don't say anything."

Daisy drew an imaginary zipper across her lips.

"Now that I think of it, he did say one thing that was strange," said Myrtle. "He said one of the paintings in the library was a forgery."

"A forgery?"

"Yes. And I'm not sure what to make of that."

"Did you mention it to Mr. Mitchell?" asked Daisy.

"I did, when I found him after Thomas left. He said Thomas was mistaken; that all the paintings were originals—that he should know since he was there when Mr. Amyx donated them."

"Mr. Mitchell studied art at Adelaide."

"Yes, and Thomas *taught* art at the École des Beaux-Arts."

"So, who do you think is right?" asked Daisy.

Myrtle shook her head. "I don't know. Oh, but there *was* one more thing. Thomas wants to paint me—a full portrait."

Daisy was quiet for a minute. "Clothed . . . or . . . ? I mean, you know, it's not like he hasn't seen you . . . ."

Myrtle merely smiled.

CHAPTER TWENTY-TWO

"Mrs. Darling," said Pierre, as he watched his landlady pour him another cup of coffee, "this oatmeal is delicious. I know it has apples in it, but there's another flavor I can't determine."

"Yah, dat's ginger," said Mrs. Darling as she moved to Myrtle's cup. "Makes it quite tasty, don't it?"

"It's amazing," said Daisy. "Almost as good as when you put thimbleberries in."

"Miss O'Hearn, I got a favor to ask of you," said Mrs. Darling. "I was wondering if you'd mind setting da noon meal out. I got fried chicken in da ice box—it's good cold—along with potato salad and some hard-boiled eggs. And I could show you how to make da coffee."

"Won't you be here for lunch?" asked Henri.

"Miss Tully has been kind enough to agree to drive me over to Marquette, once breakfast is over and I've cleared da table."

"What's in Marquette?" asked Daisy.

"I'm going to go visit Mr. Pfrommer."

"What?" exclaimed Henri. "Why in the world would you want to do that?"

"Yeah," said Daisy. "Why do you want to visit the man who killed that young girl and nearly killed Myrtle if it hadn't been for George?"

"I know he done terrible tings," said Mrs. Darling, setting the coffee pot on the wooden hot pad. "But he lived under my roof for almost turty years and never gave me no trouble, and I kind of feel sorry for him.

I'm pretty sure he don't have nobody else to visit him, so I tought I should go."

"I never met Mr. Pfrommer," said Pierre, "but I think what you're doing is admirable."

"I guess I do, too," said Daisy.

"I still think it's a mistake," said Henri, taking a bite of bacon.

"But you all wouldn't mind having a cold meal?" asked Mrs. Darling. "I promise I'll have someting special for dinner."

"Since you put it that way . . ." said Daisy.

*****

Booker Falls had been known to have a foot or more of snow on the ground by the first of October, but this day was sublime: a little cool, the sun was shining, and a light breeze wended its way in from the southwest—a perfect day for a drive.

Myrtle had been a little apprehensive when Mrs. Darling approached her about the possibility of driving her to Marquette to visit Mr. Pfrommer. She had experienced the same feelings Henri expressed—not only was the old man responsible for, not one, but two murders; he had also tried to choke her to death.

Just thinking about it, she felt a tightening of his cravat around her neck.

But Mrs. Darling had always been so kind to her, bringing her tea, sometimes with cookies, and never asking for anything in return—she didn't see how she could refuse. So she had said yes.

Now, as they drove past the same woods and farms she passed a number of times before when she went to Marquette to visit Mrs. Sinclair, she didn't feel nearly as uneasy.

As they rounded Dead's Man Curve, Myrtle remembered what Daisy told her the time she had accompanied her, that the white stripe that ran down the middle of the road was the first ever painted on a highway in the United States.

That woman knows more trivia than anyone I ever met, thought Myrtle.

Coming into Marquette on Highway 41, they followed it through the city until they came to Front Street, where they turned right. A little further on they came to Hampton Street and took a left over to Lakeshore Boulevard. Henri had told her she could continue on Front Street if she wanted to, but going by way of Lakeshore would be more scenic.

Myrtle had not seen Lake Superior on her two previous trips, so it was an easy decision.

"Look at that, Mrs. Darling," said Myrtle, glancing out at the unending expanse of water. "Isn't it beautiful?"

"I guess," replied the old lady, unimpressed. "You see one lake, you've seen dem all."

Myrtle laughed. It was the same expression her landlady used when she passed up going to the Fourth of July parade the past summer.

"No, no. They're all different," said Myrtle. "They all have their own individual soul, their own heart."

"Dearie, it's water. Don't try to make it someting it ain't."

*****

"Oh, my!" exclaimed Mrs. Darling when they reached the Marquette Branch Prison. "Look how big it is! It looks like a castle."

Constructed of local sandstone, gray and red, with arches and tower battlements, the place did indeed resemble a castle.

A little over thirty years old, the Administration Building was a three-story structure with a hipped roof and a central square tower that soared almost ninety feet into the air. The corners were octagonal, each capped with a spire.

Myrtle found a place to park the Model N, and she and Mrs. Darling entered through the main door. Myrtle had called the previous day and arranged for the visit. Initially, she had decided she wouldn't go into the visiting area with Mrs. Darling, as she wasn't sure how she might react to seeing her old housemate.

Then she changed her mind. Mr. Pfrommer had always been kind to her and Penrod. She wanted to know how he was faring. It would be the first time she'd seen him since that day she barely escaped with her life. Unlike Paul Momet's trial, she had not attended any of Mr. Pfrommer's.

She and Mrs. Darling both gasped, unable to mask the shock they felt when Mr. Pfrommer joined them.

He had always carried himself like a gentleman, sure of who he was: refined, well-mannered, his posture impeccable. Now, he appeared wearied, broken, his spirit gone.

Absent, too, was the magnificent set of muttonchops he had sported for the past thirty years.

When he sat down across from the two women they saw that his eyes were sunken, dark circles under them.

"Miss Tully, Mrs. Darling, it vas so good of you both to come," he said in a voice no more than a whisper.

"Dear Mr. Pfrommer," said Myrtle, "how are you doing?"

An unnecessary question, she realized at once. It was apparent he was not doing well at all.

"It has been an experience," said the old man.

"You shaved off your whiskers," said Mrs. Darling.

Mr. Pfrommer allowed a slight smile to cross his lips. "Vell, I did not exactly shave dem off."

"What do you mean?" asked Myrtle.

"Some of das other prisoners did it."

"Without your permission?" asked Myrtle.

"Yah," replied Mr. Pfrommer, nodding.

"Why would dey do dat?" asked Mrs. Darling.

"I am not popular among the inmates here," answered Mr. Pfrommer. "Dey do not treat me kindly."

"Why not?" asked Myrtle.

"Memories of das war are still fresh in deir minds. Although most of dem did not participate in it."

Myrtle sat back in her chair. "Because you are German."

"Yah. Because I am German."

"Oh, I'm so sorry," said Mrs. Darling, wringing her hands.

"Do you still play your violin?" asked Myrtle, hoping to change the subject to a more enjoyable topic.

"I vas for a few days after I got here. Den, no more."

"Why not?" asked Mrs. Darling. "You loved playing. And it was so beautiful."

"It vas not my choice. Vun of das prisoners took my violin from me und broke it against das vall."

Mrs. Darling started to cry. "Dat's so unfair," she said. "I'm so sorry."

"But how are you doing?" asked Mr. Pfrommer, sitting up a little straighter. "Both of you? Und Constable de la Cruz, and Miss O'Hearn? Is erybody vell?"

"We are all in good health," answered Myrtle.

"Und Penrod? How is my sveet dog doing?"

"He's as peppy as ever," said Myrtle.

"Und news? Vat's happening in town?"

"Oh, you won't believe it—" Mrs. Darling started to say before she felt Myrtle squeeze her hand.

"Quiet as ever," said Myrtle. No need to talk about murders. Not with a man who was here in prison for having committed two himself.

"Oh, right," said Mrs. Darling. "Quiet as ever."

She reached into the basket she'd brought with her and took out the pie she'd baked. "I brought this for you—your favorite: thimbleberry."

Mr. Pfrommer looked at the pie and a tear came to his eyes. "Mrs. Darling, you are wery kind. But I cannot take it."

"Won't they allow you to have it?" asked Myrtle.

"It's yust dat . . . vell, as soon as I valk out of dis room it vould be taken by das other prisoners. It is best you take it back home and enjoy it."

No one spoke for a moment before Mr. Pfrommer broke the silence.

"Miss Tully," he said, looking at Myrtle, "I do not know if you can ever forgive me for vhat I tried to do to you. It vas a moment of desperation on my part. I cannot tell you how sorry I am."

Tears flowed freely down his cheeks. He looked down at the table between them.

"I am so sorry," he said again.

Myrtle took Mr. Pfrommer's hands in hers. "Of course, I forgive you. Can you ever forgive me?"

Mr. Pfrommer looked back up. "Forgive you? Forgive you for vhat?"

"I am the reason you're in here. If I hadn't pursued the matter of that young girl's death, you wouldn't be here."

Mr. Pfrommer shook his head. "Oh, no. You did das right thing. You have done nutting for vich I should forgive you. I deserve to be here."

"Is dere anyting we can do for you?" asked Mrs. Darling. "Anyting we can get you?"

Mr. Pfrommer shook his head. "Nein. They vould take vateffer you sent me. Best I yust try to stay out of deir vay.

"Miss Tully, do you know vhat happened to my vatches?"

"I'm pretty sure Henri has them locked up in his office."

"I vould like you to have dem. You could sell dem. Mr. Abramovitz vould give you a fair price, I'm sure."

"Mr. Pfrommer, I couldn't—"

"Please," said Mr. Pfrommer. "I cannot have dem in here. Best somevone else gets pleasure from dem, yah?"

Myrtle nodded. "Very well. I'll talk to Henri when we get back."

"Time's up."

They all turned to look at the guard who had entered the room.

"Vill you come again?" asked Mr. Pfrommer.

"We will try," said Myrtle, as the guard took the old man by the elbow. "We will certainly try."

Though she knew the possibility of that happening was highly unlikely.

*****

The drive back to Booker Falls from Marquette was a quiet one, each woman deep in her own thoughts.

They were almost to town when Myrtle said, "It's my fault."

"What is, dearie?"

"That Mr. Pfrommer is in that horrible place. It's all my fault. He's old—he wasn't going to hurt anyone anymore."

She wiped a tear from her eye.

"He tried to kill you," said Mrs. Darling.

Myrtle couldn't argue with that.

CHAPTER TWENTY-THREE

Having dinner with her fellow boarders was always a special treat for Myrtle. Working at the library until six-thirty each evening meant she was able to join them only on her two days off, Sunday and Monday. Mrs. Darling always went out of her way to make sure the menu was a little bit special for at least one of those meals, including an item she knew was a favorite of Myrtle's.

Tonight's dinner consisted of bell peppers stuffed with elk meat, with side dishes of fried corn and a cucumber salad, followed by tapioca pudding.

"Mrs. Darling, you've done it again!" exclaimed Myrtle, as she eyed the bowls of food on the table before her. "This is a marvelous meal."

"I hope you enjoy it, dearie," said the old lady, beaming.

"You know, we only get special meals like this when you eat with us," whispered Daisy once Mrs. Darling had left the room. "Not that all the other meals aren't delicious. But Henri and Pierre and I want to thank you for inspiring Mrs. Darling to new heights."

"Here, here," said Pierre, lifting his water glass.

"How is Mr. Pfrommer doing?" asked Daisy.

Myrtle frowned. "Not too well, I fear. Being in a place like that at his age is hard. And he says the other prisoners are making it hard on him, too."

"Did he enjoy the pie Mrs. Darling baked for him?" asked Daisy.

Myrtle laid her spoon down as large tears started to roll down her cheeks.

"What is it?" asked Henri. "What's wrong?"

"He wouldn't take it," said Myrtle between sobs. "He said as soon as he left the room we were in they'd take it from him."

"Oh, I'm sorry," said Pierre, placing his hand on Myrtle's.

"Henri, can't you do something?" asked Daisy. "Call the warden, or something?"

Henri shook his head. "I'm afraid I have little influence at the prison."

After a few moments, Myrtle's sobs subsided and everyone was quiet. Henri started to take a bite of his pepper when Pierre spoke up.

"Henri, how's the investigation going?"

"Oh, I almost forgot," answered Henri, wiping his mouth with his napkin. "We got the fingerprint results back from the state police in Marquette. There were four sets taken off the safe. One belonged to Rudy— Mr. Folger. One was Mrs. Folger's: not unusual, since she sometimes filled in for Mrs. Pennyworth at the office. The third matched a set taken from Mrs. Pennyworth's coffee cup. We assume they are hers, but we won't know for sure until she returns from Chicago."

"And the fourth?" asked Myrtle.

"We don't know," said Henri. "Could be the killer's, but we don't have anything to match them to yet."

"How about Mr. and Mrs. Finnegan?" asked Myrtle.

"I'm going by tomorrow morning to get their prints," said Henri. "I'll send them over to Marquette and we should hear back in a few days."

"And Mickey?" said Myrtle.

Henri shrugged. "He won't give me his prints."

"Won't give you his prints?" said Daisy. "Can't you make him?"

"'Fraid not," answered Henri.

"I bet I can get them for you," said Myrtle, digging into her pepper.

"And how about the Steinmyers?" asked Daisy. "Leonard took prints from those crime scenes too, didn't he?"

Myrtle looked at Daisy. She hadn't had any indication from her housemate she'd even known Leonard was back in the area. Myrtle had thought it best not to bring up the subject, in case he had not looked her up when he was in town.

"Got the results on those, too," said Henri. "Other than Nathan and Miss Wasserman, the only other prints found in either room was a set we believe might belong to Lars, but until I can locate him we can't verify that."

"Not Mr. Li's prints?" said Myrtle.

"No," said Henri. "I have Mr. Li's prints. Took them when Leonard and I picked him up. They were not found in either bedroom."

"How about the chip?" asked Myrtle. "The gambling chip. Any prints on it?"

"Leonard said they weren't able to get a print from it."

*****

After dinner Myrtle brushed her teeth, then went to find Daisy, who was in her room, busy typing.

"I didn't know you knew Leonard had been in town," said Myrtle.

"Oh, sure," said Daisy.

She doesn't' seem too concerned, thought Myrtle.

"He stopped by the newspaper office the day he was here to get the fingerprints," said Daisy.

"You didn't say anything."

"Wasn't much to say—except he's married."

Myrtle's jaw dropped. "Married? When did he get married?"

"Met some gal down in Flint; a whirlwind romance, way he tells it. Anyway, I wished him well and that was that."

Myrtle couldn't believe Daisy was being so blasé about the whole thing. "Well . . . how do you feel? Are you okay?"

"Oh, sure. I guess I got over Leonard some time ago. I'm happy for him."

Myrtle shook her head. "All right, if you're okay, then, I guess . . . well, I guess it's okay."

"It's okay," said Daisy.

*****

Myrtle's usual Monday morning routine was to walk downtown to Paige Turner's New, Used, and Rare Books Store, to see what new additions Paige had brought in the previous week. Today, however, she didn't stop there, but continued on to Alton Woodruff's barbershop.

"Miss Tully," said Alton, as she entered. Myrtle had discovered that everyone now seemed to know who she was—a celebrity of sorts.

"Is Mr. Mulhearn back there?" asked Myrtle, nodding towards the back door.

"Why, um . . ." Alton stammered.

"Never mind. I shall see for myself."

Before Alton could protest, Myrtle swept through the door to the back room.

At nine o'clock in the morning, the place wasn't busy—but neither was it empty. One man sat by himself at a table, a half-empty bottle of whiskey in front of him, while at another, three men, one of whom was Mickey McInerney, were drinking beer and playing fifteen-two.

Myrtle hadn't actually expected to find Mickey there. She had planned to ask Joker for a favor, but this was a better opportunity to obtain what she was looking for.

She walked over to where Mulhearn was wiping out glasses and eyeing her warily. He wasn't used to having women in the place, and for sure not this early in the morning.

"Mr. Mulhearn," said Myrtle "those three men at the table there playing cribbage—I want to buy them a round."

Joker looked at her and narrowed his eyes. *What was her game?*

Myrtle opened her purse and took out a fifty-cent piece. "This should cover it, should it not?"

Whatever her game was, thought Joker, *she had money*. That was all he needed to know.

"If you will pour their glasses, I will deliver them," said Myrtle.

Joker poured the glasses, set them on the counter and picked up the money.

"A tray, please?" said Myrtle.

Taking a tray out from under the counter, Joker placed the three glasses on it.

"Thank you," said Myrtle.

"Drink up fellows," said Myrtle when she reached the table. "A fresh round on the house."

She watched as each man chugged down the remainder of the beer before him. Then she set the fresh glasses down and removed the empty ones, being careful to pick Mickey's up by the rim.

She walked back to Joker and set the tray on the bar.

"I like this glass," she said to him, holding up Mickey's empty glass. "I think I'll keep it. You don't mind, do you?"

Before Joker could answer, Myrtle was through the door, through the barbershop and out onto the sidewalk, being careful not to put her own prints on the glass as she crossed the street to Henri's office.

*****

"What is this?" asked Henri.

Myrtle stood on the other side of the desk, beaming.

"Don't touch it," she said.

Henri's brow furrowed. "Don't touch it? Why not? What's so special about an empty beer glass? I'd be more excited if it was filled with beer."

"That," said Myrtle, triumphantly, "contains Mickey McInerney's fingerprints."

Henri looked at the glass. "His fingerprints? Where did you get it?"

"Alton Woodruff's barbershop. Well, Joker Mulhearn's bar, to be more precise."

"Joker . . . ? Why were you there at this time of the morning? Why would you *ever* be there at any time, for that matter?"

"I planned to ask Mr. Mulhearn for a favor," Myrtle answered. "To secure a glass for me that Mickey had drunk from. But I didn't have to because Mickey was there. *This* is the glass he drank from. And you will find his prints on it."

Henri shook his head. Miss Myrtle Tully was certainly different than any other woman he had ever known.

CHAPTER TWENTY-FOUR

The bank had been closed since the deaths of Rachel and her father.

While Nathan had no interest in returning to work there, he realized it needed to be reopened. He'd enticed Bindi Chatham, the bank's head cashier for over thirty years until her retirement two years ago, to return and run it until he found a permanent replacement.

He had thought—albeit briefly—of 'borrowing' some money from the vault to pay Yung Li and get him off his back. The drawback to that was that he might get caught—and Nathan had no desire to spend any time in jail or prison.

He decided instead to see if he could get the reading of his father's will accomplished quickly. With the proceeds from the estate he could easily take care of the debt he owed Mr. Zhāng.

The problem was that both executors—Rudolph Folger, the primary executor, and Rachel, the secondary executor—were now deceased. Nathan had set an appointment with Judge Hurstbourne to see if he could be appointed the executor himself.

Although Judge Hurstbourne was only ten years older than Nathan, and despite the fact the judge and Isaiah had both been members for over thirty years of the poker club that met at George's house, Nathan had been in the judge's company only a handful of times, mostly on social occasions.

Judge Hurstbourne stood as his secretary, Mrs. Marley, ushered Nathan into his chambers.

The younger man hesitated for a moment before approaching the desk; he forgot how imposing the judge was. At six feet four and weighing over two hundred and sixty pounds, he filled the small room from which he transacted his business.

"Mr. Steinmyer," said Judge Hurstbourne, extending his hand.

Instinctively, Nathan took the judge's hand and found his own nearly swallowed up in it.

"Judge Hurstbourne," said Nathan.

"Please, have a seat. Frightfully sorry to hear about your sister and Isaiah. I understand from Mr. McIntyre we have a suspect in custody. Now, what can I do for you today? Would you care for a drink?"

"Uh, no, sir, thank you," said Nathan, as he sat down. "I hadn't heard someone was arrested."

"Not arrested exactly. Held for questioning. The Chinaman—Constable de la Cruz has him in custody for questioning. I believe I'll have a nip, if you don't mind," continued the judge, turning to the sideboard behind him.

Nathan shook his head. He wasn't about to remind the judge it was only ten o'clock in the morning.

Judge Hurstbourne poured a stiff drink, then turned back and sat down.

"Now, then," he said, as he sipped his drink, "what can I do for you?"

"It's about the will."

"Ah, yes, the will. Your father's will, I presume."

"Yes, sir. I was hoping that since Mr. Folger—he was the primary executor of my father's will, you know—and my sister, who was the secondary executor, are both dead, you might appoint me as the executor."

Judge Hurstbourne eyed Nathan. He didn't particularly like the man. Felt as though he had abandoned his family when he took off ten years before and headed west.

"Appoint you as the executor, eh?" said the judge.

"Yes, sir."

Judge Hurstbourne smoothed his mustache and took another sip of his drink. Opening the bronze humidor on his desk, he extracted a Yankee Girl cigar and held the tube under his nose, eyes closed in appreciation, as he breathed in the aromatic fragrance of the tobacco.

He opened his eyes, took the bullet punch cutter attached to his watch chain and carefully clipped the end from the cigar, then sighed deeply as his mouth closed around it. Removing a match from the miniature bronze boot holder that sat next to the humidor, he scraped it along the holder, causing it to flare forth, then brought it to the cigar's tip and lit it, at the same time inhaling.

He held the smoke for a moment, then exhaled.

He looked at Nathan.

"Well, son," he said, "that's not going to happen."

Nathan leaned back, surprised. This wasn't what he had expected.

"Temple Jacob over in Houghton contacted me when they heard of your father's and sister's deaths," continued the judge. "Isaiah told them the congregation was named as a beneficiary in his will, so when they learned that both of the executors were dead, they asked me to be the executor. I told them I would be honored to serve in that capacity."

Nathan hesitated a moment while he took in this unexpected—and unwelcomed—news.

"Do you suppose," he then asked, "if they knew I was back they might accept me as the executor?"

"They do know you're back," said Judge Hurstbourne, taking another puff on his cigar, "and they were very explicit they did *not* want you as the executor."

Now Nathan was more shocked than disappointed. "Did they say why not?"

"They did not, nor did I ask."

Nathan thought for a moment. "Then can the reading be done in the next few days?"

"Your family members have been dead less than a week. I have set the reading of your father's will for the fifteenth of this month."

"The fifteenth? But that's . . . that's—"

"Eleven days from now," said the judge.

Nathan squirmed in his chair.

"May I ask why it will take so long?"

"I wanted someone from Mr. Folger's office to be present. I asked Mrs. Folger, but she declined. Said she was still in mourning. Mrs. Pennyworth is scheduled to return from her trip on the fourteenth, and has agreed to be present. Now, is there anything else?"

For a moment, Nathan didn't stir. This was not at all the way he wanted this to go.

Then he shook his head. "No, sir, I guess not."

Judge Hurstbourne stood and extended his hand. "Then good day, Mr. Steinmyer. I will see you here in my chambers in eleven days—twelve o'clock sharp."

CHAPTER TWENTY-FIVE

Myrtle jumped when she heard the first BONG of the grandfather clock in the dining room. Six more quickly followed, announcing it was seven o'clock—time for breakfast.

Even after a year of hearing the clanging of the clock every hour on the hour, she was still startled when it happened. Daisy said it took her three months to get used to it: Myrtle doubted she ever would.

In the past, when Mr. Pfrommer was still a boarder at the house, breakfast had always been served precisely at seven. And lunch at noon. And dinner at five. Mr. Pfrommer was particular about when he ate.

The schedule was a little more relaxed now. Still, Myrtle didn't want to be too late; it made it seem as though she was inconsiderate of the other boarders' time.

She threw on a sweater and dashed down the stairs. Sure enough, everyone was at their place and Mrs. Darling was pouring coffee. As soon as she walked in, both Henri and Pierre jumped up. Pierre held her chair for her.

"Good morning, all," said Myrtle, cheerfully. "Sorry I'm late."

"A late night?" asked Pierre.

"A too-early morning," answered Myrtle, buttering her toast. Turning to Henri, she asked, "Is Mr. Li still in jail?"

"Yah, Jake says I may have to release him, though. He said he'd think seriously about charging him with

Miss Steinmyer's murder if he could confirm it was his gun that was used to kill her."

"Why can't he?" asked Pierre.

"There's no way to do that," said Henri.

"Of course, there is," said Pierre, cutting his sausage link and thrusting a piece into his mouth.

"How?" asked Henri. "What do you mean?"

Pierre looked at him as though the answer were obvious. "With the bullets."

"With the bullets? How with the bullets?" asked Henri.

"Why, you inspect them—one from the gun and the other from the body. If they match they came from the same gun."

Henri was starting to get a little perturbed. "What do you mean, *match*?"

Pierre lay down his knife and fork, picked up his napkin and wiped his mouth.

"Gun barrels are rifled; they have grooves that run down the length of them. That makes the bullet spiral as it passes through the barrel, which provides for greater accuracy in its flight. But the grooves are never perfect: there are always some flaws. Consequently, as the bullet goes through, it picks up small scratches. Because of the flaws, the inside of every barrel is unique, which makes the marks on the bullet unique also. By comparing the marks on one bullet to that of another bullet, one can tell if they've been fired from the same gun."

For a moment the other three just stared at Pierre.

Then Myrtle spoke up.

"You teach literature and French. How do you know so much about guns?"

"I know little about guns," said Pierre. "But I do know about this particular subject. When I was living in Boston, I had occasion to attend a trial before the

Supreme Court—the state Supreme Court. That was..."
Pierre looked up at the ceiling, his brow furrowed, "in
1903 as I recall. Yes, that's right—1903. Or was it
1902? Anyway, it was right after the turn of the
century. Oh, and I remember now—the case was
Commonwealth vee Best."

"Get on with it, man," said Henri, impatiently.
"What about the bullets?"

"The question was how to tell if two bullets that
killed a man were fired from a particular gun, in this
case a rifle."

"Just like these cases," said Daisy.

"Except we have a pistol, not a rifle," said Henri.

"I'm sure the type of weapon would have no
bearing," said Pierre.

"Were they able to determine if the same gun fired
the bullets?" asked Myrtle.

"They were," said Pierre. "Mr. Holmes—"

"Mr. Holmes?" said Daisy.

"Oliver Wendell Holmes—I'm sure you've heard of
him? He's on the Supreme Court? The United States
Supreme Court? Anyway, at that time he was Chief
Justice of the Massachusetts Supreme Court. He had
someone fire a bullet from the gun into a wad of cotton.
Then, using a magnifying glass, he examined that bullet
against the two bullets taken from the deceased and
determined that the same gun fired all the bullets. The
man was found guilty of murder."

"What you're saying then," said Myrtle, "is, if Henri
fired a bullet from Mr. Li's gun and used a magnifying
glass to compare it to the one taken from Miss
Steinmyer's body, he could tell if it was the gun that
was used to kill her?"

"Exactly," said Pierre.

"Wait a minute," said Myrtle. "Wouldn't it be possible to also tell if the same gun was used to kill both Mr. Folger *and* Miss Steinmyer?"

"I don't see why not," answered Pierre, picking up his knife and fork again. "You have the bullets from both crimes, do you not? All you have to do is compare them."

He cut another piece of sausage and put it into his mouth.

Myrtle looked at Henri for a moment, then at Daisy. "Come on," she said, getting up.

"Where are we going?" asked Daisy.

"To get your magnifying glass, and then Henri and I are going to go find a wad of cotton."

"What about the library?" asked Henri.

"You call Mr. Mitchell, tell him I'm sick in bed. Can't even talk. Come on, Daisy!" she shouted, disappearing up the stairs.

*****

"I guess there's no doubt about it," said Henri, looking up. He held Daisy's magnifying glass in one hand.

On the table in front of him sat three bullets: two from the bodies of Rudolph Folger and Rachel Steinmyer, and a third fired from Yung Li's gun.

"No," said Myrtle, "there sure isn't."

She had inspected all three bullets, then turned the glass over to Henri. For ten minutes he had been scrutinizing each bullet, trying to match up the stripes along their sides. Two matched: the ones which killed Folger and Rachel. What didn't match was the one from Yung Li's gun.

"He didn't do it," said Myrtle, slumping down into a chair.

"At least not with this gun." Henri picked up Yung's gun and turned it over.

"Not with any gun," said Myrtle. "He wasn't even in town when Mr. Folger was killed, and the same gun was used on him as was used on Miss Steinmyer."

"But he still might have killed *Mr*. Steinmyer," said Henri.

Myrtle shrugged. "Maybe. But I'm not sure there's enough evidence to support that. The poker chip is no good—it was found in Miss Steinmyer's room, and Captain Wysocki said they couldn't get a fingerprint off of it. And that was *before* Mr. Steinmyer was killed. Leonard also said he couldn't lift any fingerprints off the pillow used to smother him. All you have is motive and no alibi. But what we do know is that in all probability the same person killed both Mr. Folger and Miss Steinmyer."

"Unless your theory of murder by proxy proves out."

"Yes, that's still a possibility—but, then, it would almost have to be Mrs. Folger and her brother."

"Except Mickey's prints weren't the ones on the safe."

"Doesn't mean he didn't do it," said Myrtle.

"First of all let's see what Jake has to say about letting Mr. Li go."

*****

"I don't see how you can keep him," said Jake, after Henri told him what he and Myrtle had discovered. "As Miss Tully says, the evidence is too thin. You're going to have to let him go."

"You know as soon as I do he'll flee town," said Henri.

"Can't be helped. But at least now we know we're probably not looking for more than two killers."

*****

Henri unlocked his desk drawer and handed the gun to Yung Li.

"I am free to go?" asked the Chinaman.

Henri nodded. "Yes."

"But I don't have to leave town?"

Henri squinted. "What do you mean, you don't *have* to leave town. Why would you stick around?"

"My business here is not finished," said Yung, as he tucked the gun into his belt.

"Wait a minute. When I asked you the other day what you were doing here, you said you were a tourist. What's this about 'business'"?

"I *was* a tourist—now I have business."

Henri wasn't sure what to say. He assumed Yung would leave town right away. Now that he said he wasn't going to, he didn't know how comfortable he felt about that. Yet, he wasn't sure he had the authority to make him leave.

"What kind of business?" he asked.

"Personal business."

Henri stared at him. "Don't get in any trouble," he said, "or you'll end up right back in here."

"No trouble." Yung nodded, then turned and left.

*****

Jake picked up the bottle of scotch and poured four glasses, then passed one each to Henri and George. Mindful of their last meeting, he also handed one to Myrtle.

"I'm curious, Mr. McIntyre," she said. "How do you manage to come by liquor during prohibition?"

"It's for medicinal purposes," Jake answered.

Myrtle arched her eyebrows. "Medicinal purposes, huh?"

"That's right—I suffer from dry mouth."

They all laughed.

Jake sipped his drink, then said, "Okay, then, let's see what we got."

In light of the new information about the gun used in two of the murders, he had asked Henri, Myrtle and George to join him to update their information.

"We can forget about Mr. Li as a suspect," said Henri.

"Except possibly in the case of Mr. Steinmyer," said George.

Henri shook his head. "No, I'm pretty sure he had nothing to do with that. When I told him he was free to go, he said he was staying around for a while—no doubt to try to collect money from Nathan. If Mr. Li really was guilty of anything, I think he'd clear out of town as quick as he could."

"We now have another connection between Mr. Folger's case and Miss Steinmyer's," said Myrtle.

"Right—the murder weapon," said Jake.

"Except we don't have the gun itself yet," added Henri.

"Can we assume then that the same person committed both murders?" asked George.

"Unless you buy Myrtle's possible theory of murder by proxy," said Henri. "In which case Mickey killed Rudy and Mrs. Folger killed Miss Steinmyer. However, I just got back the results of Mickey's fingerprints— they weren't the ones on Rudy's safe."

"That doesn't mean he didn't do it, though," said George.

"That's what I said," said Myrtle.

"Henri," said Jake, "have you been able to locate Mr. Jørgensen?"

"He seems to have disappeared. He hasn't been at work since before Rudy's murder and I haven't found anyone who's seen him around for a while. I'm beginning to think he's not a viable suspect, though, since we know now that the same gun used to kill Miss

Steinmyer was also used to kill Rudy, and there's no obvious connection of Lars to him."

"Okay," said Jake, "keep looking. Were you able to get copies of the Steinmyers' wills? Oh, and Rudy's?"

"Yes," said Henri. "Besides a small bequest to Mrs. Pennyworth, Rudy left his whole estate to Mrs. Folger. Now, here's something strange," added Henri. "Turns out Rudy was the attorney for the Steinmyer family. Mrs. Folger volunteered that information. I asked her, since Mrs. Pennyworth was still out of town, if she could procure the copies of the wills for me. She told me later that she found Miss Steinmyer's will, but not her father's."

"That's odd," said Myrtle.

"She said she would contact Mrs. Pennyworth and ask her if she knew where Mr. Steinmyer's was. In the meantime, though, I approached Nathan. He had copies of both wills, and loaned them to me. I jotted down the particulars and returned the documents to him."

"What did they say?" asked Jake.

"We might have to remove Nathan's name from the suspect list," said Henri.

"Why?" asked Myrtle.

"In Mr. Steinmyer's will, other than a few bequests to Miss Wasserman, Mrs. Chatham—"

"Wait," said Myrtle. "Who is Mrs. Chatham?"

Henri explained her involvement with the bank, then continued. "And to Temple Jacob over in Houghton, the rest of the estate was to be divided equally between Nathan and Miss Steinmyer, with Nathan getting control of the bank and his sister possession of the house. Oh, and Miss Wasserman was to be allowed to continue to live in the house the rest of her life."

"What about Miss Steinmyer's will?" asked Jake.

"She left everything to Miss Wasserman."

"What if Miss Steinmyer died before her father?" asked Jake.

"According to Mr. Steinmyer's will," said Henri, "were that to happen, Miss Wasserman would get the house and Temple Jacob would get what Miss Steinmyer would have received."

Jake rubbed the back of his neck. "So . . . Nathan stood to gain nothing from his sister's death, only from his father's."

"Looks that way," said Henri.

"And his father was already dying," said Jake. "Why would Nathan have any motive to kill him?"

"To speed up the process of getting his inheritance," said Myrtle.

"But did he need the money so badly that he would take the chance of getting caught for murder?" asked George. "I mean, all he had to do was wait. And not for very long, evidently."

"There is the matter of Mr. Li being in town to collect the money Nathan owes," said Jake.

"Yes," said Myrtle, "there is that."

"I'm sorry," said Henri, "but I can't see Nathan taking that risk merely to speed up the process. In my conversations with Mr. Li, I took him to be a reasonable man, who I think would have been willing to wait and let nature take its course. I just don't see Nathan doing this."

CHAPTER TWENTY-SIX

Feeling queasy, Daisy left the newspaper office early and headed home to the boarding house, hoping to snitch a glass of sherry from the bottle Mrs. Darling kept in the kitchen for special guests. She thought it might perk her up.

Glass in hand, she was about to climb the stairs to her room, where she planned on settling in with her new copy of Sherwood Anderson's *Winesburg, Ohio*, when she heard the whistle of Mr. Littlefield, the letter carrier, making his second delivery of the day.

Better go, she thought. If no one answered the door, he'd put the mail back in his pouch and they wouldn't get it until tomorrow, since this was his second delivery of the day.

She turned around and opened the front door.

"Miss O'Hearn," said Mr. Littlefield, in his usual cheerful voice. "Just the one I was hoping to see."

Eugene Littlefield had been the letter carrier in Booker Falls since home delivery was first established fifteen years before, in 1905. Thanks to walking over twenty miles a day, six days a week while making deliveries, even at the age of sixty-nine he still sported the trim body he'd brought to the job when he left his previous employer of thirty years, the Duluth, South Shore and Atlantic Railway, where he'd served as an engineer, making runs from St. Ignace to Duluth, Minnesota.

He would still be making those runs had not his wife, Hilda, the town's postmistress, insisted he take the letter carrier job when it came open.

"I'm tired of having you home just one or two days a week," she'd said, "and besides," she added, gesturing, "there's plenty of fixin' needs doin' 'round here."

Though he'd argued against leaving the railroad, he found delivering mail to be an unexpected joy.

At each house he came to he would blow his whistle. If no one came to the door, he'd knock on it. If still no one came, he'd return the mail to his pouch and deliver it on his next round, either later that day, or his first round the following morning.

When someone did answer—and someone almost always did—it presented an opportunity to chat and catch up on the neighborhood gossip, which he later that evening shared with Mrs. Littlefield.

He was also not averse to accepting the frequent invitations he received to have a piece of pie or cake, and a cold drink in the summer or a hot one in the winter.

Three years ago he had been hailed as a hero for saving the life of the widow Malvern. She hadn't responded to either his whistle or the knock on the door any of the four times he'd been by in a two day period. He knew the only time she ever left the house was for an occasional foray six blocks into town to pick up groceries at Finnegan's.

He'd forced his way in through the front door and found her lying at the foot of the stairs with a broken leg. Leaving his mail pouch behind, he'd sprinted into town and returned with Dr. Sherman.

After successfully getting Mrs. Malvern into the doctor's carriage, he'd completed his rounds.

It was the one time in his decade and a half on the job he'd ever been late in delivering the mail.

Mr. Littlefield was, indeed, held in high esteem by the residents of Booker Falls, not least among them Daisy O'Hearn.

"Mr. Littlefield," said Daisy, "how has this day treated you?"

"Like a rare jewel in da crown of da queen of England," said Mr. Littlefield, grinning. "And I venture to say it will be a wonderful day for you, too. I got da package you been waitin' for."

When he drew a box from his pouch and handed it to Daisy, her eyes got big.

"Is this it?" she asked, her voice barely a whisper.

"I presume it is," said Mr. Littlefield. "And dis here box is for you, too." He handed her a second box.

"Yippee!" cried Daisy. "I can't wait to show this to Myrtle!"

Setting both boxes on the floor, she grabbed Mr. Littlefield in a bear hug. "Oh, thank you, thank you," she said.

Embarrassed, Mr. Littlefield replied, "Just doing my job, Miss O'Hearn."

Daisy closed the door as Mr. Littlefield walked back down the path, then picked up both boxes and dashed upstairs to her bedroom.

Minutes later, she was back in the foyer. She grabbed the glass of almost forgotten sherry and repeated her previous dart up the stairs.

*****

She was sitting in the parlor, staring out the front window when she saw Myrtle walking up the road to the house. She watched as she came up the path and onto the porch. Rushing to the door she threw it open just as her housemate reached for the handle, causing the younger girl to fall back in surprise.

"Daisy!" exclaimed Myrtle. "My goodness! You scared me half to death!"

"It finally came," said Daisy, ignoring Myrtle's remarks. "It's here—it's here at last!"

Myrtle was thoroughly confused. What in the world was she talking about?

"What's here?" asked Myrtle. "And may I please come in? It's dreadfully cold out here."

"Oh, sorry," said Daisy, backing up into the foyer. "Come upstairs," she said, quivering with excitement. She grabbed Myrtle's coat and began to drag her towards the stairs.

"Could I get a cup of tea first? I just walked two miles in the freezing cold. I need to warm up."

A disappointed look came over Daisy's face. "Oh, all right, I suppose. But make it snappy. Meet me in my room."

She watched as Myrtle headed for the kitchen, then she sprinted up the stairs.

Moments later Myrtle entered Daisy's bedroom, embracing a steaming cup in both hands.

"Now, what is the hoopla all about?" she asked.

"This," answered Daisy, triumphantly. She held up what appeared to be a black cardboard box, about the size of a toaster.

"What is that?" asked Myrtle, bending her head to get a better view of the object.

"A camera! It's a camera! I bought a camera!"

"A camera?" said Myrtle, incredulously. "I've never seen a camera that looked like that before."

"It's a Kodak Brownie. Ain't it a beaut?"

"What are you going to do with it?"

Daisy looked at Myrtle. "Do with it? Why, take pictures, of course—photographs."

"Of what?"

"Of *what*? Of everything! People, buildings, flowers, Penrod, my *foot*?"

"Your foot?"

"Just an example. How about the waterfalls—Booker Falls waterfalls? I could take a picture of it."

"Can you take a picture of me?" asked Myrtle.

"You're a people."

"Okay, go ahead."

"I can't, not right now. I can take pictures indoors, but it's too late today—there's not enough light. Tomorrow morning—before you leave for the library. I'll take your picture then."

"How much did this cost?" asked Myrtle, setting her cup down and taking the camera from Daisy's hands, turning it over, checking it out.

"Two dollars and eighty-six cents."

"I guess that's not too bad."

"I might be able to make some money with it, too."

"How?"

"By taking people's pictures and selling them to them."

"Pretty ingenious."

"Tomorrow morning," said Daisy. "Before you leave."

*****

"I'm getting my picture taken today," said Myrtle, entering the dining room.

Henri and Pierre both stopped eating and looked at her.

"Where?" asked Henri.

"Daisy," said Myrtle. "She bought a camera. And she's going to take my picture before I leave for the library."

"I want to see this," said Pierre.

"Me, too," added Henri.

"See what?" asked Mrs. Darling, entering the room.

"Myrtle's getting her picture taken," said Henri, rising to help Myrtle with her chair.

Mrs. Darling looked at Myrtle. "Getting her picture taken?"

"By me," said Daisy. "As soon as we finish breakfast."

Twenty minutes later the five of them gathered on the front porch. Daisy positioned Myrtle in front of the door and told the others to stand aside. Holding the Brownie at her stomach, she looked down into the viewfinder, waiting until Myrtle was centered, then pressed the shutter lever.

"That's it," said Daisy, looking up.

"Dat's, it?" asked Mrs. Darling. "Let's see da picture."

"Oh, you can't see it until the film is developed," said Daisy.

"When will that be?" asked Myrtle, disappointed. Like Mrs. Darling, she thought she'd be able to see her photograph right away.

"Not until I've shot all the frames on the film," said Daisy.

"How many are there?" asked Pierre.

"A dozen or more."

"Den take some more," said Mrs. Darling.

"What?" said Daisy.

"Us," said Mrs. Darling. "Take a picture of each of us—of all of us."

Daisy's face brightened. "Why didn't I think of that?"

For the next fifteen minutes, Daisy took pictures of all of them, individually, and as groups. She had Pierre take the final picture, of her, Myrtle, Henri and Mrs. Darling.

"Can you develop da film now?" asked Mrs. Darling.

"She probably has to send the whole camera back to the company," said Henri. "I know how this works.

They develop the film, then return the camera along with the pictures."

"Really?" said Myrtle. Was she *ever* going to see her picture?

"That's how some of them work," said Daisy, grinning. "But I also bought a developing machine when I bought the camera, so I can develop them myself. But I still have a few more frames to shoot, and I have some ideas about what I want to take pictures of. I'll let you all know when I've developed the film. You can see the pictures then."

CHAPTER TWENTY-SEVEN

As much as Myrtle wanted to stay in bed, her conscience wouldn't allow it.

The last time she had been in church—not counting the ice cream social at St. James'—was earlier in the summer, when she and Daisy had traveled to Chicago for Daisy's mother's funeral.

It wasn't that she didn't like to go to church—it was just much easier not to, to sit on the front porch and read a book, drinking the thimbleberry tea Mrs. Darling kept bringing her, or forcing herself to drink the dandelion tea, when that was the flavor of the day.

Her parents had been faithful church goers when they were alive. Maybe that was the problem; Myrtle had resented going to Mass every Sunday, but in her household *not* going was not an option.

She wasn't sure what was pressuring her today. Perhaps it was that so many people had died—been killed, to be more accurate—in the last few weeks that got her to thinking about the afterlife.

Still not fully committed, she got out of bed, put on her robe and slippers and padded out into the hallway to the bathroom. As she stood looking at herself in the mirror she noticed a crucifix on the wall behind her. She could swear that in the year she'd been living in this house she had never noticed that crucifix before.

That was the sign. She brushed her teeth and drew a comb through her hair; fortunately, she had taken a bath the previous night.

Returning to her room, she dressed, then headed downstairs for breakfast. For a change, she wasn't the last one there. In fact, she beat both Pierre and Daisy by a few minutes.

"You look pretty spiffy this morning," said Daisy, when she appeared and took her place at the table.

"I'm going to church," said Myrtle.

Daisy looked up. "Just how secure is that ceiling?" she asked.

Henri and Pierre, who had also sat down by now, both laughed.

Myrtle even smiled. "It's not that bad," she said. "At least I go to church sometimes. You never go."

"But at least I'm consistent," said Daisy, taking a drink of her orange juice.

*****

Myrtle had forgotten how much she enjoyed church. It was comforting to become immersed in the Latin liturgy and the music and the sermon.

The few times she had been in St. Barbara's before, she had admired the eight stained-glass windows, four along each side of the narthex. She knew they were representations of some sort of events, but of what, she had no idea. Today, she decided to stay and study them, one by one.

As she stood gazing at one window, the picture of a roughly drawn cross on a stone wall, she became aware of someone next to her.

When she turned to see who it was, she saw Father Fabien standing there.

"Miss Tully, I haven't seen you in a while, eh?" he said in a kindly voice.

Myrtle blushed. Not what you want to hear from your parish priest.

"Yes, Father, well I've been . . . I've been . . ."

"No need to explain to me, my child. But if you do feel the need to explain, you have my permission to go over my head."

Myrtle laughed. She liked Father Fabien. He wasn't like the priests she'd known at St. Louis Cathedral in New Orleans, where her family had attended. He was more like a real person.

She nodded. "I will bear that in mind, Father."

"You find the windows interesting, yah?"

"I do. But I'm afraid I don't understand what they represent. They're very different from what I'm used to seeing in church. Do they have some connection with St. Barbara?"

Father Fabien nodded. "They do. Would you like me to explain them to you? Do you have a moment?"

"Oh, yes, I'd like that."

He led Myrtle back to the first window.

"St. Barbara lived some sixteen hundred years ago," he said. "She was the daughter of a rich man, a pagan. Because she was so beautiful, her father put up a tower in which to hide her from the public."

The window depicted a tall stone tower with one window. Behind and to the right of the tower was a night scene with a myriad of twinkling stars, on the left, a day scene of wooded hills, a flowing river and meadows blanketed with flowers.

"From her one window Barbara could see the scene portrayed above, during the day and at night. Over time, she came to believe the idols her father believed in could not have created such beauty, that there must be a more powerful entity. She decided to devote her life to this God she had found. Eventually, her father relented and let her leave the tower when she wanted to."

In the second window, a young woman sat on the edge of a well with two other women. They were studying pamphlets.

"In the city she met young Christian girls who shared their faith with her," said Father Fabien.

"In this window," he continued, pointing at the third window, "a priest, disguised as a merchant, instructed her further in the Christian faith and baptized her."

When they reached the window where Father Fabien had found Myrtle, she asked, "What's the story with the cross?"

"Ah, this is where the mysticism comes in, eh? While Barbara was learning about Christianity— unbeknownst to her father—he was having a luxurious bathhouse constructed. He ordered the workers to put in two windows, but while he was out of town on business, Barbara had a third window installed, forming a Trinity of light. Then, on one of the marble walls she traced a cross with her finger, and the cross became deeply etched into the material, as if by some sort of metal instrument. Later, her footprints were found embedded in the stone steps. From then on the bathhouse water was said to have healing powers."

They crossed the nave to window number five.

"When Barbara's father returned from his trip and Barbara told him about her newfound faith he became enraged and tried to kill her. She ran away from him to a hill, which mysteriously opened up a crevice, providing her a place to hide. When Dioscorus—that was Barbara's father—found her, he beat her and handed her over to the city's prefect, who had her beaten even more."

Father Fabien pointed to window six which portrayed a violent scene of a woman being beaten by three men using rawhide whips.

"A Christian woman named Juliana was in the crowd watching. She was so inspired by Barbara's voluntary martyrdom she began to belittle the men.

They took her and tortured her along with Barbara. Then they were led through the streets, naked—"

"But those women have robes on," Myrtle interrupted, staring at the seventh window which showed two women, the one from the previous windows, and a new one, both attired in dazzling robes, walking through a jeering crowd of people.

"Yah, because the Lord sent an angel to cover them with the robes," said Father Fabien.

"And does the final window portray what I think it does?" asked Myrtle, shuddering slightly.

The same two women from window seven lay on the ground, their detached heads next to them.

"Yah, it does. Both Barbara and Juliana were beheaded, and both later sainted by the Church."

"Fascinating," said Myrtle. "Father, thank you for explaining all this to me."

"Now, Miss Tully," said Father Fabien as they walked to the front door, "don't be a stranger."

"I shan't, Father," she said, hoping she wasn't telling her priest a falsehood.

*****

When Myrtle left the church she noticed George across the street. He was sitting on a bench in front of the Lutheran church.

She grinned. She'd seen him sitting there once before, last Christmas Eve, when he'd offered to walk her home, and she had accepted.

He had asked her out her second day in town. Though she thought him exceedingly handsome, she had declined. She *had* said, 'perhaps another time' and over the ensuing months he'd broached the subject again, eventually getting her to agree to dinner.

When she discovered it was to take place at his house—she knew he lived alone—she was indignant at first, until it was made clear that Mrs. Delahanty had prepared the meal and would be present the whole evening.

Their second date had been a trip to Red Jacket to see a vaudeville show, Harvey's Greater Minstrels, followed by dinner at the Michigan House. In addition, they had, over the past year, danced together on numerous occasions at the various events in town.

Lately, though, George's seeming lack of attention had led Myrtle to believe he had lost interest.

Perhaps not.

"Miss Tully," said George, doffing his homburg.

One thing about George Salmon: he was always nattily dressed and exceedingly polite.

"Mr. Salmon. How are you this fine day?" asked Myrtle.

"Well, thank you. That was a fine service, wasn't it?"

"Indeed it was."

"Miss Tully, I was wondering if you would care to join me for lunch."

Myrtle looked at George and smiled. "As you may know, Mrs. Darling provides lunch for all of her boarders; as well as breakfast and dinner."

"I thought you might appreciate a change of venue."

"Are we talking lunch at your home?" asked Myrtle, mindful of their previous dinner date.

"No, I was thinking of Miss Madeline's. Their special today is fried green tomatoes."

Involuntarily, Myrtle licked her lips. She did love fried green tomatoes! She cocked her head for a moment, then said, "I suppose the other boarders could get along without me this one day. Yes, Mr. Salmon, I would love to have lunch with you."

*****

Miss Madeline's Eatery was the best restaurant in town. In fact, other than the Juicy Pig, which specialized in anything porcine—bacon, pork, sausage, ham, pickled pigs feet, snout—and catering mainly to the miners who lived in Greytown, it was the *only* restaurant in town.

Photographs of people and town buildings from the past thirty years covered the walls. Inside, above the front door, hung a stuffed moose head. A huge fireplace held a blazing fire.

And presiding over it all was the owner, Miss Madeline, whose charm and exuberance belied her eighty plus years of life.

While Myrtle enjoyed the luxury of eating out at Miss Madeline's, it was, unfortunately, just that—a luxury. And since all her meals at Mrs. Darlings' were included in her monthly rent, she seldom indulged herself. In fact, in her year in Booker Falls, she could count on one hand the number of times she'd eaten there.

Mona, Miss Madeline's eighteen-year-old granddaughter, arrived at their table to take their order.

"Mayor Salmon, Miss Tully," said Mona, flashing a big smile.

"Good morning, Mona," said George.

"Our special today is fried green tomatoes," said Mona.

"So I heard," said Myrtle, studying the menu. "How is the meatloaf?" she asked, looking up.

"Made with my grandma's own loving hands," said Mona. "I highly recommend it."

"Then I will have that . . ." said Myrtle, ". . . along with the fried green tomatoes."

"And mashed potatoes, gravy and biscuit?" asked Mona.

Myrtle nodded her head, resignedly. "Why not."

Mona looked at George. "And your usual, Mr. Mayor?"

George grinned. "You know me all too well, Miss Ackerson. Yes, fried chicken and I, too, will have the mashed potatoes and gravy and biscuit—and tomatoes."

"How 'bout drinks?" asked Mona.

"Coffee, please," said Myrtle.

"Tea, if you don't mind," said George.

*****

An hour later, Myrtle and George both leaned back. They had each finished off a huge piece of chocolate cake.

"I am stuffed," said Myrtle, dabbing at her mouth with her napkin.

"Me, too," said George. "Weren't the tomatoes delicious?"

"Best I ever had."

Myrtle looked at a painting on the wall behind George.

"Isn't that one of Mr. Mitchell's?" she asked, pointing. She had seen enough of Frank's pieces—at George's home, the Steinmyer's residence, in Frank's and Henri's offices—that she recognized his style. His work tended to be very dark, and his primary subject was the Booker Falls waterfalls.

George turned and looked. "Oh, yes, that's Frank's work all right. Although I don't think he does justice to the falls."

"I wouldn't know," said Myrtle, wondering if she dare ask for another piece of cake.

"You've never seen the falls?" asked George.

Myrtle shook her head. "I don't even know where they are."

"Not too far off the road you took when you first arrived. I have an idea. You're not at the library tomorrow; how about driving out there with me?"

Myrtle hesitated. One date—and she certainly considered this lunch a date—with George on one weekend was one thing. But two?

Still, she would love to see what the falls looked like.

Putting the idea of more cake out of her mind, she said, "I suppose that would be all right."

George beamed. "Excellent! We shall make a picnic of it."

"A picnic?" Myrtle clapped her hands together. "What shall I bring?"

"Oh," said George, "you don't have to bring a thing. Mrs. Delahanty will be delighted to prepare us a scrumptious meal."

Myrtle looked at the painting again.

"George, I just noticed something about that painting."

George turned to look at the painting.

"Oh, what is that?" he asked.

"There's no red in the picture—just mostly dark green and other dark colors, with a little bit of yellow. Thinking back now, I don't remember seeing any red in his other works, either."

George turned back to Myrtle.

"Very observant. And you're right. Frank doesn't like the color red—associates it with the devil. He never uses it in any of his paintings."

"But he uses red ink sometimes when he writes."

George shrugged. "What can I tell you? He told me once he thought red ink was sensual, romantic."

"How very odd."

"Well," said George, "Frank himself is a bit odd."

CHAPTER TWENTY-EIGHT

Later that day when Myrtle stepped out from her room into the hallway of the boarding house, she heard a clicking sound coming from Daisy's room, located across from her own. Curious, she peeked through the open doorway and saw her fellow boarder, oblivious to Myrtle's presence, pounding away furiously on her Underwood typewriter.

Myrtle folded her arms and leaned against the doorframe.

Being nineteen years Daisy's junior, she had come to think of her housemate as more like an older sister. And over the past year, since Myrtle had arrived in Booker Falls, the two of them had become fast friends.

It was Myrtle in whom Daisy confided that she had stabbed her husband to death—or so she thought, finding out later he had recovered, only to die a few years later in a construction accident.

And it was Myrtle who made all the arrangements for their trip to Chicago to attend Daisy's mother's funeral, at a time when the fate of her husband was still unknown, and Daisy was afraid to be spotted by his family, whom she thought was out to avenge his death.

Daisy was the one in whom Myrtle confided regarding her relationship with Henri; their first kiss—and then their second one!

But the two women could not have been more different.

Whereas Myrtle was slight, weighing no more than a hundred and ten pounds, if that—'no more than a wisp of a thing,' was the way Mrs. Darling described her when they first met—Daisy was tall, nearly six feet, and strong, with an athletic build.

She was a Chicago girl, her father a construction worker, her mother a stay at home wife. She had graduated high school, then gotten a job washing dishes at Shenanigan's, a local diner. Later she found a better job, cleaning offices, one of which was that of the managing editor of the *Examiner*, a local paper. Impressed not only with Daisy's conscientious work, but also her knowledge of Chicago's south side, where she lived, he gave her a job in the mail room. From there, she soon worked her way up to the reporting staff, the position she held when she fled Chicago, fearful she had killed her husband.

New Orleans had been Myrtle's home. Her father, a career politician, had held positions first in the parish where they lived, and later in state government. Her mother, an accomplished musician, was among the first violinists hired by the New Orleans Symphony Orchestra when it formed in 1910.

Unlike Daisy's public school education, Myrtle, coming from a staunch Catholic family, attended a private boarding school: the Academy of the Sacred Heart—also known as 'The Rosary'—graduating the same year her mother began with the symphony.

Over her parents' objections, the day after she graduated she entered the Ursuline Convent to become a nun.

That lasted less than a year. It wasn't that Myrtle became disillusioned. Rather, the mother superior saw early on that her charge was too much a woman of the world to live a cloistered life.

So Myrtle left Ursuline and went to work at AT&T as a telephone operator.

Six years later, she answered General John Pershing's call for young, bilingual women fluent in both English and French, to come to Europe and operate the telephone exchanges for the Allied Expeditionary Forces.

Now, here she was in Booker Falls, the assistant librarian at the Adelaide College library.

"How's the book coming?" asked Myrtle, walking into the room and flopping down on the bed.

Daisy had told Myrtle a year earlier of her plans to write a novel about the murder of Yvette Sinclair.

"Great!" exclaimed Daisy. "I'm about three fourths of the way done."

"Are you using real people's names?" Myrtle wasn't sure she wanted her name in the book.

Daisy shook her head. "Nope, can't do that. It's a matter of privacy. Although I'd use yours if you wanted me to."

"Heavens, no!" said Myrtle. "Please, do not!"

"'Fraid of the notoriety?" Daisy grinned. "It *would* make you famous, you know."

"I don't need to be any more famous than I am," said Myrtle. She rolled over on her stomach. "I've been meaning to ask you: why did you decide to write this book, anyway?"

"Remember I told you I ran across some old accounts at the newspaper in Traverse City when I was working there?"

Myrtle nodded. "That's right. I remember now. But had you always wanted to write?"

Daisy smoothed the hair back from her forehead. "I enjoyed working at the paper in Chicago, but I always had it in the back of my mind to do more, to maybe write a book—a novel, ya know?"

"And now you are."

"But now I know *why* I wanted to write a novel. I've been doing a lot of thinking, now that my mother and Mike are both gone."

"About what?"

"Dying."

"Dying?" Myrtle rolled back over and sat up. "That's pretty morbid, isn't it?"

"I was thinking that, after I'm dead—who would remember me?"

"That's not going to be for a long time," said Myrtle. "And if you should die before me, I'll remember you." She placed her hand on Daisy's arm.

"Thanks," said Daisy, smiling. "And I'll do the same for you."

Myrtle broke out laughing. "But it's going to be a long time for both of us."

"Do you remember your grandparents?"

"My grandparents? Sure," said Myrtle. "Why do you ask?"

"How about your great-grandparents?"

Myrtle scrunched up her eyes. "My *great-*grandparents? No, I don't remember them. I'm not sure any of them were still alive when I was born. Maybe— I'm not sure."

"Do you think anybody who's alive today remembers your great-grandparents?"

Myrtle shrugged. "I don't know. Probably not."

"That's the thing," said Daisy. "Unless you're somebody famous, such as Abraham Lincoln or Jesus or Florence La Badie or—"

"I'm sorry," said Myrtle. "Who?"

"Florence La Badie. The famous actress? She died a few years ago?"

Daisy could tell from the blank look on Myrtle's face she had no idea who Florence La Badie had been.

"Okay, maybe she's not a good example," said Daisy. "But the thing is, unless you're somebody famous, when you die, seventy-five or a hundred years later there won't be anybody still alive who remembers who you are—who you'd been. It's like you never existed.

"I figure if I can become a famous writer, then people will remember me long after I'm gone—like Dante or Shakespeare or Jane Austen. I don't want to just be lost to time."

"Hmm," said Myrtle. "I guess you're right. Personally, I figure when I'm dead, I wouldn't know if anybody remembered me or not. But, enough of death talk."

"We missed you at lunch today," said Daisy. "Mrs. Darling asked where you were."

"I'm sorry. I should have called her to tell her I wasn't coming. I had lunch with George."

Daisy sat up straight in her chair. "You did? Lunch with George?"

"He was waiting for me after church and invited me to Miss Madeline's. They had fried green tomatoes."

"Ooh, I love fried green tomatoes. So it was a date?"

"I suppose you could call it that," said Myrtle. "And we're going on a picnic tomorrow—to see Booker Falls. You know, the falls themselves?"

"Good for you, kiddo. Is this the start of something big?"

Myrtle grinned. "It's a little too early to know. I was on my way downstairs to see if I could get Mrs. Darling to brew me a cup of tea. You ready for a break?"

"Sure," said Daisy, getting up. "As long as it's not dandelion."

CHAPTER TWENTY-NINE

Myrtle had just finished getting dressed when she heard a car horn beep. She knew immediately who it was: George loved the sound of his car horn.

Earlier that year he had purchased an automobile in Jackson while on a trip there. A brand new four-door Briscoe with a convertible top and leather-covered seats, it was George's pride and joy. As mayor, he drove it in the Fourth of July parade down Main Street, waving and smiling—and blowing the horn.

It was the second automobile to find a home in Booker Falls, following Myrtle's car in which she had arrived the year before.

"Myrtle, your date is here!" shouted Daisy, whose room looked out onto the road below.

As Myrtle came bouncing down the stairs she met Henri, who was on his way up.

"George is here," he said, a frostiness to his voice.

"Yes, I know," said Myrtle.

"You're going out with him?"

"That's right. We're going on a picnic to the falls."

Henri raised his eyebrows. "Well, have fun," he said, heading up the stairs.

Myrtle had a feeling from the way he said it that Henri really didn't want her to have fun.

"Wha! You look terrific!" said George when Myrtle exited the house.

Over time, Myrtle had accepted Daisy's entreaties to be more fashionable in her dress. Today she was wearing a pair of checked wool knee-length knickers

Thank you for your purchase of *Trifecta of Murder*. If you feel so inclined, I would request you write a review for Amazon. Here are the guidelines.

Important: Before you can post a review, you need to have an Amazon.com account that has successfully been charged for the purchase of a physical or digital item. Free digital downloads don't qualify. You don't need to have purchased the product you're reviewing. There's a 48-hour waiting period after your first physical order has been completely shipped, or your digital item has been purchased, before you'll be able to submit your review. If you've purchased a digital gift for someone else, the 48-hour waiting period doesn't begin until the gift has been redeemed.

To submit a review:

1. Go to Amazon.com
2. After "All" type in Kenn Grimes
3. Click on picture of book
4. Click on # customer reviews
5. Write your review
6. Click **Submit**.

with a tweed shirt, knee-high socks, and lace-up shoes. A chocolate-colored newsboy cap covered her curly, auburn hair.

George was no less smartly dressed, in a pair of white slacks, a navy blue blazer, black and white saddle shoes and a straw boater hat.

"You look pretty sharp yourself," said Myrtle. "Are we ready?"

*****

George pulled the car off the road onto a patch of cleared land and parked it.

"We'll have to walk in from here," he said.

Myrtle waited for him to come around to her side to assist her out of the car. Six months ago she would have been out before him, but another thing Daisy had impressed on her was that men like to feel they're needed—even when they're not.

From the back seat, George took a blanket and the picnic basket Mrs. Delahanty had prepared for them. He took Myrtle's hand.

"This way," he said.

"Wait," she said. From the front seat next to where she'd been sitting she picked up the Kodak brownie.

"What's that?" asked George.

"You'll see," said Myrtle, smiling.

Five minutes later, they emerged into a wooded setting. Myrtle gasped.

"Oh, George, it's beautiful!" she exclaimed.

At the base of a thirty-two-foot waterfall sat a medium-sized pond with a large grassy area off to one side. Tall red, silver, and boxelder maples formed a canopy that cast a sense of mystery over the whole area.

"Let's put the blanket over there," said George, indicating a sliver of grass where the sun's rays managed to squeeze themselves through the mantle overhead.

Myrtle plopped down on the blanket George had spread and removed her cap.

"What delicacies did Mrs. Delahanty prepare for us?" she asked, as George began to remove the contents of the basket.

"Ham sandwiches. Potato salad. Hard-boiled eggs."

"Oh, I love hard-boiled eggs," said Myrtle. "Did she include salt and pepper?"

"Yah, she did," said George. He handed two silver shakers to Myrtle.

"Are these fish on the sides?" she asked, turning the shakers around in her hand.

"Yah," said George, grinning. "Salmon."

"I should have known," said Myrtle.

"And, see here." George held up a bottle of wine.

"We shall have a glorious feast!" exclaimed Myrtle.

While George uncorked the bottle and poured two glasses, Myrtle laid out the food and two cloth napkins on the tablecloth Mrs. Delahanty had thoughtfully included.

"Oh, George, look!" whispered Myrtle.

George looked up to see a large moose amble out from the trees. He stopped at the pond's edge and looked around. Myrtle was sure he could see them, but he paid them no mind, rather, dropped his head and began to drink.

"Shhh," said Myrtle, as she picked up the camera and slowly got to her feet.

Lowering the brownie to her waist, she adjusted the crosshair until the moose was centered. Then she pushed down the lever.

The sound caused the moose to look up and, seeing George and Myrtle for the first time, dash off into the woods.

"Did you get it?" asked George.

"I think so," said Myrtle.

"So that's a camera?" said George.

"It's Daisy's. She let me borrow it. While I'm standing here I'm going to take a picture of the falls, too."

Once again she adjusted the camera and clicked the shutter.

"Okay, that's done," she said, placing the Brownie back on the blanket. She sat down and George handed her a glass of wine.

"That was something," he said.

"I almost ran into a moose on my way into Booker Falls that first day," said Myrtle. "I wonder if this was the same one."

"We have a lot of moose up here. I doubt it. But tell me about almost running into this particular moose."

"I had just passed the sign welcoming me to town when all of a sudden this moose walked right out into the middle of the road. I had to put on my brakes to keep from hitting him. I sat there for a while, but he didn't seem inclined to move. Finally, I got out and gave him an apple, threw another into the woods and he went after it. Then I got back in my car and we were on our way."

"We?"

"Penrod. I had Penrod with me."

"That was brave of you," said George.

"Or very stupid."

"To bravery," said George, lifting his wine glass.

"Or stupidity," said Myrtle, laughing and touching her glass to George's. "Let's eat. I'm famished."

Thirty minutes later, Myrtle cleared the remains of their lunch, folded up the tablecloth and put everything back into the picnic basket.

From a pocket on the side of the basket George took out a small book.

"Are you going to read to me?" asked Myrtle.

"If you will allow me."

"What is it?"

"*A Dream of Fair Women.*"

"By Tennyson."

"Yah," said George, thumbing through the pages.

"I love him," said Myrtle. "Read away to your heart's content."

*****

An hour later, George laid the book aside. "I fear that's all my voice can take," he said.

"It was beautiful. Thank you so much. George, I know the town got its name from the falls, but where did the falls get its name?"

"You don't know?"

Myrtle shook her head.

"The story I got from Mr. Koskinen . . . do you know Mr. Koskinen?"

Myrtle shook her head again. "I don't think so."

"Mr. Koskinen is the oldest resident of Booker Falls: ninety-four. He told me once he came to the Keweenaw in 1845 to prospect for copper. He never found any, but he befriended a man named Ezra Booker, who had come here from New York for the same reason.

"This Booker fellow told Mr. Koskinen he'd been fired from his job as an accountant back in New York and decided to head west to seek his fortune. He'd been here for a few years when Mr. Koskinen met up with him. Seems Booker hadn't been any more successful at finding copper than Mr. Koskinen had been.

"But he did discover one thing—these falls. Which he named after himself: Booker Falls. And that's the whole story."

"Whatever happened to Mr. Booker?"

"Mr. Koskinen said he saw him the day he set out to go back to New York. He had sold his claim to the Joshua Mining Company. He was never heard from again. I need to stretch. What say we take a walk over to the pond?"

Myrtle extended her hand, which George took and, together, they walked the short distance to the pond.

"Be careful of the . . ."

Before George could finish, Myrtle found herself slipping on a wet rock. As she started to go down George pulled her to him, holding her tightly. She turned her face to him and started to thank him—when he kissed her.

Myrtle's eyes got big.

"I'm sorry," he said, when he let her go. "I shouldn't have done that."

"It's okay," said Myrtle, not quite sure what she *should* say.

George looked at her. "Then would it be 'okay' if I kissed you again, eh?"

"I . . . I think it might be," said Myrtle, smiling.

*****

"So you slipped on the wet rock, George caught you, and then he kissed you?"

Myrtle had just finished telling Daisy about her day at Booker Falls.

"That's what happened," said Myrtle.

"Excuse me if I'm wrong, but isn't that pretty much how it happened the first time you kissed Henri—you fell down the stairs, except he didn't catch you, you fell on him; and then *he* kissed you?"

Myrtle grinned. "I guess pretty much."

"That's a pretty neat racket you got going there, kiddo," said Daisy, laughing. "But, seriously, you're dating two men—anything serious about either one?"

Myrtle scratched her head. "That's a good question. I really like both of them. George is such a gentleman, so refined. I always feel very special, somehow, when I'm with him, like he raises me up a little."

"Raises you up?"

"Makes me feel more . . . I don't know . . . sophisticated, I guess."

"Sophisticated."

"Yes. I mean, my family was fairly well off, and I went to good schools and all. I'm well educated, I have good manners, but I'm . . . I'm . . ."

"Different," said Daisy, smiling.

Myrtle smiled back and nodded. "Yes—different. I guess I don't always act like proper young ladies should—not that I'm that young anymore. But with George, I feel I almost have to, because he's so...so..."

"Refined was the word you used."

"That's it—refined."

"And how about Henri?" asked Daisy.

"Ah, yes, how about Henri," said Myrtle. "When I'm with Henri I feel like I can be more myself. Henri's more—I don't know—common? I'm not sure I like that word, but it's the one that comes to mind. And I don't mean it in a bad way. He's just really down to earth."

"You haven't said a word yet about the physical attraction."

Myrtle smiled. "Well of course they're both very attractive—"

"Which one kisses better?"

Myrtle feigned a pained look. "Why, Miss O'Hearn, shame on you for asking such a delicate question."

"Delicate, shmelicate. Which one kisses better, that's what I want to know."

"Well, George is a very smooth kisser and—"

"Smooth?"

"Gentle. He's a gentle kisser."

"Sounds boring." Daisy scrunched up her mouth.

Myrtle shook her head. "Oh, no, not at all! Just because he's gentle doesn't mean there's no spark there."

"And Henri?"

"Henri's kisses are more like electric shocks going through my body."

Daisy sat up straight. "Okay, now this is getting interesting. Tell me more."

"I don't know, it's just like, well, when Henri kisses me, first I feel the shock, my body gets all warm, and then I just go limp, like a rag doll. He kisses hard, like he really means it. And I kiss him back just as hard."

"Is there anything else you want to tell me?"

"Like what?"

"If it's gone past the kissing stage?"

Myrtle smiled. "No."

"No, it hasn't gone past the kissing stage?"

"No, I don't want to tell you."

"Well tell me this, then—if you had to choose one over the other. . . .?"

Myrtle just smiled again.

CHAPTER THIRTY

Myrtle was surprised when she entered Frank's office to hear him whistling. In the year she had worked with him, she had never heard him whistle or even hum.

"Good morning, Miss Tully," he said, when he saw her. "How are you this fine morning?"

"I'm well, Mr. Mitchell, thank you," answered Myrtle. "You seem to be in good spirits today."

"I am," said Frank. "I am. An old friend has moved to town and has approached me with a business proposal which could prove quite lucrative."

"That sounds like good news."

"And did you have a good weekend?"

Myrtle was somewhat taken aback. This was the first time her boss had ever asked about her life outside the library.

"Why, yes . . . yes I did. I attended the service at St. Barbara's and Father Fabien explained the significance of the windows to me."

"Beautiful works of art," said Frank.

"And yesterday Mr. Salmon and I went on a picnic to your favorite spot."

Frank's brow furrowed. "My favorite spot?"

"The falls—Booker Falls: the ones you put into your paintings."

A smile lit up Frank's face. "Ah, yes, they are lovely. My favorite subject."

"So I have noticed," said Myrtle.

"Well, I shall be about my business. Much to do today," said Frank.

Read your dime novels and drink your Southern Comfort, thought Myrtle.

"By the way," said Myrtle, "I heard about you and Miss Blanchard."

Frank's face hardened. "What do you mean?"

"That you are fond of her and, apparently, she of you. I think it's wonderful."

In truth, Myrtle wasn't sure how wonderful it was, but she was not about to tell Frank that.

Frank's countenance softened. "Thank you, Miss Tully. I appreciate that."

*****

Myrtle looked up when Frank approached the desk an hour before closing time.

"Miss Tully, I'm leaving now. I shall see you tomorrow."

"Have a good evening, Mr. Mitchell."

Moments later, Myrtle heard a ruckus outside. One of the students, Allison, came rushing in.

"Miss Tully, Miss Tully, come quickly! It's Mr. Mitchell! Some men are beating up on him!"

Myrtle reached under the counter and pulled the derringer from her handbag. Running as fast as she could, she dashed out the front door and found Frank on the ground, surrounded by a group of five men, kicking and pummeling him.

She raised the gun in the air and fired, which brought an immediate halt to the attack. All the men turned to look.

"I have one more bullet in this gun," Myrtle yelled. "And it will be for the next man who lays a hand on Mr. Mitchell. Now, get out of here!"

The startled men stared at Myrtle for a second, shocked by this slip of a woman who had threatened them, then turned and fled back to the car waiting for them at the road.

By this time, a number of the male students had come outside. Myrtle called them over.

"Help Mr. Mitchell back inside," she said. "I'll call the constable."

While they waited for Henri to arrive, Myrtle attended to Frank's wounds as best she could with the help of another student, Mary, who had served as a nurse during the war.

"What happened?" asked Henri when he arrived.

Myrtle filled him in on the details.

Henri turned to Frank. "Do you know who they were? Did you recognize them?"

Frank shook his head. "I didn't recognize them. But I know who they are."

"Who?" asked Myrtle and Henri, together.

"I don't know their names, but they said they were with the Klan."

"The Klan?" said Myrtle.

"The Ku Klux Klan," said Henri. "I've heard from Leonard there are some over in Marquette."

"These men must have been from there," said Myrtle. "They had an automobile."

"Did they say why they did this?" asked Henri.

Frank took a deep breath. "Because I'm seeing Eloise."

"That's what I suspected," said Henri.

"They said they'd kill me the next time if I didn't stop seeing that 'Nigger.' That's what they called her— a nigger."

"What are you going to do?" asked Myrtle.

Frank looked at her. "I'm not going to stop seeing her. In fact, I'm going to ask her to marry me."

*****

When Myrtle returned to the boarding house that evening, she went straight to Henri's room.

"What is it?' he asked, opening his door.

"I need to talk," said Myrtle. "I'm unsettled about what happened today."

"Let's go downstairs," said Henri.

"Would you like something to drink?" he asked when they reached the parlor.

"A sherry," replied Myrtle. "I would like a sherry."

Moments later, Henri returned from the kitchen, a drink in each hand.

"You said you felt unsettled," he said, handing one of the glasses to Myrtle, who had taken a seat in one of the overstuffed chairs.

"Yes. I don't understand why those men would do that . . . yes, I do. And I guess that's what I'm upset about."

"What do you mean?"

"I know about the Klan."

"You do?" said Henri, surprised.

"I'm from the south, remember? My great-grandparents were slave owners. And my grandparents after them. Some of their coloreds, after they were set free, continued on as servants for my parents. I grew up with Mama Chessy caring for me. She'd been born a slave on my great-grandfather's plantation in 1838. My grandfather was a member of the Klan."

Henri's surprise gave way to shock.

"Your grandfather was a Klan member?"

Myrtle nodded. "I remember my parents talking about it. They still had the robe and hood he wore. But I never expected that sort of thing still went on today."

"Leonard said they've noticed some Klan activity over in Marquette, where we think these fellows came from. Nothing big yet, but the state police are keeping a close eye on the situation. I telephoned him and told him what happened here."

"But I don't understand," said Myrtle. "You and I have gone out together, and no one has said anything."

"I remember when you first came to town you didn't much care for me."

Myrtle felt her face redden. "Yes, but . . . but that wasn't because . . . because you were . . . you were . . . ."

"Yes it was," said Henri. "At least part of it— because I'm colored." He smiled. "I'm sure there were other reasons, too, but that was definitely part of it. And our situation is different. I'm the constable. And I'm a mulatto. I'm not dark-skinned like Eloise."

"But do you think there's any resentment, bad feelings—I don't know what else to call it—about you and me?"

"I've heard some rumblings," said Henri.

"Oh?" Now it was Myrtle's turn to be surprised— and a little frightened.

"But I'm not worried," said Henri. "I don't care what people say."

"What have you heard?"

"Nothing to be concerned about, trust me."

They were both silent for a minute before Myrtle spoke.

"I think Mr. Mitchell's situation is compounded by the age difference between him and Eloise."

"You're right," said Henri. "He's old enough to be her father."

"Her *grandfather*," said Myrtle.

"In a way you have to admire him for that," said Henri, grinning.

Myrtle shook her head. "You men are all alike."

CHAPTER THIRTY-ONE

Mrs. Darling was surprised when Henri asked her to accompany him to Mr. Abramovitz's pawn shop.

"Why in da world would I want to go dere?" she asked.

"He has some desk lamps and I need a new one for my office. I need a woman's input on which one I should buy."

Mrs. Darling looked at him as though he had gone crazy. "A lamp's a lamp, eh? Ya can't pick one out by yourself?"

Henri tried to look as helpless as possible. "Please?" he pleaded.

"Oh, all right den," said Mrs. Darling, unenthusiastically.

"I'll ring the bell," said Henri.

Mrs. Darling's eyes lit up.

Henri had recently purchased a Packard Town Car, only the third automobile in Booker Falls following Myrtle's and George's.

Befitting his role as the county constable, he had installed a twelve-inch high bell on the front of the hood that could be rung using a chain that ran to a lever next to the steering wheel. The word "POLICE" painted on either side of the vehicle made it clear that it was to be used for official business.

"All da way into town, den," said Mrs. Darling, grabbing her coat.

*****

"How 'bout dis one?" asked Mrs. Darling, holding up a brass and iron lamp that looked as though it would be more appropriate in a factory work setting than a constable's office.

Henri hunched his shoulders. "I think I'm looking for something a little more . . . I don't know . . . attractive?"

"Attractive is it?" said Mrs. Darling. "What? You planning a spread in *House Beautiful*?"

"Nah, it's just . . . it's . . ."

"All right, all right, den. Eh, how's about dis one? Dis little naked boy one?"

She pointed to a bronze cherub holding up the column of the lamp.

Henri shook his head. "A little too risqué, I think."

Mrs. Darling sighed. "I ain't got all night. Mr. Abramovitz, you got anyting else Mr. de la Cruz here might want to look at?"

Mr. Abramovitz stroked his goatee. "Could be. Vait right here."

He disappeared into the back of the store and emerged moments later holding a copper lamp with a curved base and a fringe of colored tubes dangling from the bronze shade.

"No, no," said Mrs. Darling. "Dat's too 'girlie.'"

Henri's eyes lit up. "No, I like this. I think it's exactly what I'm looking for."

Mrs. Darling looked at Henri disgustedly. "Den why did you drag me along if you din't want my advice?"

Henri ignored his landlady. What could he say? Instead he turned to Mr. Abramovitz. "How much?"

"Two und a quarter."

Henri removed a two-dollar bill from his wallet and handed it the old man. Then he reached into his pocket, took out a handful of change, chose a shiny, brand new Standing Liberty quarter and gave it to Mr. Abramovitz also.

"I guess we can go now," said Henri.

*****

When they reached Main Street, Henri turned the car right instead of left, the normal route back to the boarding house.

"Where you taking me now?" asked Mrs. Darling, growing more impatient by the minute.

"I have to stop at the Polar Bear," said Henri. "Mr. Peletier said he had something for me to pick up."

Mrs. Darling sighed. "Make it fast, den, will you? Don't dawdle. I got work to do, ya know?"

"Won't be a minute," said Henri.

Henri parked the car in front of the court house and hurried across the street.

For over forty years The Polar Bear had been a popular spot in Booker Falls, serving ice cream, sodas and hot dogs. In 1904, after a trip to the World's Fair in St. Louis, Barnabas Peletier, owner of The Polar Bear, introduced the ice cream cone to Copper Country. Four years later, he followed that by offering banana splits.

The interior appeared just as it first had in 1878: two glass chandeliers set in a copper-colored tin ceiling that ran the length of the room. Each chandelier was eight feet in diameter. A parquet floor, a deeper brown than the ceiling, accommodated half a dozen booths on one side of the room and an oak counter on the other with ten stools. Metal tables ran down the middle.

A favorite attraction was the Welte-Mignon player piano at the back which held over a hundred songs.

Mrs. Darling watched as Henri darted into the shop, then reappeared almost immediately.

"Mrs. Darling," he said excitedly, opening the car door for her. "You have to come see this."

"What? What is it?"

"Just come—quickly."

Reluctantly, Mrs. Darling got out of the car and followed Henri across the street. She was anxious to get home and pluck the chicken for tomorrow night's dinner.

She waited as Henri opened the door and then they walked in—to a chorus of 'Happy Birthday.'

She stepped back, startled, and looked around. There were Myrtle and Daisy and Pierre and George, along with Paige Turner and Madeline Ackerson, owner of Miss Madeline's Eatery, Isabell Dougherty, and most of the other store owners in town.

Even Mr. Abramovitz had left his shop and sneaked across the street while Mrs. Darling sat waiting in the car.

For a moment, Mrs. Darling stood there, gaping. Then a flood of tears came.

Myrtle and Daisy rushed to her side and wrapped their arms around their landlady.

"Mrs. Darling, don't cry," implored Myrtle. "It's your party—your birthday party."

"I know," said Mrs. Darling through her tears, "I ain't never had no birthday party before."

"Well, you got one now," said Daisy. "Come on over and sit down."

No sooner did Mrs. Darling slide into the booth than Sally, the waitress, deposited a giant banana split in front of her.

"Just the way you like it," she said.

Mrs. Darling stared at the concoction before her: three generous scoops of ice cream—vanilla, chocolate and strawberry—topped by strawberry and peach preserves, pineapple and chocolate syrup, three maraschino cherries and under it all a fresh, ripe banana, split down the middle.

After never having set foot in The Polar Bear in her first sixty-seven-years of life, she had been taken there by Myrtle and Daisy during Mr. Pfrommer's trial, where she'd had her first banana split. From that point on, they'd become one of her favorite desserts.

On one occasion she even persuaded Myrtle to drive over fifty miles to Red Jacket to the Great Atlantic & Pacific Tea Company to purchase the fruit, as it was not available at the time in Booker Falls.

"Oh, my," said Mrs. Darling, eyeing her treat.

"Now, Mrs. Darling, as always, if you can't finish that, I am happy to help," said Daisy.

Mrs. Darling gave Daisy a dismissive look: she had never yet not finished a banana split.

While Mrs. Darling indulged herself, everyone else was doing the same. She finished scooping the last spoonful of syrup from the bottom of the dish and wiped her mouth with her napkin.

"My, dat was tasty," she said.

"And now . . ." said Daisy, as Sally approached the table with a birthday cake filled with a blazing candle representing every year of Mrs. Darling's life. Sally set the cake down, then backed away to allow the rest of the partygoers to crowd around.

". . . time to make a wish."

Mrs. Darling took a deep breath and, with a little help from both Myrtle and Daisy, succeeded in extinguishing every candle.

While Daisy removed the candles, Myrtle cut the cake and handed slices to the others as they presented their plates.

When the last person had been served, Henri said, "And we have something for you."

He held out a small box which Mrs. Darling tentatively took. She opened it and a broad grin spread across her face when she saw the contents: a pair of dangly earrings, each with two turquois globes, one half-way down the gold chain, the other hanging at the bottom.

"I love dem!" exclaimed Mrs. Darling.

Myrtle knew she would. The first day she met her new landlady one of the things that impressed her most were the oval drop earrings—black onyx stones outlined in gold filigree—swinging with abandon from her ears. Myrtle came to find out that Mrs. Darling had an extensive collection of dangling earrings, and was almost never seen without a set on.

Mrs. Darling reached up and removed the ones she was wearing and replaced them with the new ones. "How do they look?" she asked.

"Wait a minute," said Myrtle, rooting in her purse. She pulled out a silver-plated case and handed it to Mrs. Darling. "Take a look."

Mrs. Darling opened the case and stared into the mirror inside.

A broad grin spread across her face.

"Dere perfect," she said. "But now I got to get home. I still got a lot of work to do, eh?"

"Not before I take a lot of pictures," said Daisy, holding up her camera.

CHAPTER THIRTY-TWO

Norma Pennyworth gave a sigh of relief when the carriage in which she was riding with Margaret Folger turned the corner and her home came into view.

The past three weeks had been a trying time. The trip to Chicago by train had been long and arduous. Then had come the shocking realization that her mother was considerably more ill than her letters had led Norma to believe, so ill that a little over two weeks after arriving, Norma laid her to rest in Graceland Cemetery.

As if that were not enough, three days after leaving Booker Falls, Norma received a telegram informing her that her employer, Mr. Folger, had been murdered.

It had not taken Norma long to handle her mother's meager estate; everything had been left to her.

Yesterday she boarded the northbound Chicago and Northwestern train and, after several stops and transfers, arrived in Houghton, where Margaret had come for her.

Norma Pennyworth's home was one of those gray, non-descript houses in Greytown, the lower-class section of Booker Falls Myrtle drove through when she first arrived in town, so named because every structure was painted the same dull gray, with a slighter darker gray trim.

More than that, though, was the color of the sky: a dullish brown-gray filled with the smoke that poured from every chimney, pressing down like a pall, smothering the whole area.

Each home was the same: two-story, dormer windows, a small front porch. Some boasted a fence, many of wood, the more elegant ones of wrought iron. Most yards, though, were open to the neighborhood kids—of which there seemed to be no end—who treated everybody's home as their own.

Overhead, like fishnet, stretched a plethora of electric lines, overlaid in places by the few telephone lines scrapping for their own space.

Like many of the other families who lived there, Norma and her husband had relied on the Joshua Mining Company for their income. Now, however, with her husband gone these past five years from lung cancer, the casualty of more than a quarter of a century toiling in the mines, she had had to find another way to support herself. She was grateful to Mr. Folger for the job.

But now he was dead. She wasn't sure what she would do next.

As the carriage pulled up in front of her house, Norma saw a familiar face staring at her through the wrought iron fence that enclosed the front yard: Duke, her five-year-old German Shepherd, whom Mrs. Wellman next door had been looking after.

"Duke!" said Norma, grabbing her valise and climbing down from the carriage.

Duke responded by placing his front paws on top of the fence and voicing his approval at his mistress's return with a series of raucous barks.

Norma turned back to the carriage. "Mrs. Folger, I can't thank you enough for everything you've done. And I'm sure you know how sorry I am about Mr. Folger's passing."

Margaret nodded. "I know. And I, likewise, about your mother."

Norma watched as Margaret drove away. Then she opened the gate, bent down, kissed Duke, and went inside.

*****

Duke's soft growl pulled Norma from an uneasy sleep. She'd been dreaming she heard strange noises coming from the house—or inside the house. She wasn't sure which.

When she opened her eyes, she saw what had disturbed the dog: the silhouette of a man framed in the doorway of her bedroom.

The soft growl suddenly turned ferocious.

Norma pulled the bed sheets up under her chin and watched the intruder bolt from the room, slamming the door shut as Duke lunged towards him.

She sprang out of bed and ran to the window in time to see the man running down the street away from her house.

Then she hurried downstairs and called for the constable.

*****

"We've had a number of burglaries in town the last several weeks. It's possible that's who was here," said Henri, who was sitting at Norma's kitchen table, a cup of coffee in front of him.

He had come as soon as he'd received the call.

"Now that don't make sense. Everything I got dat's worth anything is downstairs: my silver, a few pieces of artwork. And they ain't even worth much. Why would he have passed by all dat to come up to my bedroom, eh?"

"It's primarily paintings that have been stolen, but perhaps he was after your jewelry. Do you keep it upstairs?"

"Yah," said Norma. "But it ain't worth much neither."

"Whoever it was, I guess he didn't know you had a dog."

"Thank goodness for Duke," said Norma, patting the dog's head.

"I'll ask around, see if any of your neighbors noticed anything suspicious, but I doubt we'll find the scoundrel. I also doubt he'll be back, now that he *does* know about Duke.

"You going to be at the reading of Mr. Steinmyer's will tomorrow?" asked Henri.

"Yah," said Norma. "I'll be dere."

*****

The nicest thing that could be said about the Booker Falls courthouse was that it had been built strong enough to withstand three earthquakes since the turn of the century. That it was constructed for utilitarian, rather than aesthetic, purposes, was obvious.

Unlike the other downtown buildings erected of wood or brick or Jacobsville Sandstone, the courthouse was constructed of concrete. And unlike many of the town's structures whose exteriors boasted bold colors, it was gray—as gray as an Upper Peninsula sky in the dead of winter.

The interior was no more pretentious than the outside, devoid of any adornments such as paintings or murals or statuary.

The first floor consisted of county offices, including George's, Jake's and Henri's, along with the two-cell jail. A long hallway ran the length of the upper level. On one side were more offices and meeting spaces, and Judge Hurstbourne's chambers. On the opposite side of the hallway was a court room that could seat fifty spectators.

Today an overcast sky and a constant rain made the structure appear even more foreboding.

Nathan hurried through the courthouse door into the lobby. He removed his dripping wet Macintosh and shook the water from his hair. Miss Wasserman had cautioned him that rain was on the way. He was glad he had taken her advice to wear a slicker. He wished he'd thought of an umbrella, too.

He hurried upstairs and through the two giant doors which led to the courtroom. He was taken aback when he walked in and saw Henri and Myrtle there.

She had talked Frank into letting her have an hour for lunch instead of her usual half hour.

Nathan had expected to find the others who were present: Miss Wasserman, Mrs. Chatham, Mrs. Pennyworth and a representative from Temple Jacob, whom he didn't know, along with Judge Hurstbourne.

"Mr. Steinmyer, you are late," said the judge.

Nathan looked at his watch: two minutes past noon.

"Yes, your honor, my apologies."

"Well, sit down, then," said Judge Hurstbourne. "Let's get this done."

He picked up the will Nathan had delivered to him several days before and began to read.

"This is the last will and testament of me, Isaiah Samuel Steinmyer, of Booker Falls, Michigan. First, I appoint my attorney, Rudolph Folger, sole executor of my will. Should he not be able to fulfill said duties, I appoint my daughter, Rachel Ruth Steinmyer, as secondary executor."

Judge Hurstbourne looked up. "As I explained to young Mr. Steinmyer here, inasmuch as neither of the executors is alive to fulfill their duties, I have chosen to act as the executor at the request of Temple Jacob. Miss Wasserman and Mrs. Chatham have agreed to this . . ." he looked at Nathan, who remained silent ". . . as did Mr. Steinmyer."

The judge looked back down and continued reading. "To my faithful housekeeper of these past thirty-eight years, Mildred Wasserman, I leave a bequest in the amount of five thousand dollars. To my faithful employee of twenty-five years, Bindi Chatham, I leave a bequest in the amount of two thousand dollars. To my congregation, Temple Jacob of Houghton, Michigan, I leave a bequest in the amount of five thousand dollars.

"To my son, Nathan Ezekiel Steinmyer, I leave sole ownership of the Booker Falls Bank and Trust. To my daughter, Rachel Ruth Steinmyer, I leave the house at Fourteen Thimbleberry Road, Booker Falls, Michigan. The balance of my estate including all personal effects is to be divided evenly between the aforementioned Nathan Ezekiel Steinmyer and Rachel Ruth Steinmyer, with the exception of five thousand dollars, to be set in a trust to be administered by my attorney, Rudolph Folger.

"In addition to the above, the aforementioned Mildred Wasserman may continue to reside in the home at Fourteen Thimbleberry Road for the remainder of her life while the property remains in my family. If the home should pass out of my family prior to Miss Wasserman being called home to her maker, she shall receive the balance of the funds remaining in the above mentioned trust. Should she pass from this life while still in residence at the above mentioned home, the trust will go to Temple Jacob.

"Should my son predecease me in death, the assets of the Booker Falls Bank and Trust shall go to my brother, Benjamin Hezekiah Steinmyer, of Menominee, Wisconsin, and his share of my estate to Temple Jacob.

"Should my daughter predecease me in death, the home at Fourteen Thimbleberry Road shall go to Mildred Wasserman, and the remainder of her share of the estate shall go to Temple Jacob.

"In witness whereof I have to this will set my hand the day and year first above written. Isaiah Samuel Steinmyer. Signed and declared by the said Isaiah Samuel Steinmyer the testator as his last will and testament in the presence of us present at the same time who in his presence at his request and in the presence of each other have hereunto subscribed."

Judge Hurstbourne removed his glasses and looked up. "The witnesses were a Mrs. Ruth Sheldon and Mr. Malcolm Middleton."

He cast his eye over the half dozen people seated in the gallery. "Are there any questions?"

Mrs. Pennyworth stood. "Clarence, I did not hear you read da date of da will."

Henri and Myrtle looked at each other. Clarence? They were to discover later from Mrs. Darling that Norma Pennyworth and Clarence Hurstbourne had at one time been engaged before going their separate ways. Judge or no, to Norma Pennyworth, Clarence Hurstbourne was still just 'Clarence.'

Judge Hurstbourne smiled. Knowing how exact Norma was, he would have expected no less.

"I believe you're right, Mrs. Pennyworth," said the judge. He looked down at the paper before him, then back up. "The will is dated the seventh day of February, nineteen and ten."

"In dat case," said Mrs. Pennyworth, "I do not believe you have Mr. Steinmyer's most recent will."

CHAPTER THIRTY-THREE

For a moment, no one spoke. Even Judge Hurstbourne was speechless. Then he asked, "And what makes you say that, Nor . . . Mrs. Pennyworth?"

"Because I got da latest will right here," said Mrs. Pennyworth, holding up a sheet of paper.

"Your honor—" Nathan started to say. But Judge Hurstbourne held up his hand.

"Mrs. Pennyworth, could you bring that up here, please?" asked the judge.

Norma walked to the bench and laid the paper in front of the judge. "As you can see," she said, "dis will is dated da twenty-first of last month."

Judge Hurstbourne picked up the paper and read it, then laid it back down. "I was under the impression no copy of the will could be found at Mr. Folger's office."

"I know dere was a copy in da safe when I left," said Norma. "I suppose dat might be what was taken when Mr. Folger was murdered."

"And where did this copy come from?" asked the judge.

"It has been in my possession since Mr. Steinmyer come into Mr. Folger's office three weeks ago today."

Judge Hurstbourne looked at Nathan. "Mr. Steinmyer, were you aware of the existence of this will?"

Nathan hesitated a moment before answering. "No, sir, I was not," he said.

Mrs. Pennyworth turned to face Nathan. "Dat is a lie," she said.

"And you know this how?" asked the judge.

Norma turned back to Judge Hurstbourne.

"When Mr. Steinmyer was in da office, him and Mr. Folger had a heated exchange. I did not hear what was being said, but I could tell dey was arguing. When Mr. Steinmyer left, Mr. Folger come out and told me he had given Mr. Steinmyer a copy of da updated will—da one you have dere, Clarence—and Mr. Steinmyer was not happy.

"Mr. Folger had already given two copies of da will to Miss Steinmyer, one for her and one for her father."

"Apparently those copies went missing also," said the judge, glaring at Nathan.

Norma continued. "Mr. Folger went over to da mining company—"

"The Joshua Mining Company?" asked Judge Hurstbourne.

"Yah," said Norma. "You know, he is deir attorney and he has . . . had . . . an office dere. Dey have one of dose newfangled machines—I tink it's called a Rectigraph? It makes copies. Anyway, Mr. Folger had made da first tree copies dere for da Steinmyers, and dat day he went back and made a fourth copy. He gave it to me and said I should keep it someplace safe."

"Did he say why he thought you should have a copy?" asked the judge.

Norma looked back at Nathan. "He did not trust da young Mr. Steinmyer. And it looks like he was right."

"Now, just a minute!" shouted Nathan, springing up from his seat.

Mr. Steinmyer!" cried Judge Hurstbourne. "Be quiet and sit down!"

Abashed, Nathan sank back into his seat.

"Now," said the judge, "Mr. Steinmyer, do you still contend you had no knowledge of this new will."

"I do!" said Nathan, defiantly. "I am not the liar—Mrs. Pennyworth is!"

"Sir," said Judge Hurstbourne, "I have known Mrs. Pennyworth for forty years. I do not believe she would lie about this, nor would she have any reason to. I do not know you as well, and if I had to choose between you and Mrs. Pennyworth as to who is telling the truth, believe me, sir, it is an easy choice. Let's hear the reading of the new will now, shall we?"

Norma returned to her seat and Judge Hurstbourne began to read. "This is the last will and testament of me, Isaiah Samuel Steinmyer, of Booker Falls, Michigan."

He looked up. "It is dated September twenty-first of this year.

"First, I appoint my attorney, Rudolph Folger, sole executor of my will. Should he not be able to fulfill said duties, I appoint my daughter, Rachel Ruth Steinmyer, as secondary executor.

"To my faithful housekeeper of these past forty-eight years, Mildred Wasserman, I leave a bequest in the amount of ten thousand dollars. To my faithful former employee of thirty-three years, Bindi Chatham, I leave a bequest in the amount of five thousand dollars. To my congregation, Temple Jacob of Houghton, Michigan, I leave a bequest in the amount of twenty thousand dollars. To my son, Nathan Ezekiel Steinmyer, I leave a bequest of twenty-five dollars."

Henri and Myrtle looked at one another.

Twenty-five dollars? Myrtle mouthed.

"Five thousand dollars shall be placed into a trust to be administered by my attorney, Rudolph Folger.

"The remainder of my estate, including the Booker Falls Bank and Trust, the home at Fourteen Thimbleberry Road, Booker Falls, Michigan, and all personal effects, is to be left to my daughter, Rachel Ruth Steinmyer.

"In addition to the above, the aforementioned Mildred Wasserman may continue to reside in the home at Fourteen Thimbleberry Road for the remainder of her life while the property remains in my family. If the home should pass out of my family prior to Miss Wasserman being called home to her maker, she shall receive the balance of the funds remaining in the above mentioned trust. Should she pass from this life while still in residence at the above mentioned home, the trust will go to Temple Jacob.

"Should my daughter predecease me in death, the home at Fourteen Thimbleberry Road shall go to Mildred Wasserman, and the remainder of her share of the estate shall go to Temple Jacob.

"In witness whereof I have to this will set my hand the day and year first above written. Isaiah Samuel Steinmyer.

"Signed and declared by the said Isaiah Samuel Steinmyer, the testator, as his last will and testament in the presence of us present at the same time who in his presence at his request and in the presence of each other have hereunto subscribed."

Judge Hurstbourne looked up. "This time the witnesses were Mrs. Pennyworth and Mrs. Ackerson."

Myrtle turned to Henri and whispered, "He didn't leave Nathan anything."

"Twenty-five dollars," whispered Henri.

Nathan jumped up from his seat.

"This is ridiculous! That will never hold up in court. It was written the day after the bank was robbed. The day after my father suffered a heart attack. He wasn't in his right mind. He wasn't of sound mind and certainly not of sound body. I shall get a lawyer and I will get that will thrown out!"

He turned and stormed from the room.

Everyone sat for a moment, shocked.

Then Judge Hurstbourne said, "Mr. Gartner, I will see that a draft is sent to Temple Jacob within a week. And Miss Wasserman, you and I will sit down and go over what all this means for you. Mrs. Pennyworth, I thank you for bringing the new will to our attention."

"You're welcome, Clarence," said Mrs. Pennyworth.

*****

Nathan stepped out of the courthouse into what had now become a downpour. He saw Yung Li across the street, standing under the Polar Bear awning, puffing on a cigar and eyeing him.

Pulling the collar of his coat up around his neck, Nathan hurried across the street towards the barber shop: he desperately needed a drink.

Yung flipped the half-smoked cigar into the current of water rushing down the street and started to follow Nathan. He stopped when he saw Henri and Myrtle emerge from the courthouse, then turned and headed back the other way.

*****

"Wow, that was a surprise," said Myrtle as she climbed into Henri's automobile.

"I'll say," answered Henri, "and I don't think Nathan was any too happy about it."

"You know what this means?" asked Myrtle.

Henri nodded. "We need to look more closely at Nathan as a suspect."

"And not just for one or two of the murders, but for all three."

"I'll talk to Jake about meeting again tonight. But right now I need to get you back to the library."

"Yes, I suppose Mr. Mitchell will be having conniptions that I've been gone this long."

*****

Myrtle walked over to the front door of the library and peeked out the small window in the middle of it. She was thankful to see Henri's car out front. The rain was still coming down in torrents.

He had called and said Jake wanted to meet at eight to discuss the new situation regarding the Steinmyer will. He suggested he pick Myrtle up and they could get a bite to eat at Miss Madeline's beforehand.

Myrtle was happy to oblige.

"I swear, I wonder if this rain is ever going to stop," said Myrtle, when she was safely in the car and out of the downpour.

"This is the first time we've had any since the night Miss Steinmyer and her father were murdered."

"I believe you're right," said Myrtle.

Twenty minutes later, they were luxuriating in the warmth of the blaze in the huge fireplace at Miss Madeline's. Henri was wolfing down his pot roast.

"I think," said Myrtle, cutting a chunk of meatloaf, "there's a good possibility Mr. Steinmyer committed all three murders."

Henri took a sip of hot chocolate. "You may be right. The thing is: how to prove it? We don't have the murder weapon. Miss Wasserman said she saw Nathan coming down the hallway when she ran out after hearing the gunshot, and he was coming *towards* Miss Steinmyer's room, not going away from it."

"There's still the fingerprint on the safe."

"I talked with Jake about that. Since Mrs. Pennyworth confirmed that Nathan was in Rudy's office the day they met, even if it is his fingerprint, it wouldn't necessarily prove anything."

The meeting with Jake and George was a short one. They both agreed Nathan now had to be the prime suspect. They also agreed there was not enough evidence yet to even charge him with the crimes, let alone obtain a guilty verdict.

"I'll get a search warrant from Judge Hurstbourne tomorrow," said Jake. "We'll go over that house with a fine tooth comb."

CHAPTER THIRTY-FOUR

Henri told Myrtle he would drop her back home at Mrs. Darling's, and then he had to return to his office.

She ran from the car to the house, cold rain pelting her from above, mud grabbing her feet from below.

Throwing open the door she rushed through the foyer into the comforting warmth of the parlor where a fire was going full force in the fireplace. Daisy was there, reading. She looked up as Myrtle came into the room.

"That is nasty weather out there," she said, laying the book aside.

"Tell me about it," said Myrtle, taking off her raincoat and shaking her hair.

"Oh, oh," said Daisy.

Myrtle looked at her. "What? What's wrong?"

Daisy pointed to the carpet behind Myrtle where a set of muddy footprints led from the foyer to where Myrtle stood.

"Oh, no," cried Myrtle. "Did I do that?"

"You see anyone else in the room besides you and me?"

"I have to clean that up right away. If Mrs. Darling..."

"Too late," said Daisy.

"Hello, dearie, heard you come in. Tought you could use a cup of tea. Oh, look what's happened here," she said, noticing the muddy prints.

"Oh, Mrs. Darling," said Myrtle, "I'll . . ."

"Oh, now don't fret yourself," said Mrs. Darling. "Happens all da time. Dis old carpet has seen worse dan dat. I need to get a real sidewalk put in. Now you sit right down and enjoy your tea. We'll just let dat dry, and den I'll get it up with da vacuum."

Myrtle plopped down in an easy chair and sipped her tea.

"She really is a darling," she said.

"Amen to that," said Daisy. "I heard the reading of the Steinmyer will today was a real shocker."

Myrtle nodded. "I think everyone was surprised—everyone except Nathan. Well, except that he was found out. I'm sure he knew there was a new will, regardless of what he says. And I guess he was surprised, too, that Mrs. Pennyworth had a copy."

"Do you think he killed his father and sister—and Mr. Folger?"

"It seems that way to me. But right now Henri doesn't believe there's enough evidence. Mr. Steinmyer had motive, all right. And he was right there in the house when the two deaths occurred. What I don't know is his alibi for when Mr. Folger was shot."

"Henri says he claims he was home all evening. Miss Wasserman couldn't confirm it, but she couldn't say he wasn't, either."

"Something will turn up, I'm sure."

*****

Myrtle found it hard to sleep that night. She kept running over in her mind what had transpired at the courthouse. *Did* Nathan Steinmyer know there was a second will, as seemed likely? And what happened to all the copies other than the one produced by Mrs. Pennyworth? Did he destroy them? Tossing and turning, she dozed off into a restless sleep in which she dreamt of walking into the house and leaving muddy footprints everywhere: the parlor, the dining room, up the stairs, down the hall, in her bedroom, up the bedroom walls, across the ceiling, back and forth until everything was covered in mud.

Suddenly the scene shifted: she was in the Steinmyer home. As she walked through the living room with Henri, she looked behind her; more muddy boot prints following them like a carpet being rolled out. She looked up and saw prints on the ceiling two stories above. As they started up the stairs the prints went before them, appearing even before she and Henri could step where they were.

She sat straight up in bed, wide awake. "That's it!" she exclaimed. "Why didn't I see it before?"

Jumping from the bed she threw on her robe and ran down the hall to Henri's room.

"Henri," she said in a loud whisper, knocking softly on the door. "Henri, wake up, wake up."

"He's not there."

Myrtle turned and saw Pierre peeking out from around his door. "He's not here. He was called out for a robbery a little while ago."

"Darn!" muttered Myrtle.

She turned and ran back to Daisy's room. "Daisy, wake up," she said, not as quietly now.

Moments later, Daisy opened the door, her eyes half closed. "What? What is it?"

"I know what's been bothering me about that night," said Myrtle, the words tumbling out.

"What night?"

"The night the Steinmyers were killed."

"What about it?"

"I'm sure the killer was already in the house."

"What do you mean?"

"Henri and I tracked in mud when we got there. Miss Wasserman cleaned it up. She said she had done the same thing earlier when Nathan arrived home. But she didn't say anything about doing it between then and when we arrived. If she didn't, that means the killer was already in the house."

"Uh, huh." Daisy still wasn't sure what Myrtle was rambling about, nor did she much care—she just wanted to go back to bed.

"Go back to sleep now," said Myrtle. "I'll talk to Henri in the morning."

*****

Myrtle was the first to arrive for breakfast the next day, followed closely by Pierre and Daisy.

But no Henri.

"Mr. Longet, do you know where Henri is?" asked Myrtle.

Pierre set his coffee cup down. "I ran into him as I was coming out of the bathroom. He was off again to speak with the man who called last night regarding a break-in at his home."

"Shoot," said Myrtle. "I wanted to talk with him."

She wolfed down her bacon and eggs, then excused herself and made a hasty exit.

Upstairs in her room she stood gazing out at the big barn at the back of the lot, trying to gather her thoughts.

Should she go see Miss Wasserman on her own?

Or should she wait for Henri to return and tell him about her dream, and what she now felt certain to be true: that Nathan Steinmyer killed all three of the victims?

And how long before Henri returned? He could be gone for the day. Maybe she should go by his office to see if she could catch him there.

But what if she were wrong? She had been sure her boss, Frank Mitchell, had killed Yvette Sinclair, only to discover it was her friend, Mr. Pfrommer, who lived down the hall from her.

She'd leave a message with Mrs. Darling asking her to have Henri come by the library when he returned.

She could talk to him then. He'd know what to do.

*****

By noon, Myrtle still hadn't heard from Henri.

Frank had stepped out for lunch, so Myrtle decided to use the phone in his office to call Henri's office.

"I don't think he's there," said Maribel, when Myrtle asked to be connected.

"Do you know where he is?"

"Mr. McIntyre called him a few minutes ago; they was heading over to the Steinmyer home."

Drats! thought Myrtle. She would have wanted to go along. "If you hear from him, would you have him stop by the library?"

"Okay," said Maribel. "Will do."

By the time it came to leave work, Myrtle still had had not heard from Henri.

Locking the library door before her, she took off, walking as fast as she could. She was sure Henri and Mr. McIntyre had gone to the Steinmyer home to search for a gun. Had they found it? Had they found anything?

When Myrtle arrived home, she first checked the parlor, then the dining room: no Henri. She dashed upstairs to his room and knocked on the door.

No answer.

Downstairs she found Mrs. Darling in the kitchen.

"Oh there you are, dearie," said her landlady. "I tought you come in, but den you was gone. I got a nice sandwich for you here, and some hot chicken soup."

"Mrs. Darling, do you know where Henri is?" asked Myrtle, sitting down to the kitchen table.

Mrs. Darling set the sandwich and soup in front of her and Myrtle started eating.

"Yah. Ebenezer Humphries' cow got out and is a'wandering around out dere on da road. Henri went out to help get it back in da barn 'fore somebody come along in dere carriage and run into it."

"Did he say if he and Mr. McIntyre found anything when they were at the Steinmyer home today?"

"Yah, he said dey din't find nothing. He was real disappointed."

"Do you have any idea when he'll be back?"

"He just left about ten minutes ago. It's a way out to da farm, so I reckon it'll be a while 'fore he gets back."

Myrtle bit her lip. What should she do?

Finally, she decided. What could it hurt to go speak with Miss Wasserman, to know for sure about the muddy foot prints? If she had indeed cleaned some up between when Mr. Steinmyer came home and her and Henri's entrance, then her theory that the killer— namely Nathan—was already in the house wouldn't hold water.

*****

Myrtle parked the Ford on the street in front of the Steinmyer home and switched off the engine.

She stepped down from the car and walked around to the back of the house. Myrtle hoped to find Miss Wasserman in the kitchen. She preferred Mr. Steinmyer not know she was there, and hoped he hadn't seen her through a window as she approached the house.

A soft knock on the door brought the housekeeper.

"Miss Tully! What a surprise! What brings you by? Constable de la Cruz and Mr. McIntyre, they was by this morning."

"I know," said Myrtle. "I just had a few more questions about the night Miss Steinmyer and her father were murdered. Is Mr. Steinmyer here?"

"Oh, I'm afraid he stepped out for a bit."

Good! thought Myrtle.

"Actually," said Myrtle, "you're the one I wanted to speak with."

"Well, come in," said Miss Wasserman. "I got water going for some tea, if you'd like some."

"Tea would be fine."

As she entered the kitchen, Myrtle heard a whistling sound, similar to that of a steam engine, but much quieter.

"What is that noise?" she asked.

"Oh," said Miss Wasserman, hurrying to the stove, "dat's da tea kettle."

"A tea kettle that whistles?"

"Yah, it's new. Just come out a few years ago. Tells you when da water's hot."

"What won't they think of next," said Myrtle.

"Have a seat, ducky. I'll have your tea in a jiffy."

Moments later, Miss Wasserman set a cup in front of Myrtle, then her own across the table.

Myrtle picked up her cup, blew across the steaming liquid, and took a sip. She looked at Miss Wasserman, who was doing the same.

"Wow, this is delicious," said Myrtle, her eyebrows raised. "What flavor is this?"

"It's licorice," said Miss Wasserman. "I get it from Mr. Kinnamon."

"Mr. Kinnamon?"

"Yah. He's a traveling salesman. Comes tru town ever four or five months. Always has a lot of good tings you can't get hereabouts."

"I didn't know traveling salesmen still existed."

"Oh, yah, but not so much anymore, ya know. Now, den, ducky, what was it you wanted to ask me?"

"The night Mr. Steinmyer and his daughter were killed," said Myrtle, "were there any foot prints or boot prints on the floor *after* you heard the gunshot and before Constable de la Cruz and I arrived and traipsed them across the room?"

Miss Wasserman thought for a moment. "No, like I said, I cleaned up some earlier from Mr. Nathan—I never could get dat boy to take off his dirty boots or shoes. But after we found Miss Rachel dead, I hadn't even gone downstairs until you and da constable arrived."

Then Nathan must be our man, thought Myrtle.

"I see. Well, thank you, Miss Wasserman."

"Does da constable have any idea who did dis terrible ting?"

"There are still a number of suspects." Myrtle took another sip of tea. She certainly wasn't going to tell Miss Wasserman that Nathan was at the top of the list. "I suppose I should be getting off. Thank you for your time."

Miss Wasserman stood and headed for the door to the hallway. "Here, you can go out da front way, if you're not superstitious."

Myrtle smiled. Her mother wouldn't have gone out a different door than she came in. *Bad luck*, she'd always say.

"No, I'm not superstitious."

As they passed by the small room where she and Henri had talked with Miss Wasserman the night of Rachel's murder, Myrtle wondered: if she *was* wrong, and it wasn't Nathan who did it, could this be the room where the killer might have hidden?

"Miss Wasserman, do you mind if I peek in here for a second?" asked Myrtle.

"No, ducky, not at all."

The room was as Myrtle remembered it: the long table, the eight chairs, the small table with the menorah and that horridly bad painting at the end of the room, one of Frank Mitchell's poorly done renderings of Booker Falls' waterfalls.

"That picture is crooked again," said Myrtle.

"Oh, yah, it gets like dat sometimes. It's da safe behind it what does it. Whenever anybody gets in da safe, da picture's always whopper-jawed afterwards."

Myrtle's eyes lit up: *a safe*?

"Did Constable de la Cruz or Mr. McIntyre know about this safe?" asked Myrtle.

"I don't tink so. At least, they didn't say nothing. I wasn't with them when they was looking around."

Myrtle walked to the end of the room and removed the picture. Behind it, set into the wall, was a safe, measuring approximately two feet by two feet.

Myrtle turned to Miss Wasserman. "I, uh, I don't suppose you know the combination, do you?"

Miss Wasserman shook her head. "No, ducky, I don't."

A disappointed look came over Myrtle's face.

Just then the teakettle began to whistle. Miss Wasserman turned to go get it.

"But it's written on da back of da picture," she said as she exited the room.

Myrtle turned the painting over. *Sixteen, left, four. Thirty-two, right, three. Nine, left, two. Twenty to the right.*

She set the painting down on the table behind her, removed a pair of gloves from the beaded purse she'd taken to carrying and slipped them on. Hands shaking, she tried the combination. When she moved twenty to the right, the dial stopped and Myrtle felt the door give.

She turned the handle and the door swung open, revealing the one item inside: a gun.

Reaching in, she removed it, turning it over in her hand.

"What are you doing?"

Startled, Myrtle turned around to find Nathan standing at the door, his face contorted in rage.

"What are you doing?" he asked again, threateningly.

In spite of the tremble in her hands, Myrtle tried to remain calm. "Is this the gun you used to kill Mr. Folger and your sister?"

Nathan growled, grabbed the menorah from the table and moved towards her. "You'll never know," he snarled.

Myrtle raised the gun and pointed it at him. "Don't come any closer. I know how to use this."

Nathan stopped and smiled. "It works better if it's loaded."

Myrtle released the cylinder: empty. She laid the gun on the table and picked up her bag. "Stop now!" she said.

"Or what?" asked Nathan, coming closer and raising the menorah above his head. "Do you propose to beat me off with your bag?"

He took another step, then stopped, a shocked look on his face as he saw the derringer in Myrtle's hand, pointed at him.

"Don't come any closer," said Myrtle, her voice wavering. "I'm warning you."

Nathan's features relaxed; he laughed and started to advance but stopped again when he heard the report of the gun and felt a piercing pain in his shoulder. Looking down he saw a red stain start to spread over his white linen shirt.

"Why, you—"

He lunged towards Myrtle who flattened herself against the wall and fired once more. Nathan looked down again and saw the bullet had found its mark in the middle of his chest.

The menorah slipped from his hand, crashing at his feet.

He looked back up at Myrtle, then slumped to the floor, collapsing on top of the menorah.

"What happened?"

Myrtle looked at the door and saw Miss Wasserman standing there.

"Call the doctor," said Myrtle. "And see if you can get hold of Constable de la Cruz."

CHAPTER THIRTY-FIVE

Both Henri and Dr. Sherman arrived at the Steinmyer home within minutes of the housekeeper's phone calls. Nathan lay unconscious on the floor. Miss Wasserman had applied bandages to both of his wounds.

Myrtle had reloaded the derringer, just in case.

She explained what happened and showed Henri the gun she'd removed from the safe.

Dr. Sherman made a quick assessment of Nathan's injuries and decided they were not life threatening. He and Henri carried Nathan to Henri's car and transported him to the doctor's office where he was laid out on the operating table, his right wrist handcuffed to the table's metal leg.

Before they'd left the Steinmyer home, Henri had called George to come by and drive the still shaken Myrtle back to the boarding house. He'd then asked the next door neighbor to come over and stay with Miss Wasserman.

News of the shooting spread quickly through town. When Daisy heard it she left the newspaper office and ran all the way to the boarding house.

Now she, along with Myrtle, George, and Mrs. Darling waited in the parlor for Henri to arrive, anxious to hear what he had to report.

Myrtle jumped up when Henri entered the parlor. "Is he all right?" she asked, concern in her voice.

Henri removed his hat and coat and sat down. "He'll live," he said, accepting the cup of tea Mrs. Darling offered him.

"Thank God!" said Myrtle, relieved. She sank back down into her chair.

"Did he say anything?" asked Daisy.

"He made a full confession," said Henri, sipping the tea.

Myrtle's head jerked back. "A full confession? To everything?"

"To everything. He admitted to knowing about the new will, and knew if it had been allowed to stand he'd end up with nothing, well, twenty-five dollars. And with Yung Li waiting to collect on the gambling debt, he couldn't allow that to happen.

"He knew in order to hide its existence, he'd have to get rid of his sister as well as Mr. Folger, because they both knew about the new will. He'd even thought of getting rid of Mrs. Pennyworth, but he hadn't counted on her leaving town. He did break into her house a few nights ago, but the dog scared him off.

"He hadn't planned on killing his father, but when he realized he was still alert enough to tell someone that there was a newer will, he knew he had to kill him, too. So he smothered him, hoping his death would look like an accident."

"But thanks to Myrtle, that didn't happen," said Daisy.

Henri frowned at her. "I'm sure Doc Sherman would have come to the same conclusion on his own.

"Anyway, Rachel had told him about Mickey's gun being in my desk drawer, so he'd broken in and stolen it, thinking that would throw suspicion on Mickey. And when Yung Li showed up in town that gave Nathan the opportunity to try to pin his sister's death on him. He purposely left the gambling chip in her room where it could be found.

"After he shot Miss Steinmyer, he ran out of her room, rushed downstairs and placed the gun into the safe he'd left open, then raced back upstairs in time to see Miss Wasserman coming out of her room.

"Later that night, after everybody left and Miss Wasserman had gone to bed, Nathan went into his father's room and smothered him."

"He might have gotten away with everything if Mrs. Pennyworth hadn't had a copy of the new will," said George.

"And if Myrtle hadn't found the gun," said Daisy.

"About that," said Henri, staring at Myrtle. "What were you thinking, breaking into that safe?"

"First of all," said Myrtle, "I didn't technically break into the safe, since I had the combination."

"If you didn't have the authority to open the safe, that's the same as breaking in," said Henri.

"I sort of thought Miss Wasserman gave me permission. Otherwise, why would she have told me where the combination was?"

Henri shook his head. "You're lucky Jake isn't going to charge you with trespassing and attempted robbery."

"Attempted robbery?" exclaimed Daisy. "She cracked the case! She's a hero! She should get a medal."

"I'll settle for not going to jail," said Myrtle. "I'm surprised he was willing to make a full confession."

"He knew that now, not only did we have a motive, we also had the murder weapon—which I'm sure it will turn out to be—as well as his prints on the gun—which I'm also sure we'll find. I explained to him how it was possible to confirm that the bullets that killed Mr. Folger and Miss Steinmyer both came from his gun.

"He questioned whether or not the gun could be used as evidence, since we didn't have a warrant, but when I pointed out to him that Myrtle wasn't a law enforcement officer, it didn't matter if I had a warrant or not, since I wasn't the one who found the gun.

"I think the real reason he decided to confess was that he knew Michigan doesn't have the death penalty, and the worst he could get would be life in prison, which appealed to him much more than what Mr. Li might do if Nathan couldn't pay what he owed.

"And, I have one more piece of news: Lars Jørgensen showed up. It seems he's been in Omaha."

"Omaha?" said Daisy. "What's he been doing in Omaha?"

Henri chuckled. "The day before Mr. Folger was killed, Lars got drunk and fell asleep in one of the rail cars. When he woke up, he found himself in Omaha. He's been working his way back here ever since."

"Well, okay, then," said Daisy, "It's sure been an exciting couple of weeks. And Myrtle solved another murder—three murders this time. This could become a habit."

"Let's hope not," said Myrtle. "I think Booker Falls has seen more than enough murders to last it for a long time."

EPILOGUE

YUNG LI—*Monday, October 18, 1920*

As Yung Li left the post office, which doubled as the telegraph office for Booker Falls, he nearly collided with Henri, who was on his way in.

"Still here, I see," said Henri. "More 'sightseeing' or do you still have business to transact?"

"No sightseeing," said Yung Li. "And no more business to transact."

"You're leaving town?"

Yung Li nodded. "Yes, I am leaving now."

"Back to San Francisco?"

Yung Li shook his head. "No, no San Francisco. Chicago."

"Chicago?" said Henri, surprised. "More sightseeing? Or, business?"

"Neither. I am moving there."

Henri looked perplexed. "Moving there?"

"Yes. San Francisco is no longer safe for me and my family."

Henri nodded. "Because you weren't able to collect the money Nathan owed your boss."

"Mr. Zhāng does not take kindly to not getting what is owed to him. I have wired money to my wife. She and my children will leave tomorrow and meet me in Chicago."

"You're driving there?"

"No, first I will return the automobile to the man in Houghton I got it from when I arrived there. Then I will take the train to Chicago and meet my family."

"And what will you do when you get there?"

"When I arrived in Chicago a few weeks ago, I met a man in the train station who was waiting for someone. He said he was from New York and had arrived in Chicago himself a few months earlier. I guess he was in his early twenties, but he appeared much older. We struck up a conversation, and he told me he worked at a club, The Four Deuces, I think he called it. He said he was sure he could get me a job there, too, if I wanted to leave San Francisco. At the time I gave it little thought, but now I think it is best way."

"What kind of work will you be doing?" asked Henri.

"He said he was a bouncer. I would be, too."

Henri grinned. "You know what a bouncer does?"

"Yes," said Yung, "he throws people out who are acting up."

"And you'd be happy doing that?"

This time it was Yung who grinned. "More happy than what I am doing now, yes."

"What's the fellow's name?"

"I know you Americans think we Chinese have strange names, but yours are just as strange, Mr. de la Cruz. His name is Alphonse—Alphonse Capone.

*****

THE FINNEGANS—*Tuesday, October 19, 1920*

Agnes Finnegan picked up the teakettle from the burner and poured the steaming liquid into two mugs, each holding a teabag. She took a spoon from the silverware drawer and swirled the water around, watching as it began to darken.

Then she picked up both cups and carried them to the kitchen table, where she placed one in front of her husband, who was sitting, hands folded, waiting for her.

She took a seat across from him and proceeded to dunk the teabag in her cup, up and down, up and down, up and down—considerably more times than was necessary. Concern showed on her face, and there was a slight tremor in her hand.

The Finnegan home, while not as extravagant as some of the other residences in their neighborhood was, nevertheless, one of the best maintained, thanks to J. P.'s practice of having it re-painted every three years and Agnes' passion for gardening and flowers, which rendered the grounds a true feast for the eyes.

Unfortunately, the perfection that existed outside the house did not reflect the turmoil that had engulfed the interior over the past twelve months, a year during which Agnes had looked elsewhere for fulfillment of her sexual needs in the person of Rudolph Folger, and J. P. had moved into a room above his store.

But now Folger was dead. And J. P. had moved back into the house.

"Joseph, I'm sorry for everything," said Agnes, breaking the silence, but not looking up.

J. P. looked at her. "Yah, me, too," he said. His cup remained untouched.

Agnes looked up. "You ain't got nothing to be sorry for. I'm da one to blame."

"I'm sorry I couldn't be the husband you needed, that you had to go outside our marriage."

"I shouldn't of done it," said Agnes. Tears began to roll down her cheeks. "You been a good husband, a good father. You're a good provider."

She looked back down at the cup. The water was darker now. "I shouldn't of done it," she said again. "Can you ever forgive me?"

J. P. stared at her for a moment. "I gotta know something: if he was still alive, would you still be with him?"

Agnes' head jerked up. Her eyes were red. "No! No! I met him da night he got killed and told him it was over. I been to confession dat day and Father Fabien said he couldn't give me absolution unless I quit seeing Rudy. I didn't want to burn in Hell! So I told Rudy it was over between us. No, I wouldn't be with him now."

"You know, until they arrested Nathan, I thought you killed Folger," said J. P. "I saw you go in the building with him that night. I never saw you come out. I went down to the store and when I heard the gunshot, I figured you'd killed him."

Agnes laughed. "Dat's funny."

"What's funny?"

"Because I done thought you done it."

"I wanted to. Even tried to hire someone to do it. But he never did—too drunk, I reckon, eh. I'd gone down to get my gun. I was going to go over and shoot the bastard myself. But then I heard the shot, and figured you'd done it."

Agnes shook her head. "No, he was still alive when I left. I knew you was in your room, 'cause I saw the light on. I figured you'd watched me leave, then walked across the street and shot him dead."

"I guess we're both lucky someone else did it for us, eh?" said J. P.

"I guess so. So am I forgiven?"

J. P. nodded. "You know, I still ain't able to get it up."

"Don't make no difference. I still love you. And I promise—I ain't going looking again."

*****

MARGARET FOLGER—*Wednesday, October 20, 1920*

Margaret removed her hat, laid it on the seat beside her, leaned back and took a deep breath.

Three days ago she had released Jessica, giving her two month's salary and a good letter of reference. She had sold off most of the furnishings in the house on Gossamer Street and placed the rest in storage. Then she put the property up for sale, turning the task of selling it over to Mr. Hodgens at the Booker Falls Premier Real Estate and Auction Company.

She had driven to Houghton, accompanied by Mrs. Pennyworth. There, she made a gift of both the horse and the carriage to her late husband's former secretary to do with as she wished.

"You may keep it or sell it," she said. Margaret knew that with Rudolph gone, Norma no longer had employment and could use the money.

She then purchased a ticket at the Douglas House and boarded the first trolley heading north.

Margaret watched as the houses and farms, the trees and woods and ponds of the Keweenaw Peninsula rumbled by outside the car window.

She was on her way to Mohawk, retracing the route she had taken almost a month earlier. But this time it was different. Then, she had been pondering how best to extricate herself from a marriage that had turned sour, that had resulted in her husband having an affair with another woman. She had considered two alternatives: filing for a divorce . . . and having Rudolph murdered.

She had decided on the former.

But then the decision was made for her, when Nathan Steinmyer shot her husband in the back and killed him.

She watched as the conductor came down the aisle towards her. She opened her handbag, took out the ticket and placed it in the man's waiting hand. He handed her back a transfer ticket, which she placed back in her handbag.

She had no idea what had become of Mickey. She hadn't seen him since the day the constable came by the house to talk to both of them, the day after Rudy's body was found. She heard he'd been seen around town for a few days after that, but then he had seemed to disappear.

Wherever he is, she thought, *I hope he stays there.*

At the Arcadia station, Margaret watched a young woman in her twenties board with two tow-headed girls, twins, no more than three years old.

"I imagine they're a handful," said Margaret, as the trio settled into their seats.

"Yah, for sure," said the young woman. "My name's Florence."

Margaret introduced herself and the two of them struck up a conversation. Shortly, the sign for Electric Park came into view.

"Do you know what dat is?" asked Florence.

Margaret looked out the window. "Yah," she said, and proceeded to repeat what she had been told on her previous trip.

"You've been dere, den?" asked Florence.

"No," said Margaret, shaking her head. "But I plan to."

"We're going to Albion," said Florence, doing her best to keep the girls in their seats. "How far are you going?"

"All the way," answered Margaret. "All the way to the end—to Mohawk."

"Is Mohawk your home?"

Margaret smiled and looked out the window.

"It is now."

*****

MILDRED WASSERMAN—*Thursday, October 21, 1920*

Mildred watched as Henri held the ladder on which George was standing.

"Are you sure you want to do this?" asked George. He knew Miss Wasserman was in her seventies.

"Yah, I do," said Mildred. "I ain't about to sit around doing nutting and shriveling up. Besides, what else am I going to do with a house dat's got eight bedrooms?"

George looked again at the sign he held in his hands, the one he was about to hang above the front entrance of the house: WASSERMAN'S ROOM & BOARD.

"I already got my first boarder," said Mildred.

"You do?" said Henri.

"Yah, a nice young fellow named Herman Hutchinson came by yesterday. Said Hilda at da post office told him I was fixing to open da boarding house. He's a little feller, not as tall as I am, and I ain't but about five three. He's a painter."

"A painter?" said George, struggling to get the eye hook onto the "S" hook screwed into the upper beam. "Does he paint houses, then?"

"Oh, no. He's what you call an artist—he paints pictures."

"Pictures, huh?" said George, succeeding in getting the second eye hook in place.

"I wouldn't think that pays very well," said Henri, as George descended the ladder.

"I don't know 'bout dat," said Mildred. "Gave me da first month's rent. Rented out da space above da carriage house, too. Said it would be his studio."

"Studio, huh?" said Henri. "Maybe he *is* a really good artist."

"Hopefully better than Frank," said George, laughing.

Henri's eyebrows arched. "Who isn't?"

"Dis fellow says he knows Mr. Mitchell," said Mildred. "Says dey was in school together."

"Did he just get into town?" asked George.

"Oh, no. He's already been here a while, now. Been staying over at da Walther Building."

"I wonder why Frank never mentioned him," said George.

"I don't know," said Mildred. "But I do know one ting: dat's a mighty fine looking sign. Now, you boys come on inside. I tink I remember where Mr. Steinmyer used to keep his peach brandy."

THE END

THE NEXT BOOK IN THE SERIES
A New Booker Falls Mystery
Paint the Librarian Dead
Here's a sample:

CHAPTER ONE

"Frank Mitchell?"

Frank turned to find a large man in front of him, a man he remembered seeing once before. Before Frank could say or do anything, he felt the sharp stab of the knife as it slid in between the fourth and fifth rib of his left side.

The man pulled the knife back out and stood for a minute, watching as Frank doubled over and dropped onto the snow-covered sidewalk.

"Don't be messing around with that nigger no more," the man said.

Then he turned and walked back to his car, parked in front of Oosterman's Men's Wear, got in, and drove off.

*****

Snow and sub-freezing temperatures had gripped the town of Booker Falls for the past five days.

The college library had been closed since Friday, the result of a broken boiler. It wasn't scheduled to be repaired for another week, until after Christmas.

Consequently, Myrtle Tully, who held the position of assistant librarian, was on a paid holiday, and making the most of it.

She'd spent the morning at Paige Turner's New, Used and Rare Books Store, then met Daisy O'Hearn, her best friend and fellow boarder at Mrs. Darling's Boarding House, for lunch at Miss Madeline's Eatery, a rare treat for both of them. Normally they would have eaten at the boarding house. After all, all their meals were included in the monthly rent they paid, and neither was in a position to spend money they didn't have to.

This afternoon Myrtle had ridden with Henri de la Cruz, who also called the boarding house home, out to see the old logging camp northeast of town, where Louis Amyx, the founder of Adelaide College, had worked for the Joshua Mining Company, overseeing the production of the timber used to build the homes in Greytown, that part of Booker Falls where most of the men who worked the various mines in the area resided.

At first she had declined his invitation.

"Henri, it's cold out. I'd much rather just sit here by the fire and read this new book Paige got in yesterday."

"What's it called?" asked Henri, taking the book from Myrtle's hand. *The Mysterious Affair at Styles*? And who's Agatha Christie?"

"It's a murder mystery. You know how I love murder mysteries," said Myrtle, giving him a wink. "This is Miss Christie's first book. But from what I've read so far, it certainly won't be her last."

"We'd be going in the sleigh."

Myrtle's eyes lit up. "In the sleigh?"

Myrtle loved the sleigh!

She had had the pleasure of riding in Henri's sleigh twice before, the first when she and Henri went to interview Paul Momet last December about the unsolved death of Yvette Sinclair, a young woman who had been murdered some twenty-eight-years before and whose case had been reopened; and later that same month when he had given her a lift to St. Barbara's Catholic Church to attend Christmas Eve Mass.

"Did you put the Packard away?"

At Henri's urging, Myrtle had reluctantly put her own car, a thirteen-year-old Model N Ford, away for the winter in the big barn out behind the house, where it shared space with the two carriages, one belonging to

Mrs. Darling and the other to Henri, as well as Henri's sleigh.

Jessie and Hank, the two horses who pulled all of these conveyances, also called the barn home.

Henri, who was in his fifth year as county constable, had decided to keep his car out a while longer, in case it was needed for police business.

"No, I just thought a sleigh ride would be fun. Besides, the roads out there will probably be unpassable in a car. I think there must be at least three feet on the ground by now."

So Myrtle had found herself at the logging camp, where Henri was giving her the grand tour.

"You've been here before?" asked Myrtle.

"Yah. A couple of times with old Mr. Koskinen."

"Mr. Koskinen? The one who's ninety-four?"

"Do you know him?" asked Henri.

Myrtle shook her head. "No, George told me about him when we were at the falls, and I asked how they got their name."

"I see." Henri's tone had an unmistakable frostiness to it. He had known about the picnic she and George had gone on to see the falls after which the town was named. And though he knew he had no claim on her, even though they had gone out several times—had even shared a few kisses, maybe more—he wasn't all that keen she was also seeing George Salmon, the town mayor and his best friend.

"So, what's that building over there?" asked Myrtle, pointing to a large building leaning precariously to one side. She hadn't missed Henri's annoyance, and hoped to change the subject.

"According to Mr. Koskinen, that was the camp office and store. The foreman and the log scaler lived on the top floor. At the store, the loggers could buy stuff like socks, and tobacco and some clothes—and sewing material. They didn't have anybody around but themselves to mend something when they tore it."

"What's a log scaler?"

"He's the fellow who would measure the cut timber for volume and determine its quality. Then he figured out how much it would be worth."

"Is that bigger building the barn?" asked Myrtle.

"No," said Henri. "That was the bunkhouse. It could hold over seventy men. The cookshanty was attached to it, where the meals were prepared and eaten. As you can see, it's fallen over now. The barn is over there."

Henri pointed to the far side of the camp.

"That's where they kept the horses and oxen and hay and some equipment. Next to it was the blacksmith shop."

"I imagine logging was hot, sweaty work," said Myrtle.

"I suppose to some extent. But all the work was done in the winter, so they sure didn't have to worry about summer heat."

"In the winter? But that's the worst weather. Why would they only work in the winter?"

"That way they could drag the logs on sleds—the horses and oxen would—over the snow to the river banks. They'd leave them there 'til spring, when they could float them downstream."

Myrtle looked up at the towering trees that stretched above them, their branches laden with snow.

"I guess these have all grown back since they stopped taking the lumber out," she said.

"Yes and no," said Henri. "These trees *have* grown up since then, but they aren't the same kind of trees that were here when logging was going on."

"What do you mean?"

"When logging was at its peak here, all the trees were white pine. They're the only kind they were taking out. But when those were all gone, that allowed the trees you see here now—aspen, sugar maple, jack pine—to spring up in their place."

Henri looked up at the sky. "It's getting dark. We'd better be getting back."

*****

The snow, which had let up somewhat while Myrtle and Henri were exploring the logging camp, had started up again. By the time they arrived back at the main road, it was coming down hard, the temperature had dropped considerably, and the sun had disappeared.

"I really appreciate this foot warmer," said Myrtle, pulling the collar of her skunk fur coat up around her neck. On her head she wore a full fur Russian hat she'd purchased a few days before in town at de Première Qualité Women's Wear Shop.

Henri remembered from their previous sleigh rides together that Myrtle had found the foot warmer, a small metal box with hot coals placed inside, to be especially welcome. By now, the coals were almost out, but the container still provided a modicum of warmth.

The moon was about eighty per cent visible and, with no clouds to hide them, a myriad of stars filled the night sky.

"Henri, it is so beautiful out here," said Myrtle, snuggling down under the lap robe Henri had also thoughtfully brought along. Brightly colored flowers— red, yellow, white, purple—spilled forth from a cornucopia set on a dark background. She remembered Henri had said it belonged to his mother.

She leaned her head back. "Look at those stars," she said. "I've never seen so many."

"You know what Mrs. Darling would say, don't you?" asked Henri.

Myrtle turned to him. "No. What would Mrs. Darling say?"

"You see one star, you've seen dem all."

Myrtle howled with laughter.

Almost seventy years of age, Mrs. Darling, though pleasant, kind and considerate, was not one to mince words.

Myrtle remembered having heard her on two occasions utter words to the effect of what Henri had just quoted: one, regarding the Fourth of July parade, which the old lady had chosen to forego—"*You see one parade, you've seen dem all*"—and the second time on their trip a few months ago when the two of them had traveled to Marquette to visit a former boarder at Mrs. Darling's boarding house, now in prison there, and Myrtle had attempted to get Mrs. Darling to look at Lake Superior.

"*You see one lake, you've seen dem all,*" her landlady had replied.

"I'm sure you're right," said Myrtle. "That's exactly what she would have said. But I think they're wonderful."

The trip from the logging camp back to the boarding house took them past the library. A solitary light above the front entrance was the only illumination.

When they were within about fifty yards of the building, the front door burst open and a man ran out, carrying a large object that appeared to be a painting. Within minutes he disappeared around the corner of the building, heading towards the area where there was a garden with a pond and a grotto.

"Henri, did you see that?" asked Myrtle.

"Yah," said Henri, urging Jessie to a faster gait. When they reached the library both of them sprang from the sleigh, following the tracks around the side of the building the man had left in the snow-covered ground. The only light here was that provided by the moon, which was more than sufficient to allow them to see footprints leading to the edge of the pond, which was now frozen over.

"He must have gone across the pond and run into the woods," said Henri.

But when they reached the far side of the pond, there was no sign of any tracks.

"Where did he go?" asked Myrtle, looking around.

"I don't know," answered Henri. He started to walk around the pond, first to the point where it ended at the grotto, then back to the other side.

Nothing.

"He couldn't have just disappeared," said Myrtle.

"I sure don't know where he went," said Henri. He walked over to the woods. He didn't expect to find tracks there either, but he didn't know where else to look.

"Nothing there," he said, returning to Myrtle's side. "That was a painting he was carrying, wasn't it?"

"It must have been. I don't know what else it could have been."

"Let's go inside and see what's missing," said Henri. "You have keys?"

Myrtle nodded.

The Adelaide College Library was the repository for a dozen paintings bequeathed by Louis Amyx, the founder of the college, upon his death in 1888. All the works were by French artists, including two by Pierre-Auguste Renoir and Paul Cézanne.

Six of the works hung on the west wall of the library, while the east wall held the other six.

Inside, Myrtle turned on the lights and quickly scanned both walls. Nothing was missing.

"They're all here," she said.

"Does the library have any other paintings?" asked Henri. "Any that would be worth stealing?"

"No, this is all . . . except . . ."

"Except?"

"There is one more piece, upstairs at the head of the staircase: the painting of Mrs. Hutchinson. Her husband built the library."

Myrtle quickly climbed the spiral staircase, Henri close on her heels. When they reached the top they stopped.

"Looks like it's still here," said Henri.

The portrait of Betsy Hutchinson, a magnificent piece measuring some six feet in height and five feet across looked down upon them.

"Besides," he continued, "what that fellow had under his arm wasn't nearly this big." He turned to Myrtle. "You're sure there are no other pieces of art in the library?"

Myrtle shook her head. "Not that I'm aware of. Oh, wait, Mr. Mitchell has one in his office, one of his that he painted."

"I've seen that painting," said Henri. "Pretty much like the one I have in my office. I sure can't see anyone wanting to steal that."

Back downstairs they looked through the windows of the office of Frank Mitchell, the head librarian and Myrtle's boss.

The painting still hung on the wall.

"Well, okay, then, we have a mystery, don't we?" said Henri. "If that wasn't a painting the fellow had, what was it?"

"That's not the only mystery," said Myrtle.

"What do you mean?"

"Where did he disappear to?"

ABOUT THE AUTHOR

 Kenn Grimes is both an author and a screenwriter, with two published books to his credit prior to the *Booker Falls Mystery Series:* a collection of short stories, *Camptown: One Hundred and Fifty Years of Stories from Camptown, Kentucky,* published in 2005 by Arbutus Press (now out of print); and *The Other Side of Yesterday,* a time travel novel published in 2012 by Deer Lake Press.

A retired Lutheran minister who served congregations in Indiana, Kentucky, and Missouri, Kenn later owned and operated *Simply Married,* the largest wedding service on Maui, Hawaii. During his ministry he has officiated at over 4,200 ceremonies

He and his wife, Judy, also a retired minister, now split their time between their homes in Louisville, Kentucky, and Lower Northern Michigan, where they continue to do weddings.

Made in the USA
Middletown, DE
10 July 2017